Julia Quinn started writing her first book one

By Julia Quinn

JULIA QUINN

A Night Like This

PIATKUS

PIATKUS

First published in the US in 2012 by Avon Books,
An imprint of HarperCollins, New York
First published in Great Britain as a paperback original in 2012 by Piatkus
by arrangement with Avon
This paperback edition published in 2021 by Piatkus

1 3 5 7 9 10 8 6 4 2

A CIP catalogue record for this book
is available from the British Library.

ISBN 978-0-3494-3047-8

Printed and bound in Italy by Elcograf S.p.A.

Papers used by Piatkus are from well-managed forests
and other responsible sources.

Piatkus
An imprint of
Little, Brown Book Group
Carmelite House
50 Victoria Embankment
London EC4Y 0DZ

An Hachette UK Company
www.hachette.co.uk

www.littlebrown.co.uk

For Iana, one of the strongest people I know.

And also for Paul, even though
I still don't understand
why anyone might need seven sleeping bags.

1824 has been a very busy year for Daniel Smythe-Smith.

He has:

- *returned to England after three years in exile.*

- *attended the world's worst concert.*

- *kissed a complete stranger.*

- *fended off an attack by thieves on a London Street.*

- *performed the leading role in a twelve-act melodrama.*

- *barely survived a carriage accident.*

- *hunted down a madman.*

- *fallen in love.*

 And it's only April …

Prologue

"Winstead, you bloody cheat!"

Daniel Smythe-Smith blinked. He was a little bit drunk, but he *thought* someone had just accused him of cheating at cards. It had taken him a moment to be sure; he'd been the Earl of Winstead for barely a year, and he still sometimes forgot to turn when someone called him by his title.

But no, he was Winstead, or rather Winstead was he, and . . .

His head did a bob and then a weave. What was it he had been thinking?

Oh, right. "No," he said slowly, still rather puzzled by the whole thing. He raised his hand to protest, because he was quite certain he hadn't been cheating. In fact, after that last bottle of wine, it was possibly the only thing he was certain of. But he didn't manage to say anything more. In fact, he was barely able to hop out of the way when the table came crashing toward him.

The table? Holy hell, how drunk was he?

Sure enough, the table was now sideways and the cards were on the floor, and Hugh Prentice was screaming at him like a lunatic.

Hugh must be drunk, too.

"I didn't cheat," Daniel said. He lifted his brows and blinked, as if the owlish motion might remove the filmy layer of intoxication that seemed to obscure, well, everything. He looked over at Marcus Holroyd, his closest friend, and shrugged. "I don't cheat."

Everyone knew he didn't cheat.

But Hugh had clearly lost his mind, and Daniel could only stare at him as he raved, arms waving, voice rising. He brought to mind a chimpanzee, Daniel thought curiously. Minus all the fur.

"What is he talking about?" he asked, to no one in particular.

"There is no way you could have had the ace," Hugh railed. He lurched toward him, one of his arms outstretched in an unsteady accusation. "The ace should have been over . . . over . . ." He shook his hand at some spot in the general vicinity of where the table had been. "Well, you shouldn't have had it," he muttered.

"But I did," Daniel told him. Not angrily, not even defensively. Just matter-of-fact, and with a *what-else-is-there-to-say* sort of shrug.

"You couldn't," Hugh shot back. "I know every card in the deck."

It was true. Hugh always knew every card in the deck. His mind was freakishly sharp that way. He could do maths in his head, too. The complicated kind, with more than three digits and borrowing and carrying and all that rot they'd been forced to practice endlessly at school.

In retrospect, Daniel probably shouldn't have challenged him to a game. But he'd been looking for amusement, and honestly, he had expected to lose.

No one ever won a game of cards against Hugh Prentice.

Except, apparently, him.

"Remarkable," Daniel murmured, looking down at the cards. True, they were now scattered on the floor, but he knew what they were. He'd been as surprised as anyone else when he'd laid down the winning hand. "I won," he announced, even though he had a feeling he'd said as much already. He turned back to Marcus. "Fancy that."

"Are you even listening to him?" Marcus hissed. He clapped his hands in front of Daniel's face. "Wake up!"

Daniel scowled, scrunching his nose at the ringing in his ears. Really, that had been uncalled for. "I am awake," he said.

"I will have satisfaction," Hugh growled.

Daniel regarded him with surprise. "What?"

"Name your seconds."

"Are you challenging me to a duel?" Because

that was what it sounded like. But then again, he *was* drunk. And he rather thought Prentice was, too.

"Daniel," Marcus groaned.

Daniel turned. "I think he's challenging me to a duel."

"Daniel, shut *up*."

"Pfft." Daniel brushed Marcus off with a wave of his hand. He loved him like a brother, but he could be so stodgy sometimes. "Hugh," Daniel said to the furious man in front of him, "don't be an ass."

Hugh lunged.

Daniel jumped out of the way, but not fast enough, and both of them went crashing to the floor. Daniel had a good ten pounds on Hugh, but Hugh had rage, whereas Daniel just had befuddlement, and Hugh got at least four punches in before Daniel managed even his first.

And even that didn't make contact because Marcus and a few other people leapt between them, pulling them apart.

"You're a bloody cheat," Hugh rasped, struggling against the two men holding him back.

"You're an idiot."

Hugh's face darkened. "I will have my satisfaction."

"Oh, no, you won't," Daniel spat. At some point—probably when Hugh had slammed his fist into his jaw—Daniel's confusion had given way to fury. "*I* will have satisfaction."

Marcus groaned.

"The Patch of Green?" Hugh said coolly, referring to the secluded spot in Hyde Park where gentlemen sorted their differences.

Daniel's eyes leveled against his. "At dawn."

There was a hushed silence as everyone waited for either man to come to his senses.

But they didn't. Of course they didn't.

The corner of Hugh's mouth tipped up. "So be it."

"OH, BLOODY HELL," Daniel groaned. "My head hurts."

"Really," Marcus said sarcastically. "Can't imagine how that came to be."

Daniel swallowed and rubbed his good eye. The one Hugh hadn't blackened the night before. "Sarcasm doesn't become you."

Marcus ignored him. "You can still put a stop to this."

Daniel glanced around, at the trees surrounding the clearing, at the green, green grass that spread before him, all the way to Hugh Prentice and the man next to him, inspecting his gun. The sun had come up barely ten minutes earlier, and the morning dew still clung breathlessly to every surface. "It's a little late for that, don't you think?"

"Daniel, this is idiocy. You have no business shooting a pistol. You're probably still foxed from last night." Marcus looked over at Hugh with an alarmed expression. "And so is he."

"He called me a cheat."

"It's not worth dying for."

Daniel rolled his eyes. "Oh, for heaven's sake, Marcus. He's not actually going to shoot me."

Again, Marcus looked over at Hugh with concern. "I wouldn't be too sure of that."

Daniel dismissed his worries with another roll of his eyes. "He'll delope."

Marcus shook his head and walked over to meet Hugh's second in the middle of the clearing. Daniel watched as they inspected the guns and conferred with the surgeon.

Who the bloody hell thought to bring a surgeon? No one actually shot each other at these things.

Marcus came back, his expression grim, and handed Daniel his gun. "Try not to kill yourself," he muttered. "Or him."

"Will do," Daniel said, keeping his voice just jaunty enough to annoy the hell out of Marcus. He took his mark, raised his arm, and waited for the count of three.

One.

Two.

Thr—

"Bloody hell, you shot me!" Daniel yelled, looking up at Hugh with furious shock. He looked down at his shoulder, now oozing with blood. It was just a muscle wound, but good God, it hurt. And it was his shooting arm. "What the hell were you thinking?" he shouted.

Hugh just stood there staring at him like a moron, as if he hadn't realized that a bullet could draw blood.

"You bloody idiot," Daniel muttered, raising his gun to shoot back. He aimed off to the side—there was a nice, thick tree that could take a bullet—but then the surgeon came running over, blathering on about something, and as Daniel turned toward him, he slid on a damp patch, and his finger tightened on the trigger, taking the shot before he'd meant to.

Damn, the recoil hurt. Stupid—

Hugh screamed.

Daniel's skin turned to ice, and with dawning horror, he raised his eyes to the spot where Hugh had once stood.

"Oh, my God."

Marcus was already running over, as was the surgeon. There was blood everywhere, so much of it Daniel could see it seeping through the grass, even from across the clearing. His gun slipped from his fingers and he stepped forward, trancelike.

Dear God, had he just killed a man?

"Bring me my bag!" the surgeon yelled, and Daniel took another step forward. What was he supposed to do? Help? Marcus was already doing that, along with Hugh's second, and besides, hadn't Daniel just shot him?

Was that what a gentleman was supposed to do? Help a man after he put a bullet in him?

"Hold on, Prentice!" someone was pleading, and Daniel took another step, and another, until the coppery stench of blood assaulted him like a blow.

"Tie it tight," someone said.

"He'll lose the leg."

"Better than his life."

"We've got to stop the bleeding."

"Press harder."

"Stay awake, Hugh!"

"He's still bleeding!"

Daniel listened. He didn't know who was saying what, and it didn't matter. Hugh was dying, right there on the grass, and he had done it.

It had been an accident. Hugh had shot him. And the grass had been wet.

He'd slipped. Good God, did they know that he had slipped?

"I . . . I . . ." He tried to speak, but he had no words, and anyway, only Marcus heard him.

"You'd best stay back," Marcus said grimly.

"Is he . . ." Daniel tried to ask the only question that mattered, but he choked.

And then he fainted.

WHEN DANIEL CAME to, he was in Marcus's bed, a bandage wrapped tightly around his arm. Marcus sat in a nearby chair, staring out the window, which shone with the midday sun. At Daniel's waking groan, he turned sharply toward his friend.

"Hugh?" Daniel asked hoarsely.

"He's alive. Or at least he was last I heard."

Daniel closed his eyes. "What have I done?" he whispered.

"His leg is a mess," Marcus said. "You hit an artery."

"I didn't mean to." It sounded pathetic, but it was true.

"I know." Marcus turned back to the window. "You have terrible aim."

"I slipped. It was wet." He didn't know why he was even saying it. It didn't matter. Not if Hugh died.

Bloody hell, they were friends. That was the most asinine part of it all. They were friends, he and Hugh. They'd known each other for years, since their first term at Eton.

But he'd been drinking, and Hugh had been drinking, and everyone had been drinking except Marcus, who never had more than one.

"How is your arm?" Marcus asked.

"It hurts."

Marcus nodded.

"It's good that it hurts," Daniel said, looking away.

Marcus probably nodded again.

"Does my family know?"

"I don't know," Marcus replied. "If they don't, they will soon."

Daniel swallowed. No matter what happened, he would be a pariah, and it would rub off on his family. His older sisters were married, but Honoria had just made her debut. Who would have her now?

And he didn't even want to think what this would do to his mother.

"I'm going to have to leave the country," Daniel said flatly.

"He's not dead yet."

Daniel turned to him, unable to believe the plainness of the statement.

"If he lives, you won't have to leave," Marcus said.

It was true, but Daniel couldn't imagine that Hugh would pull through. He'd seen the blood. He'd seen the wound. Hell, he'd even seen the bone, laid bare for all to see.

No one survived such an injury. If the blood loss didn't kill him, infection would.

"I should go see him," Daniel finally decided, pushing back against the bed. He swung his legs over the side and had almost touched down by the time Marcus reached him.

"That's not a good idea," Marcus warned.

"I need to tell him I didn't mean it."

Marcus's brows rose. "I don't think that's going to matter."

"It matters to me."

"The magistrate may very well be there."

"If the magistrate wanted me, he would have already found me here."

Marcus considered that, then finally stepped aside and said, "You're right." He held out his arm, and Daniel took it to steady himself.

"I played cards," Daniel said in a hollow voice, "because that's what a gentleman does. And when he called me a cheat, I called him out, because that's what a gentleman does."

"Don't do this to yourself," Marcus said.

"No," Daniel said darkly. He would finish. There were some things that had to be said. He turned to Marcus with flashing eyes. "I shot to the side, because that's what a gentleman does," he said furiously. "*And I missed*. I missed, and I hit him, and now I'm going to bloody well do what a *man* does, and go to his side, and tell him I'm sorry."

"I will take you there," Marcus said. It was all there was to say.

HUGH WAS THE second son of the Marquess of Ramsgate, and he had been taken to his father's home in St. James's. It did not take long for Daniel to ascertain that he was not welcome.

"You!" thundered Lord Ramsgate, stretching out one arm to point at Daniel as if identifying the devil himself. "How dare you show your face here?"

Daniel held himself very still. Ramsgate had a right to be angry. He was in shock. He was grieving. "I came to—"

"Pay your respects?" Lord Ramsgate cut in derisively. "I'm sure you'll be sorry to hear that it's a bit early for that."

Daniel allowed himself a glimmer of hope. "Then he lives?"

"Barely."

"I would like to apologize," Daniel said stiffly.

Ramsgate's eyes, already bulbous, became impossibly huge. "Apologize? Really? You think an apology is going to save you from the gallows if my son is dead?"

"That's not why—"

"I *will* see you hang. Don't think that I won't."

Daniel did not doubt it for a second.

"It was Hugh who issued the challenge," Marcus said quietly.

"I don't care who issued the challenge," Ramsgate snapped. "My son did what he was supposed to do. He aimed wide. But you . . ." He turned on Daniel then, venom and grief pouring forth. "You shot him. Why would you do that?"

"I did not mean to."

For a moment Ramsgate did nothing but stare. "You did not mean to. *That* is your explanation?"

Daniel said nothing. It sounded weak to his own ears, as well. But it was the truth. And it was awful.

He looked to Marcus, hoping for some sort of silent advice, something to indicate what to say, how to proceed. But Marcus looked lost, too, and Daniel supposed that they would have apologized once more and departed had not the butler entered the room just then, announcing that the doctor had come down from Hugh's bedside.

"How is he?" Ramsgate demanded.

"He will live," the doctor confirmed, "provided he avoids infection."

"And the leg?"

"He will keep it. Again, if he avoids infection. But he will limp, and he may very well be lame. The bone was splintered. I set it as best I could . . ." The doctor shrugged. "There is only so much I can do."

"When will you know if he has escaped infection?" Daniel asked. He had to know.

The doctor turned. "Who are you?"

"The devil who shot my son," Ramsgate hissed.

The doctor drew back in shock, and then in self-preservation as Ramsgate stalked across the room. "You listen to me," he said malevolently, advancing until he and Daniel were nearly nose to nose. "You will pay for this. You have ruined my son. Even if he lives, he will be ruined, with a ruined leg, and a ruined life."

A cold knot of unease swirled in Daniel's chest. He knew Ramsgate was upset; he had every right to be. But something more was at work here. The marquess looked unbalanced, possessed.

"If he dies," Ramsgate hissed, "you will hang. And if he doesn't die, if you somehow escape the rule of law, I will kill you."

They were standing so close to one another that Daniel could feel the moist air that escaped Ramsgate's mouth with every word. And as he looked into the older man's glittering green eyes, he knew what it meant to be afraid.

Lord Ramsgate was going to kill him. It was only a matter of time.

"Sir," Daniel began, because he had to say something. He couldn't just stand there and take it. "I must tell you—"

"No, I'm telling you," Ramsgate spat. "I don't care who you are, or what title your godforsaken father has passed down to you. You will die. Do you understand me?"

"I think it is time we left," Marcus intervened. He put his arm between the two men and carefully widened the space between them. "Doctor," he said, nodding toward the physician as he ushered Daniel past. "Lord Ramsgate."

"Count your days, Winstead," Lord Ramsgate warned. "Or better yet, your hours."

"Sir," Daniel said again, trying to show the older man respect. He wanted to make this right. He needed to try. "I must tell you—"

"Don't speak to me," Ramsgate cut in. "There is nothing you could say that will save you now. There is no place you will be able to hide."

"If you kill him, you will hang, too," Marcus said. "And if Hugh lives, he will need you."

Ramsgate looked at Marcus as if he were an idiot. "You think I will do it myself? It's an easy thing to hire a killer. The price of a life is low indeed." He flicked his head toward Daniel. "Even his."

"I should leave," the doctor said. And he fled.

"Remember that, Winstead," Lord Ramsgate said, his eyes landing on Daniel's with venomous disdain. "You can run, and you can try to hide, but my men will find you. And you won't know who they are. So you will never see them coming."

THOSE WERE THE words that haunted Daniel for the next three years. From England to France, from France to Prussia, and from Prussia to Italy. He heard them in his sleep, in the rustle of the trees, and in every footfall that came from behind. He learned to keep his back to walls, to trust no one, not even the women with whom he occasionally took his pleasure. And he accepted the fact that he would never again step foot on English soil or see his family, until one day, to his great surprise, Hugh Prentice came limping toward him in a small village in Italy.

He knew that Hugh had lived. He received the occasional letter from home. But he hadn't expected to see him again, certainly not here, with the Mediterranean sun baking the ancient town square and cries of *arrivederci* and *buon giornio* singing through the air.

"I found you," Hugh said. He held out his hand. "I'm sorry."

And then he uttered the words Daniel never thought he'd hear:

"You can come home now. I promise."

Chapter One

For a lady who had spent the last eight years trying *not* to be noticed, Anne Wynter was in an awkward position.

In approximately one minute, she would be forced to walk onto a makeshift stage, curtsy to at least eighty members of the *crème de la crème* of London society, sit at a pianoforte, and play.

That she would be sharing the stage with three other young women was some consolation. The other musicians—members of the infamous Smythe-Smith quartet—all played stringed instruments and would have to face the audience. Anne, at least, could focus on the ivory keys and keep her head bowed. With any luck, the audience would be too focused on how horrific the music was to pay any attention to the dark-haired woman who had been forced to step in at the last minute to take the place of the pianist, who had (as her mother declared to anyone who would listen) taken dreadfully—nay, catastrophically—ill.

Anne didn't believe for one minute that Lady Sarah Pleinsworth was sick, but there wasn't anything she could do about it, not if she wanted to keep her position as governess to Lady Sarah's three younger sisters.

But Lady Sarah *had* convinced her mother, who had decided that the show must go forth. And then, after delivering a remarkably detailed seventeen-year history of the Smythe-Smith musicale, she had declared that Anne would take her daughter's place.

"You told me once that you have played bits and pieces of Mozart's Piano Quartet no. 1," Lady Pleinsworth reminded her.

Anne now regretted this, deeply.

It did not seem to matter that Anne had not played the piece in question in over eight years, or that she had never played it in its entirety. Lady Pleinsworth would entertain no arguments, and Anne had been hauled over to Lady Pleinsworth's sister-in-law's house, where the concert was to be held, and given eight hours to practice.

It was ludicrous.

The only saving grace was that the rest of the quartet was so bad that Anne's mistakes were hardly noticeable. Indeed, her only aim for the evening was that she *not* be noticeable. Because she really didn't want it. To be noticed. For any number of reasons.

"It's almost time," Daisy Smythe-Smith whispered excitedly.

Anne gave her a little smile. Daisy did not seem to realize that she made terrible music.

"Joy is mine," came the flat, miserable voice of Daisy's sister Iris. Who did realize.

"Come now," said Lady Honoria Smythe-Smith, their cousin. "This shall be wonderful. We are a family."

"Well, not her," Daisy pointed out, jolting her head toward Anne.

"She is tonight," Honoria declared. "And again, thank you, Miss Wynter. You have truly saved the day."

Anne murmured a few nonsensical words, since she couldn't quite bring herself to say that it was no trouble at all, or that it was her pleasure. She rather liked Lady Honoria. Unlike Daisy, she *did* realize how dreadful they were, but unlike Iris, she still wished to perform. It was all about family, Honoria insisted. Family and tradition. Seventeen sets of Smythe-Smith cousins had gone before them, and if Honoria had her way, seventeen more would follow. It didn't matter what the music sounded like.

"Oh, it matters," Iris muttered.

Honoria jabbed her cousin lightly with her violin bow. "Family and tradition," she reminded her. "*That* is what matters."

Family and tradition. Anne wouldn't have minded some of those. Although, really, it hadn't gone so well for her the first time around.

"Can you see anything?" Daisy asked. She was hopping from foot to foot like a frenetic magpie, and Anne had already backed up twice, just to preserve her toes.

Honoria, who was closer to the spot from which they would make their entrance, nodded. "There are a few empty seats, but not many."

Iris groaned.

"Is it like this every year?" Anne could not quite refrain from asking.

"Like what?" Honoria replied.

"Well, er . . ." There were some things one simply did not say to the nieces of one's employer. One did not, for example, make any sort of explicit comment about the lack of another young lady's musical skills. Or wonder aloud if the concerts were always this dreadful or if this year was particularly bad. And one definitely did not ask, *If the concerts are always so horrific, why do people keep coming?*

Just then fifteen-year-old Harriet Pleinsworth came skidding in through a side door. "Miss Wynter!"

Anne turned, but before she could say anything, Harriet announced, "I am here to turn your pages."

"Thank you, Harriet. That will be most helpful."

Harriet grinned at Daisy, who gave her a disdainful stare.

Anne turned away so no one would see her roll her eyes. Those two had never gotten along. Daisy took herself too seriously, and Harriet took nothing seriously.

"It's time!" Honoria announced.

Onto the stage they went, and after a brief introduction, they began to play.

Anne, on the other hand, began to pray.

Dear God, she had never worked so hard in her life. Her fingers raced across the keys, trying desperately to keep up with Daisy, who played the violin as if in a footrace.

This is ridiculous ridiculous ridiculous, Anne singsonged in her mind. It was the strangest thing, but the only way to get through it was to keep talking to herself. It was an impossibly difficult piece of music, even for accomplished players.

Ridiculous ridiculous— Ack! C-sharp! Anne flung out her right pinkie finger and hit the key just in time. Which was to say, two seconds later than it should have been.

She stole a quick glance at the audience. A woman in the front row looked ill.

Back to work back to work. Oh dear, wrong note. Never mind. No one would notice, not even Daisy.

And on she played, half wondering if she should just make up her part. It couldn't possibly make the music any worse. Daisy was flying through her section, her volume modulating between loud and extremely loud; Honoria was plodding on, each note like a determined footfall; and Iris—

Well, Iris was actually *good.* Not that it mattered.

Anne took a breath, stretching her fingers during a brief pause in the piano part. Then it was back to the keys and—

Turn the page, Harriet.

Turn the page, Harriet.

"Turn the page, Harriet!" she hissed.

Harriet turned the page.

Anne struck the first chord, then realized that Iris and Honoria were already two bars ahead. Daisy was—well, good gracious, she had no idea where Daisy was.

Anne skipped ahead to where she hoped the rest of them were. If nothing else, she'd be somewhere in the middle.

"You missed some of it," Harriet whispered.

"Doesn't matter."

And really, it didn't.

And then finally, oh *finally,* they reached a section where Anne didn't have to play for three entire pages. She sat back, let out the breath she'd been holding for, oh, it felt like ten minutes, and . . .

Saw someone.

She froze. Someone was watching them from the back room. The door through which they had entered the stage—the one which Anne was certain she'd shut with a click—was now ever so slightly ajar. And because she was the closest to the door, not to mention the only musician who didn't have her back to it, she could see a sliver of a man's face peering through.

Panic.

It burst through her, compressing her lungs, firing her skin. She knew this feeling. It didn't come often, thank God, but often enough. Every time she saw someone where someone shouldn't be . . .

Stop.

She made herself breathe. She was in the home of the dowager Countess of Winstead. She was as safe as safe could be. What she needed to do was—

"Miss Wynter!" hissed Harriet.

Anne jumped to attention.

"You missed your entrance."

"Where are we now?" Anne asked frantically.

"I don't know. I can't read music."

Despite herself, Anne looked up. "But you play the violin."

"I know," Harriet said miserably.

Anne scanned the notes on the page as fast as she could, her eyes jumping quickly from bar to bar.

"Daisy's glaring at us," Harriet whispered.

"Shhh." Anne needed to concentrate. She flipped the page, took her best guess, and brought her fingers down into G minor.

And then slid over to major. That was better.

Better being a most relative term.

For the rest of the performance she kept her head down. She didn't look up, not at the audience, not at the man watching her from the back room. She banged through the notes with as much finesse as the rest of the Smythe-Smiths, and when they were done, she stood and curtsied with her head still bowed, murmured something to Harriet about needing to tend to herself, and fled.

DANIEL SMYTHE-SMITH HADN'T planned to return to London on the day of his family's annual musicale, and indeed, his ears were wishing mightily that he hadn't, but his heart . . . well, that was another story.

It was good to be home. Even with the cacophony.

Especially with the cacophony. Nothing said "home" to a Smythe-Smith male like badly played music.

He hadn't wanted anyone to see him before the concert; he'd been gone three years, and he knew that his return would upstage the performance. The audience would probably have thanked him, but the last thing he wanted was to greet his family in front of a crowd of lords and ladies, most of whom probably thought he should have remained in exile.

But he wanted to see his family, and so as soon as he'd heard the music begin, he'd crept silently into the rehearsal room, tiptoed to the door, and opened it just a crack.

He smiled. There was Honoria, smiling that big smile of hers as she attacked her violin with her bow. She had no idea she couldn't play, poor thing. His other sisters had been the same. But he loved them for trying.

At the other violin was—good heavens, was that Daisy? Wasn't she still in the schoolroom? No, he supposed she must be sixteen by now, not yet out in society but no longer a young girl.

And there was Iris at the cello, looking miserable. And at the piano—

He paused. Who the devil was that at the piano? He leaned a little closer. Her head was down, and he couldn't see much of her face, but one thing was for certain—she was definitely *not* his cousin.

Well, now, *this* was a mystery. He knew for a fact (because his mother had told him so, many times) that the Smythe-Smith quartet was comprised of unmarried Smythe-Smith young ladies, and no one else. The family was rather proud of this, that they'd produced so many musically inclined (his mother's words, not his) female cousins. When one married, there was always another waiting to take her place. They had never needed an outsider to step in.

But more to the point, what outsider would *want* to step in?

One of his cousins must have taken ill. That could be the only explanation. He tried to remember who ought to have been at the piano. Marigold? No, she was married now. Viola? He thought he'd received a letter saying she'd married, too. Sarah? It must have been Sarah.

He shook his head. He had a ferocious lot of female cousins.

He watched the lady at the piano with some interest. She was working very hard to keep up. Her head was bobbing up and down as she glanced at the music, and every now and then she'd wince. Harriet was next to her, turning the pages at all the wrong times.

Daniel chuckled. Whoever that poor girl was, he hoped his family was paying her well.

And then, finally, she lifted her fingers from the keys as Daisy began her painful violin solo. He watched her exhale, stretching her fingers, and then . . .

She looked up.

Time stopped. It simply stopped. It was the most maudlin and clichéd way of describing it, but those few seconds when her face was lifted toward his . . . they stretched and pulled, melting into eternity.

She was beautiful. But that didn't explain it. He'd seen beautiful women before. He'd slept with plenty of them, even. But this . . . Her . . . She . . .

Even his thoughts were tongue-tied.

Her hair was lustrously dark and thick, and it didn't matter that it had been pulled back into a serviceable bun. She didn't need curling tongs or velvet ribbons. She could have scraped her hair back like a ballerina, or shaved it all off, and she'd still be the most exquisite creature he'd ever beheld.

It was her face, it had to be. Heart-shaped and pale, with the most amazing dark, winged brows. In the dusky light, he couldn't tell what color her eyes were, and that seemed a tragedy. But her lips . . .

He dearly hoped this woman was not married, because he was *going* to kiss her. The only question was when.

Then—he knew the instant it happened—she saw him. Her face jerked with a tiny gasp, and she froze, her eyes widening in alarm. He smiled wryly, shaking his head. Did she think him a madman, sneaking into Winstead House to spy on the concert?

Well, he supposed it made sense. He had spent enough time being wary of strangers to recognize the trait in someone else. She didn't know who he was, and there certainly wasn't supposed to be anyone in the back room during the performance.

The amazing thing was, she didn't look away. Her eyes held his, and he didn't move, didn't even breathe until the moment was broken by his cousin Harriet, jabbing at the dark-haired woman and presumably informing her that she'd missed her entrance.

She never looked up again.

But Daniel watched her. He watched her through every flip of the page, every *fortissimo* chord. He watched her so intently that at some point, he even ceased to hear the music. His mind played its own symphony, lush and full, sweeping toward a perfect, inevitable climax.

Which it never reached. The spell was broken when the quartet slammed out its final notes and the four ladies stood to make their curtsies. The dark-haired beauty said something to Harriet, who was beaming at the applause as if she had been a player herself, and then took off so quickly Daniel was surprised she didn't leave marks on the floor.

No matter. He'd find her.

He moved quickly through the back hallway of Winstead House. He'd sneaked out himself many times when he was a young man; he knew exactly which route someone would take to escape undetected. And sure enough, he cut her off right before she rounded the last corner toward the servants' entrance. She didn't see him right away, though, she didn't see him until—

"There you are," he said, smiling as if greeting a long-lost friend. There was nothing like an unexpected smile to set someone off balance.

She lurched with shock, and a staccato scream flew from her lips.

"Good Lord," Daniel said, clamping a hand over her mouth. "Don't do *that*. Someone will hear you."

He pulled her against him—it was the only way to keep a firm grip over her mouth. Her body was small and slight against his, and shaking like a leaf. She was terrified.

"I'm not going to hurt you," he said. "I just want to know what you're doing here." He waited for a moment, then adjusted his position so he could see her face more directly. Her eyes met his, dark and alarmed.

"Now then," he said, "if I let you go, will you be quiet?"

She nodded.

He considered this. "You're lying."

She rolled her eyes, as if to say, *What did you expect,* and he chuckled. "Who are you?" he mused.

And then the strangest thing happened. She relaxed in his arms. A little, anyway. He felt some of the tension lift away, felt her breath as it sighed into his hand.

Interesting. She hadn't been worried that he didn't know who she was. She'd been worried that he *did*.

Slowly, and with enough deliberation to make sure she knew he could change his mind at any time, he lifted his hand from her mouth. He didn't remove his arm from her waist, though. Selfish of him, he knew, but he couldn't quite bring himself to let her go.

"Who are you?" he murmured, tilting his words toward her ear.

"Who are *you*?" she returned.

He quirked a smile. "I asked you first."

"I don't speak to strangers."

He laughed at that, then twirled her around in his arms so that they were face-to-face. He knew he was behaving abominably, all but accosting the poor thing. She wasn't up to anything naughty. She'd been playing in his family's quartet, for heaven's sake. He *ought* to thank her.

But he was feeling light-headed—almost light-bodied. Something about this woman set his blood fizzing in his veins, and he was already a bit giddy at having finally reached Winstead House after weeks of travel.

He was home. *Home*. And there was a beautiful woman in his arms whom he was quite certain was *not* planning to kill him.

It had been some time since he'd savored that particular sensation.

"I think . . ." he said wonderingly. "I think I might need to kiss you."

She jerked back, not looking scared precisely, but rather puzzled. Or maybe concerned.

Smart woman. He did sound rather like a madman.

"Just a little," he assured her. "I just need to remind myself . . ."

She was silent, and then, as if she could not help herself, she asked, "Of what?"

He smiled. He liked her voice. It was comforting and round, like a good brandy. Or a summer's day.

"Of goodness," he said, and he touched her chin, tilting her face toward his. Her breath caught—he could hear the rasp of air rushing over her lips—but she did not struggle. He waited, just a moment, because if she fought him he knew he would have to let her go. But she didn't. Her eyes held his, as mesmerized by the moment as he was.

And so he kissed her. Tentatively at first, almost afraid she'd disappear in his arms. But it wasn't enough. Passion swirled to life within him and he pulled her closer, reveling in the soft press of her body against his.

She was petite, small in that way that made a man want to slay dragons. But she felt like a woman, warm and lush in all the right places. His hand ached to close around her breast, or to cup the perfect curve of her bottom. But even he would not be so bold, not with an unknown lady in his mother's house.

Still, he was not ready to let her go. She smelled like England, of soft rain and sun-kissed meadows. And she felt like the best kind of heaven. He wanted to wrap himself around, bury himself within her, and stay there for all of his days. He hadn't had a drop to drink in three years, but he was intoxicated now, bubbling with a lightness he'd never thought to feel again.

It was madness. It had to be.

"What is your name?" he whispered. He wanted to know. He wanted to know *her*.

But she did not reply. She might have done; given more time he was sure he could have teased it out of her. But they both heard someone coming down the back stairs, just down the hall from the spot where they were still locked in their embrace.

She shook her head, her eyes wide with caution. "I can't be seen like this," she whispered urgently.

He let her go, but not because she'd asked him to. Rather, he saw who was coming down the stairs— and what they were doing—and he forgot all about his dark-haired vixen.

A furious cry rose from his throat, and he took off down the hall like a madman.

Chapter Two

FIFTEEN MINUTES LATER, Anne was in the same spot she'd found herself in fifteen minutes earlier, when she'd dashed down the hall and hurled herself through the first unlocked door she'd come across. Her luck being what it was (dreadful) she had ended up in some sort of dark and windowless storage room. A brief, blind exploration revealed a cello, three clarinets, and possibly a trombone.

There was something fitting in this. She had come to the room where the Smythe-Smith musical instruments came to die. And she was stuck here, at least until the insanity in the hallway was over. She had no idea what was going on out there, except that there was a great deal of shrieking involved, rather a lot of grunting, and quite a few noises that sounded sickeningly like fist on flesh.

She could find no place to sit save the floor, so she plopped down on the cold, uncarpeted wood, leaned up against a bare patch of wall near the door, and prepared to wait out the brawl. Whatever was going on, Anne wanted no part of it, but more importantly, she wanted to be nowhere *near* it when they were discovered. Which they surely would be, given the racket they were making.

Men. They were idiots, the lot of them.

Although there seemed to be a woman out there as well—she'd be the one doing the shrieking. Anne thought she heard the name Daniel, and then possibly Marcus, who she realized had to be the Earl of Chatteris, whom she'd met earlier in the evening. He was quite besotted with Lady Honoria . . .

Come to think of it, that did sound a bit like Lady Honoria shrieking.

Anne shook her head. This was not her business. No one would fault her for staying out of the way. No one.

Someone slammed into the wall right behind her, jolting her a good two inches across the floor. She groaned and let her face fall into her hands. She was never going to get out of here. They'd find her dried-up and lifeless body years later, flung over a tuba, two flutes making the sign of the cross.

She shook her head. She had to stop reading Harriet's melodramas before bedtime. Her young charge fancied herself a writer, and her stories were growing more gruesome by the day.

Finally the pounding in the corridor stopped, and

the men slid down to the floor (she felt this; right through the wall). One of them was directly behind her; they would have been back to back had it not been for the wall between them. She could hear them breathing hard, then talking as men did, in sentences short and terse. She didn't mean to eavesdrop, but she could hardly help it, stuck as she was.

And that was when she figured it out.

The man who'd kissed her—he was Lady Honoria's older brother, the Earl of Winstead! She'd seen his portrait before; she ought to have recognized him. Or maybe not. The painting had got the basics right—his coffee brown hair and finely shaped mouth—but it did not capture him truly. He was quite handsome, there was no denying that, but no paint or brushstroke could convey the easy, elegant confidence of a man who knew his place in the world and found it quite satisfactory.

Oh, heavens, she was in deep now. She'd kissed the infamous Daniel Smythe-Smith. Anne knew all about him, everyone did. He'd dueled several years earlier and had been chased out of the country by his opponent's father. But they'd reached some sort of truce, apparently. Lady Pleinsworth had mentioned that the earl would be finally coming home, and Harriet had filled Anne in on all the gossip.

Harriet was quite helpful that way.

But if Lady Pleinsworth found out what had happened that evening . . . Well, that would be the end of Anne's governessing, for the Pleinsworth girls or anyone. Anne had had a hard enough time getting this position; no one would hire her if it got out she'd consorted with an earl. Anxious mamas generally did not hire governesses of questionable moral rectitude.

And it wasn't her fault. This time, it absolutely wasn't.

She sighed. It had gone quiet in the hall. Had they finally departed? She'd heard footsteps, but it was difficult to tell how many sets of feet had been included. She waited a few more minutes, and then, once she was certain there would be nothing but silence to greet her, she turned the doorknob and carefully stepped out into the hall.

"There you are," he said. For the second time that evening.

She must have jumped a foot. Not because Lord Winstead had surprised her, although he had done. Rather, she was astonished that he'd remained in the hall for so long in such complete silence. Truly, she hadn't heard a thing.

But that wasn't what made her jaw drop.

"You look awful," she said before she could stop herself. He was alone, sitting on the floor with his long legs stretched out across the hall. Anne hadn't thought a person could look so unsteady while sitting down, but she was quite certain that the earl would have fallen over if he hadn't been propped up against the wall.

He lifted one hand in a floppy salute. "Marcus looks worse."

She took in his eye, which was turning purple at

the perimeter, and his shirt, which was stained with blood from heaven knew where. Or whom. "I'm not certain how that can be possible."

Lord Winstead let out a breath. "He was kissing my sister."

Anne waited for more, but he clearly considered this to be explanation enough. "Ehrm . . ." she stalled, because there was no etiquette book with instruction for a night like this. In the end, she decided her best bet would be to inquire about the conclusion of the altercation, rather than whatever had occurred to cause it. "Is it all worked out, then?"

His chin dipped in a magnanimous tilt. "Congratulations will be in order very soon."

"Oh. Well. That is very nice." She smiled, then nodded, then clasped her hands together in front of her in an attempt to keep herself still. This was all terribly awkward. What was one supposed to do with an injured earl? Who'd just returned from three years in exile? And had rather a naughty reputation before he'd been run out of the country.

Not to mention the whole kissing business a few minutes earlier.

"Do you know my sister?" he asked, sounding terribly tired. "Oh, of course you do. You were playing with her."

"Your sister is Lady Honoria?" It did seem prudent to verify.

He nodded. "I am Winstead."

"Yes, of course. I had been informed of your pending return." She stretched out another awkward smile, but it did little to set her at ease. "Lady Honoria is most amiable and kind. I am very happy for her."

"She's a terrible musician."

"She was the best violinist on the stage," Anne said with complete honesty.

He laughed loudly at that. "You would do well as a diplomat, Miss . . ." He paused, waited, then pointed out, "You never did tell me your name."

She hesitated, because she always hesitated when so questioned, but then she reminded herself that he was the Earl of Winstead and thus the nephew of her employer. She had nothing to fear from him. At least not if no one saw them together. "I am Miss Wynter," she said. "Governess to your cousins."

"Which ones? The Pleinsworths?"

She nodded.

He looked her straight in the eye. "Oh, you poor, poor thing."

"Stop! They're lovely!" she protested. She adored her three charges. Harriet, Elizabeth, and Frances might be more high-spirited than most young girls, but they had good, kind hearts. And they always meant well.

His eyebrows rose. "Lovely, yes. Well-behaved, not as much."

There was some truth to that, and Anne could not suppress a tiny smile. "I'm certain they have matured greatly since you were last in their company," she said primly.

He gave her a dubious look, then asked, "How did you come to be playing the piano?"

"Lady Sarah took ill."

"Ah." There was a world of meaning in that "ah." "Do convey my wishes for a speedy recovery."

Anne was quite sure that Lady Sarah had begun to feel better the moment her mother had excused her from the concert, but she merely nodded and said that she would be sure to do so. Even though she wouldn't. There was no way she was telling anyone she'd run into the Earl of Winstead.

"Does your family know that you have returned?" she asked. She regarded him a bit more closely. He really did look quite like his sister. She wondered if he had the same remarkable eyes—a vividly pale blue, almost lavender. It was impossible to tell for sure in the dim light of the hallway. Not to mention that one of his eyes was rapidly swelling shut. "Other than Lady Honoria, of course," she added.

"Not yet." He glanced toward the public area of the house and grimaced. "Much as I adore every last soul in that audience for bringing themselves to attend the concert, I'd rather not make such a public homecoming." He looked down at his disheveled state. "Especially not like this."

"Of course not," she said quickly. She couldn't even begin to imagine the commotion were he to walk in on the post-musicale reception bruised and bloodied.

He let out a little groan as he shifted position on the floor, then muttered something beneath his breath that Anne was fairly certain she was not meant to hear. "I should go," she blurted out. "I'm terribly sorry, and . . . ehrm . . ."

She told herself to move, she really did. Every last corner of her brain was screaming at her to come to her senses and get out of there before someone came along, but all she could think was—he'd been defending his *sister.*

How could she abandon a man who did that?

"Let me help you," she said, against all better judgment.

He smiled weakly. "If you wouldn't mind."

She crouched down to get a better look at his injuries. She'd treated her share of cuts and scrapes, but never anything like this. "Where are you hurt?" she asked. She cleared her throat. "Other than the obvious spots."

"Obvious?"

"Well . . ." She pointed gingerly toward his eye. "You've a bit of a bruise there. And there . . ." she added, motioning to the left side of his jaw before moving on to his shoulder, which was visible through his ripped and bloodied shirt. " . . . and over there."

"Marcus looks worse," Lord Winstead said.

"Yes," Anne replied, biting back a smile. "You'd mentioned."

"It's an important detail." He gave her a loopy grin, then winced and brought his hand to his cheek.

"Your teeth?" she asked worriedly.

"They all seem to be in place," he mumbled. He

opened his mouth, as if testing the hinge mecha-
nism, then closed it with a groan. "I think."

"Is there someone I can get for you?" she asked.

His brows rose. "You wish for someone to know
you've been here alone with me?"

"Oh. Of course not. I wasn't thinking clearly."

He smiled again, that dry half grin that made her
feel rather squirmy on the inside. "I have that effect
on women."

Any number of retorts sprang to mind, but Anne
bit them all back. "I could help you to your feet,"
she suggested.

He cocked his head to the side. "Or you could sit
and talk to me."

She stared at him.

Again, that half smile. "It was just an idea," he
said.

An ill-advised idea, she thought immediately. She
had just kissed him, for heaven's sake. She should
not be anywhere near him, certainly not beside him
on the floor, where it would be so easy to turn to
him, and tip her face toward his . . .

"Perhaps I could find some water," she blurted
out, her words spewing forth so quickly she almost
had to cough. "Have you a handkerchief? You will
want to clean your face, I should think."

He reached in his pocket and pulled out a wrinkled square of cloth. "The finest Italian linen," he
quipped in a tired voice. He frowned. "Or at least
it once was."

"I'm sure it will be perfect," she said, taking it

from him and folding it to her liking. She reached out and dabbed it against his cheek. "Does this hurt?"

He shook his head.

"I wish I had some water. The blood has already dried." She frowned. "Have you any brandy? In a flask, perhaps?" Gentlemen often carried flasks. Her father had. He had rarely left home without it.

But Lord Winstead said, "I don't drink spirits."

Something about his tone startled her, and she looked up. His eyes were on hers, and she caught her breath. She hadn't realized how close she'd leaned in.

Her lips parted. And she wanted . . .

Too much. She had always wanted too much.

She pulled back, unsettled by how easily she'd swayed toward him. He was a man who smiled easily, and often. It didn't take more than a few minutes in his company to know this. Which was why the sharp and serious edge to his voice had transfixed her.

"But you can probably find some down the hall," he said suddenly, and the strange, captivating spell was broken. "The third door on the right. It used to be my father's study."

"At the back of the house?" It seemed an unlikely place.

"There are two entrances. The other side opens onto the main hall. There shouldn't be anyone there, but you'll want to be careful when you go in."

Anne rose to her feet and followed his directions

to the study. Moonlight filtered through the window, and she easily found a decanter. She brought the whole thing back with her, carefully shutting the door behind her.

"On the shelf by the window?" Lord Winstead murmured.

"Yes."

He smiled a bit. "Some things never change."

Anne pulled out the stopper and put the handkerchief over the vessel's opening, sloshing a healthy dose of brandy onto the cloth. The scent of it was instant and permeating. "Does that bother you?" she asked with sudden concern. "The smell?" In her last position—right before she'd come to work for the Pleinsworths—her young charge's uncle had drunk too much and then stopped. It had been monstrously difficult to be near him. His temper was even worse without the alcohol, and if he so much as smelled a hint of it, he nearly went mad.

Anne had had to leave. For that and other reasons.

But Lord Winstead just shook his head. "It's not that I *can't* drink spirits. I choose not to."

Her confusion must have shown on her face, because he added, "I have no craving for it, just disdain."

"I see," she murmured. He had secrets of his own, apparently. "This will probably sting," she warned him.

"It will *definitely* st—ow!"

"I'm sorry," she mumbled, rubbing the handkerchief lightly against his wound.

"I hope they *pour* the bloody stuff over Marcus," he muttered.

"Well, he does look worse than you do," she remarked.

He looked up, confused, and then a slow smile spread across his face. "Indeed he does."

She moved to the scrapes on his knuckles, murmuring, "I have it on the best authority."

He chuckled at that, but she didn't look up. There was something so intimate about this, bending over his hand, cleaning his wounds. She did not know this man, not really, and yet she was loath to let go of this moment. It wasn't because it was *him*, she told herself. It was just that . . . It had been so long . . .

She was lonely. She knew that. It was no great surprise.

She motioned to the cut on his shoulder and held out the handkerchief. His face and hands were one thing, but she couldn't possibly touch his *body*. "Perhaps you should . . ."

"Oh, no, don't let me stop you. I'm quite enjoying your tender ministrations."

She gave him a look. "Sarcasm does not become you."

"No," he said with an amused smile. "It never did." He watched as she slopped more brandy onto the handkerchief. "And anyway, I wasn't being sarcastic."

That was a statement she could not allow herself to examine, so she pressed the wet cloth to his shoulder and said briskly, "This will definitely sting."

"Aaaaah-*aaaaaaaaah*," he sang out, and she had to laugh. He sounded like a bad opera singer, or one of those jesters at a Punch-and-Judy show.

"You should do that more often," he said. "Laugh, I mean."

"I know." But that sounded sad, and she didn't want to be sad, so she added, "I don't often get to torture grown men, though."

"Really?" he murmured. "I would think you do it all the time."

She looked at him.

"When you walk into a room," he said softly, "the air changes."

Her hand went still, hovering an inch or so above his skin. She looked at his face—she couldn't help herself—and she saw the desire in his eyes. He wanted her. He wanted her to lean forward and touch her lips to his. It would be so easy; she need only to sway. She could tell herself she hadn't meant to do it. She'd lost her balance, that was all.

But she knew better. This wasn't her moment. And it wasn't her world. He was an earl, and she was . . . Well, she was who she'd made herself to be, and that was someone who did not consort with earls, especially those with pasts wreathed with scandal.

A bucketload of attention was about to rain down on him, and Anne wanted to be nowhere near him when that happened.

"I really do have to leave now," she told him.

"To go where?"

"Home." And then, because it seemed she ought

to say something more, she added, "I'm quite tired. It has been a very long day."

"I will escort you," he told her.

"That is not necessary."

He glanced up at her and pushed back against the wall, wincing as he rose to his feet. "How do you intend to convey yourself?"

Was this an inquisition? "I will walk."

"To Pleinsworth House?"

"It is not far."

He scowled at her. "It is too far for a lady unescorted."

"I'm a *governess*."

This seemed to amuse him. "A governess is not a lady?"

She let out an unconcealed sigh of frustration. "I will be perfectly safe," she assured him. "It is well lit the entire way back. There will probably be carriages lining the entire route."

"And yet that does not ease my mind."

Oh, but he was stubborn. "It was an honor to meet you," she said firmly. "I am sure that your family is most eager to see you again."

His hand closed over her wrist. "I cannot allow you to walk home unescorted."

Anne's lips parted. His skin was warm, and now hers was hot where he touched her. Something strange and vaguely familiar bubbled within her, and with a prickle of shock she realized it was excitement.

"Surely you understand," he murmured, and she

almost gave in. She wanted to; the girl she used to be desperately wanted to, and it had been so long since she'd opened her heart wide enough to let that girl out.

"You can't go anywhere looking as you do," she said. It was true. He looked like he'd escaped from prison. Or possibly hell.

He shrugged. "The better to go unrecognized."

"My lord . . ."

"Daniel," he corrected.

Her eyes widened with shock. "What?"

"My name is Daniel."

"I *know*. But I'm not going to use it."

"Well, that's a pity. Still, it was worth a try. Come now . . ." He held out his arm, which she did not take. "Shall we be off?"

"I'm not going with you."

He smiled rakishly. Even with one side of his mouth swollen and red, he looked like a devil. "Does that mean you're *staying* with me?"

"You've been hit in the head," she said. "It's the only explanation."

He laughed at that, then avoided it entirely. "Have you a coat?"

"Yes, but I left it in the rehearsal room. I— Don't try to change the subject!"

"Hmmm?"

"I am leaving," she stated, holding up a hand. "You are staying."

But he blocked her. His arm came out in a stiff, horizontal line, his hand connecting flat with the wall. "I might not have made myself clear," he said, and in that moment she realized that she had underestimated him. Happy-go-lucky he might be, but that was not all that he was, and right now, he was deadly serious. His voice low and fixed, he said, "There are a few things about which I will not compromise. The safety of a lady is one of them."

And that was that. He would not be budged. So with an admonishment that they must remain in the shadows and alleys where they would not be seen, she allowed him to escort her to the servants' entrance of Pleinsworth House. He kissed her hand, and she tried to pretend she did not love the gesture.

She might have fooled him. She certainly did not fool herself.

"I will call upon you tomorrow," he said, still holding her hand in his.

"What? No!" Anne yanked her hand back. "You can't."

"Can't I?"

"No. I am a governess. I can't have men calling upon me. I will lose my position."

He smiled as if the solution could not be easier. "I will call upon my cousins, then."

Was he completely ignorant of proper behavior? Or merely selfish? "I will not be home," she replied, her voice firm.

"I'll call again."

"I won't be home again."

"Such truancy. Who will instruct my cousins?"

"Not *me,* if you are loitering about. Your aunt will terminate me for sure."

"Terminate?" He chuckled. "It sounds so grisly."

"*It is*." Good heavens, she had to make him understand. It did not matter who he was, or how he made her feel. The excitement of the evening . . . the kiss they'd shared . . . these were fleeting things.

What mattered was having a roof over her head. And food. Bread and cheese and butter and sugar and all those lovely things she'd had every day of her childhood. She had them now, with the Pleinsworths, along with stability, and position, and self-respect.

She did not take these things for granted.

She looked up at Lord Winstead. He was watching her closely, as if he thought he could see into her soul.

But he did not know her. No one did. And so, wearing formality like a mantle, Anne drew back her hand and curtsied. "Thank you for your escort, my lord. I appreciate your concern for my safety." She turned her back to him and let herself in through the back gate.

It took a bit of time to sort things out once she was inside. The Pleinsworths returned only a few minutes after she did, so there were excuses to be made, pen in hand as she explained that she had been about to send a note explaining her departure from the musicale. Harriet could not stop talking about the excitement of the evening—apparently, Lord Chatteris and Lady Honoria had indeed become betrothed, in quite the most thrilling manner possible—and then Elizabeth and Frances came running downstairs, because it wasn't as if either of them had fallen asleep in the first place.

It would be two hours before Anne finally let herself into her own room, changed into her night-gown, and crawled into bed. And it would be two hours more before she could even try to fall asleep. All she could do was stare at the ceiling, and think, and wonder, and whisper.

"Annelise Sophronia Shawcross," she finally said to herself, "*what* have you got yourself into?"

Chapter Three

THE FOLLOWING AFTERNOON, despite the dowager Countess of Winstead's insistence that she did not wish to let her newly returned son out of her sight, Daniel made his way over to Pleinsworth House. He did not tell his mother *where* he was going; she would surely have insisted upon accompanying him. Instead, he told her that he had legal matters to attend to, which was true. A gentleman could not return from a three-year trip abroad without having to visit at least one solicitor. But it just so happened that the law office of Streatham and Ponce was *only* two miles in the opposite direction of Pleinsworth House. A mere trifle, really, and who could say that he wouldn't suddenly take it upon himself to visit his young cousins? It was an idea that could come to a man as easily in a carriage riding through the city as anywhere else.

The Pleinsworths' back entrance, for example.

Or the entire time he'd walked himself home.

Or in bed. He'd lain awake half the night thinking of the mysterious Miss Wynter—the curve of her cheek, the scent of her skin. He was bewitched, he freely admitted it, and he told himself that it was because he was so happy to be home. It made perfect sense that he'd find himself enchanted by such a lovely example of English womanhood.

And so after a grueling two-hour appointment with Messrs. Streatham, Ponce, *and* Beaufort-Graves (who apparently hadn't quite managed to get his name on the door yet), Daniel directed his driver to Pleinsworth House. He did want to see his cousins.

He just wanted to see their governess more.

His aunt was not at home, but his cousin Sarah was, and she greeted him with a delighted cry and a warm hug. "Why didn't anyone tell me you'd returned?" she demanded. She drew back, blinking as she got a good look at his face. "And what *happened* to you?"

He opened his mouth to reply, but she cut in with "And don't tell me you were attacked by footpads, because I heard all about Marcus's blackened eyes last night."

"He looks worse than I do," Daniel confirmed. "And as for why your family did not tell you I was back, they did not know. I did not want my arrival to interrupt the concert."

"Very thoughtful of you," she said wryly.

He looked down at her with affection. She was the same age as his sister, and growing up, it had often seemed that she'd spent as much time in his household as in her own. "Indeed," he murmured. "I watched from the rehearsal room. Imagine my surprise to see a stranger at the piano."

She put a hand to her heart. "I was ill."

"I am relieved to see that you've made a speedy recovery from death's door."

"I could barely remain upright yesterday," she insisted.

"Really."

"Oh, indeed. The vertigo, you know." She flicked her hand in the air, as if waving away her words. "It's a terrible burden."

"I'm sure people who suffer from it think so."

Her lips pressed together for a moment, then she said, "But enough of me. I assume you heard Honoria's splendid news?"

He followed her into the drawing room and took a seat. "That she is soon to be Lady Chatteris? Indeed."

"Well, I am happy for her, even if you are not," Sarah said with a sniff. "And don't say that you are, because your injuries say otherwise."

"I'm overjoyed for them both," he said firmly. "This"—his hand twirled before his face—"was merely a misunderstanding."

She gave him a dubious look, but all she said was, "Tea?"

"I would be delighted." He stood as she rose to ring for it. "Tell me, are your sisters at home?"

"Up in the schoolroom. Do you wish to see them?"

"Of course," he said immediately. "They will have grown so much in my absence."

"They'll be down soon," Sarah said, returning to the sofa. "Harriet has spies all over the house. Someone will alert them to your arrival, I'm sure."

"Tell me," he said, sitting back into a casual position, "who was that at the piano last night?"

She looked at him curiously.

"In your stead," he added unnecessarily. "Because you were ill."

"That was Miss Wynter," she replied. Her eyes narrowed suspiciously. "She is my sisters' governess."

"How fortuitous that she could play."

"A happy accident indeed," Sarah said. "I had feared the concert would be canceled."

"Your cousins would have been so disappointed," he murmured. "But this . . . what was her name again? Miss Wynter?"

"Yes."

"She knew the piece?"

Sarah leveled a frank stare in his direction. "Apparently so."

He nodded. "I should think the family owes the talented Miss Wynter a rousing round of thanks."

"She has certainly earned my mother's gratitude."

"Has she been your sisters' governess for long?"

"About a year. Why do you ask?"

"No reason. Just curiosity."

"Funny," she said slowly, "you've never been curious about my sisters before."

"That's certainly not true." He tried to gauge

how affronted he ought to appear at such a comment. "They are my cousins."

"You have an abundance of cousins."

"All of whom I missed while abroad. Absence does indeed make the heart grow fonder."

"Oh, stop," Sarah finally said, looking as if she'd like to throw up her hands in disgust. "You are fooling no one."

"I beg your pardon?" Daniel murmured, even though he had a feeling his goose was cooked.

Sarah rolled her eyes. "Do you think you are the first person to notice that our governess is absurdly gorgeous?"

He was about to think up some dry rejoinder, but he could see that Sarah was about to say, *And don't say you haven't noticed . . . ,* so instead he said, quite plainly, "No."

Because really, there was no point in saying otherwise. Miss Wynter had the kind of beauty that stopped men in their tracks. It was not a quiet sort of thing, like his sister, or Sarah, for that matter. They were both perfectly lovely, but one didn't really notice just how much until one got to know them. Miss Wynter, on the other hand . . .

A man would have to be dead not to notice her. More than dead, if such a thing were possible.

Sarah sighed, with equal parts exasperation and resignation. "It would be most tiresome if she weren't so very nice."

"Beauty does not have to be accompanied by a bad character."

She snorted. "Someone has grown quite philo-sophical while on the Continent."

"Well, you know, those Greeks and Romans. They do rub off on you."

Sarah laughed. "Oh, Daniel, do you want to ask me about Miss Wynter? Because if you do, just say so."

He leaned forward. "Tell me about Miss Wynter."

"Well." Sarah leaned forward. "There's not much to tell."

"I may throttle you," he said mildly.

"No, it's true. I know very little about her. She's not *my* governess, after all. I think she might be from somewhere in the north. She came with a ref-erence from a family in Shropshire. And another from the Isle of Man."

"The Isle of Man?" he asked in disbelief. He didn't think he knew anyone who'd even *seen* the Isle of Man. It was a fiendishly remote spot, hard to get to and with very bad weather. Or so he'd been told.

"I asked her about it once," Sarah said with a shrug. "She told me it was quite bleak."

"I would imagine."

"She does not talk about her family, although I think I heard her mention a sister once."

"Does she receive correspondence?"

Sarah shook her head. "Not that I'm aware of. And if she posts any, she does not do it from here."

He looked at her with a bit of surprise.

"Well, I would have noticed at some point," she said defensively. "At any rate, I shall not permit you to bother Miss Wynter."

"I'm not going to bother her."

"Oh, you are. I see it in your eyes."

He leaned forward. "You're quite dramatic for someone who avoids the stage."

Her eyes narrowed with suspicion. "What do you mean by that?"

"Merely that you are the picture of health."

She let out a ladylike snort. "Do you think to blackmail me? I wish you luck with that. No one believes I was ill, anyway."

"Even your mother?"

Sarah drew back.

Checkmate.

"What do you want?" she asked.

Daniel paused, the better to draw this out. Sarah's teeth were clenched just *splendidly,* and he rather thought that if he waited long enough, steam might emerge from her ears.

"Daniel . . ." she ground out.

He tilted his head as if pondering the point. "Aunt Charlotte would be so disappointed to think that her daughter was shirking her musical duties."

"I already asked you, what do you— Oh, never mind." She rolled her eyes, shaking her head as if about to pacify a three-year-old. "I might have overheard Miss Wynter this morning, planning to take Harriet, Elizabeth, and Frances for a constitutional walk in Hyde Park."

He smiled. "Have I told you recently that you are one of my very favorite cousins?"

"We are even now," she warned him. "If you say a word to my mother . . ."

"I wouldn't dream of it."

"She's already threatened to take me to the country for a week. For rest and recuperation."

He swallowed a chuckle. "She's concerned about you."

"I suppose it could be worse," Sarah said with a sigh. "I actually prefer the country, but she says we must go all the way to Dorset. I'll spend the entire time in the carriage, and then I really *will* be ill."

Sarah did not travel well. She never had.

"What is Miss Wynter's Christian name?" Daniel asked. It seemed remarkable that he didn't know it.

"You can discover that for yourself," Sarah retorted.

He decided to allow her the point, but before he could say anything, Sarah turned her head sharply toward the door. "Ah, perfect timing," she said, cutting through his words. "I do believe I hear someone coming down the stairs. Who could it possibly be, I wonder."

Daniel stood. "My dear young cousins, I'm sure." He waited until he saw one of them gallop past by the open doorway, then called out, "Oh, Harriet! Elizabeth! Frances!"

"Don't forget Miss Wynter," Sarah muttered.

The one who had walked past backed up and peered in. It was Frances, but she did not recognize him.

Daniel felt a pang in his chest. He had not expected this. And if he had, he wouldn't have thought it would make him feel quite so wistful.

But Harriet was older. She had been twelve when he'd left for the Continent, and when she poked her head into the drawing room, she shrieked his name and came running in.

"Daniel!" she said again. "You're back! Oh, you're back you're back you're back."

"I'm back," he confirmed.

"Oh, it is so lovely to see you. Frances, it's Cousin Daniel. You remember him."

Frances, who looked to be about ten now, let out a dawning, "Oooooh. You look quite different."

"No, he doesn't," remarked Elizabeth, who had come into the room behind them.

"I'm trying to be polite," Frances said out of the corner of her mouth.

Daniel laughed. "Well, *you* look different, that's for certain." He bent down and gave her a friendly chuck on the chin. "You're nearly grown."

"Oh, well, I wouldn't say that," Frances said modestly.

"She'll say everything else, though," Elizabeth said.

Frances whipped her head around like a shot. "Stop that!"

"What happened to your face?" Harriet asked.

"It was a misunderstanding," Daniel said smoothly, wondering how long it might take for his bruises to heal. He did not think he was particularly vain, but the questions were growing tiresome.

"A misunderstanding?" Elizabeth echoed. "With an anvil?"

"Oh, stop," Harriet admonished her. "I think he looks very dashing."

"As if he dashed into an anvil."

"Pay her no attention," Harriet said to him. "She lacks imagination."

"Where is Miss Wynter?" Sarah asked loudly.

Daniel gave her a smile. Good old Sarah.

"I don't know," Harriet said, glancing first over one shoulder and then the other. "She was right behind us coming down the stairs."

"One of you should fetch her," Sarah said. "She'll want to know why you've been delayed."

"Go on, Frances," Elizabeth said.

"Why do I have to go?"

"Because you *do*."

Frances stomped off, grumbling mightily.

"I want to hear all about Italy," Harriet said, her eyes sparkling with youthful excitement. "Was it terribly romantic? Did you see that tower everyone says is going to fall over?"

He smiled. "No, I didn't, but I'm told it's more stable than it looks."

"And France? Were you in Paris?" Harriet let out a dreamy sigh. "I should love to see Paris."

"I should love to shop in Paris," Elizabeth said.

"Oh, yes." Harriet looked as if she might swoon at the prospect. "*The dresses*."

"I wasn't in Paris," he told them. No need to add that he *couldn't* have gone to Paris. Lord Ramsgate had too many friends there.

"Maybe we won't have to go for our walk now," Harriet said hopefully. "I'd much rather stay here with Cousin Daniel."

"Ah, but I would rather enjoy the sunshine," he said. "Perhaps I will accompany you to the park."

Sarah snorted.

He looked over. "Something in your throat, Sarah?"

Her eyes were pure sarcasm. "I'm sure it's related to whatever it was that befell me yesterday."

"Miss Wynter says she'll wait for us in the mews," Frances announced, trotting back into the room.

"The mews?" Elizabeth echoed. "We're not riding."

Frances shrugged. "She said the mews."

Harriet let out a delighted gasp. "Maybe she has formed a *tendre* for one of the stableboys."

"Oh for heaven's sake," Elizabeth scoffed. "One of the stableboys? Really."

"Well, you must admit, it would be very exciting if she had."

"For whom? Not for her. I don't think any of them even know how to read."

"Love is blind," Harriet quipped.

"But not illiterate," Elizabeth retorted.

Daniel choked out a laugh despite himself. "Shall we be off?" he asked, giving the girls a polite bow. He held out his arm to Frances, who took it with an arch look directed at her sisters.

"Have a *jolly* time!" Sarah called out. Insincerely.

"What's wrong with *her*?" Elizabeth asked Harriet as they headed out to the mews.

"I think she's still upset about having missed the concert," Harriet replied. She looked over at Daniel. "Did you hear that Sarah missed the musicale?"

"I did," he confirmed. "Vertigo, was it?"

"I thought it was a head cold," Frances said.

"Stomach ailment," Harriet said with certainty. "But it was no matter. Miss Wynter"—she turned toward Daniel—"that's our governess," she added, her head bobbing back to her sisters, "was brilliant."

"She took Sarah's part," Frances said.

"I don't think she wanted to," Elizabeth added. "Mother had to be quite forceful."

"Nonsense," Harriet cut in. "Miss Wynter was heroic from the start. And she did a very good job. She missed one of her entrances, but other than that, she was superb."

Superb? Daniel allowed himself a mental sigh. There were many adjectives to describe Miss Wynter's piano skills, but *superb* was not one of them. And if Harriet thought so . . .

Well, she was going to fit right in when it came time for her to play in the quartet.

"I wonder what she's doing in the mews?" Harriet said as they stepped out behind the house. "Go fetch her, Frances."

Frances let out an indignant puff of air. "Why do I have to?"

"Because you *do*."

Daniel released Frances's arm. He wasn't going to argue with Harriet; he wasn't sure he could speak quickly enough to win. "I will wait right here, Frances," he told her.

Frances stomped off, only to return a minute later. Alone.

Daniel frowned. This would not do.

"She said she would be with us in a moment," Frances informed them.

"Did you tell her that Cousin Daniel is going to join us?" Harriet asked.

"No, I forgot." She shrugged. "She won't mind."

Daniel was not so sure about that. He was fairly certain that Miss Wynter had known he was in the drawing room (hence her rapid flight to the mews), but he did not think she realized that he intended to accompany them to the park.

It was going to be a lovely outing. Jolly, even.

"What do you suppose is taking her so long?" Elizabeth asked.

"She's only been a minute," Harriet replied.

"Well, now, that's not true. She was in there at least five minutes before we arrived."

"Ten," Frances put in.

"Ten?" Daniel echoed. They were making him dizzy.

"Minutes," Frances explained.

"It wasn't ten."

He wasn't sure who'd spoken that time.

"Well, it wasn't five."

Or that time.

"We can settle for eight, but I think it's inaccurate."

"Why do you talk so quickly?" Daniel had to ask.

They paused, all three of them, and regarded him with similarly owlish expressions.

"We're not talking quickly," Elizabeth said.

Added Harriet: "We always talk this way."

And then finally Frances informed him, "Everyone else understands us."

It was remarkable, Daniel thought, how three young girls could reduce him to speechlessness.

"I wonder what's taking Miss Wynter so long," Harriet mused.

"I'll get her this time," Elizabeth declared, shooting a look at Frances that said she found her to be ineffectual in the extreme.

Frances just shrugged.

But just as Elizabeth reached the entrance to the mews, out stepped the lady in question, looking very much like a governess in her practical dove gray day dress and matching bonnet. She was pulling on her gloves, frowning at what Daniel could only imagine was a hole in the seam.

"This must be Miss Wynter," he said loudly, before she saw him.

She looked up but quickly masked her alarm.

"I have heard such splendid things about you," he said in a grand voice, stepping forward to offer her his arm. When she took it—reluctantly, he was sure—he leaned down and murmured, so that only she could hear, "Surprised?"

Chapter Four

S HE WASN'T SURPRISED.

Why would she be surprised? He had told her he would be here, even when she had said she would not be at home when he called. He had told her he would be there again, even when she'd told him *again* that she wouldn't be at home.

Again.

He was the Earl of Winstead. Men of his position did as they pleased. When it came to women, she thought irritably, men *below* his position did as they pleased.

He was not a malicious man, nor even truly selfish. Anne liked to think she had become a good judge of character over the years, certainly better than she'd been at sixteen. Lord Winstead was not going to seduce anyone who didn't know what she was doing, and he wasn't going to ruin or threaten or blackmail or any of those things, at least not on purpose.

If she found her life upended by this man it would not be because he'd meant to do it. It would simply happen because he fancied her and he wanted her to fancy him. And it would never occur to him that he should not allow himself to pursue her.

He was allowed to do anything else. Why not that?

"You should not have come," she said quietly as they walked to the park, the three Pleinsworth daughters several yards ahead of them.

"I wished to see my cousins," he replied, all innocence.

She glanced at him sideways. "Then why are you lagging behind with me?"

"Look at them," he said, motioning with his hand. "Would you have me shove one of them into the street?"

It was true. Harriet, Elizabeth, and Frances were walking three across along the pavement, oldest to youngest, the way their mother liked for them to promenade. Anne could not believe they had chosen this day to finally follow directions.

"How is your eye?" she asked. It looked worse in the harsh light of day, almost as if the bruise was melting across the bridge of his nose. But at least now she knew what color his eyes were—light, bright blue. It was almost absurd how much she had wondered about that.

"It's not so bad as long as I don't touch it," he told her. "If you would endeavor not to throw stones at my face, I would be much obliged."

"All my plans for the afternoon," she quipped. "Ruined. Just like that."

He chuckled, and Anne was assaulted by memory. Not of anything specific, but of herself, and how lovely it had felt to flirt, and laugh, and bask in the regard of a gentleman.

The flirting had been lovely. But not the consequences. She was still paying for those.

"The weather is fine," she said after a moment.

"Have we already run out of things to say?"

His voice was light and teasing, and when she turned to steal a glance at his face, he was looking straight ahead, a small, secret smile touching his lips.

"The weather is *very* fine," she amended.

His smile deepened. So did hers.

"Shall we go to The Serpentine?" Harriet called out from up ahead.

"Anywhere you wish," Daniel said indulgently.

"Rotten Row," Anne corrected. When he looked at her with raised brows, she said, "I am still in charge of them, am I not?"

He saluted her with a nod, then called out, "Anywhere Miss Wynter wishes."

"We're not doing maths again?" Harriet lamented.

Lord Winstead looked at Anne with unconcealed curiosity. "Mathematics? On Rotten Row?"

"We have been studying measurement," she informed him. "They have already measured the average length of their strides. Now they will count their steps and compute the length of the path."

"Very nice," he said approvingly. "And it keeps them busy and quiet as they count."

"You have not heard them count," Anne told him.

He turned to her with some alarm. "Don't say they don't know how?"

"Of course not." She smiled; she could not help herself. He looked so ridiculous with his one surprised eye. The other was still too swollen to register much of any emotion. "Your cousins do everything with great flair," she told him. "Even counting."

He considered this. "So what you are saying is, in five or so years, when the Pleinsworths have taken over the Smythe-Smith quartet, I should endeavor to be far, far away?"

"I should never say such a thing," she replied. "But I will tell you this: Frances has elected to break with tradition and has taken up the contrabassoon."

He winced.

"Indeed."

And then they laughed, the both of them. Together.

It was a marvelous sound.

"Oh, girls!" Anne called out, because she could not resist. "Lord Winstead is going to join you."

"I am?"

"He is," Anne confirmed, as the girls came trotting back. "He told me himself that he is most interested in your studies."

"Liar," he murmured.

She ignored the gibe, but when she allowed herself a smirky half smile, she made sure the upturned side of her mouth was facing him. "Here is what we shall do," she said. "You shall measure the length of the path as we discussed, multiplying the number of your strides times the length."

"But Cousin Daniel doesn't know the length of his stride."

"Precisely. That is what makes the lesson so much better. Once you have determined the length of the path, you must work backwards to determine the length of his stride."

"*In our heads?*"

She might as well have said they must learn to wrestle an octopus. "It is the only way to learn how to do it," she told them.

"I have great love for pen and ink myself," Lord Winstead remarked.

"Don't listen to him, girls. It is extremely useful to be able to do sums and tables in your head. Just think of the applications."

They just stared at her, all four of them. Applications, apparently, were not jumping to mind.

"Shopping," Anne said, hoping to appeal to the girls. "Mathematics is of tremendous help when one goes shopping. You're not going to carry pen and paper with you when you go to the milliner's, are you?"

Still, they stared. Anne had a feeling they had never so much as inquired about price at the milliner's, or any establishment, for that matter.

"What about games?" she tried. "If you sharpen your arithmetic skills, there is no telling what you can achieve in a game of cards."

"You have no idea," Lord Winstead murmured.

"I don't think our mother wants you to teach us how to gamble," Elizabeth said.

Anne could hear the earl chortling with amusement beside her.

"How do you intend to verify our results?" Harriet wanted to know.

"That is a very good question," Anne replied, "and one that I will answer tomorrow." She paused for precisely one second. "When I have figured out how I am going to do it."

All three girls tittered, which had been her intention. There was nothing like a little self-deprecating humor to regain control of the conversation.

"I shall have to return for the results," Lord Winstead remarked.

"There is no need for that," Anne said quickly. "We can send them over with a footman."

"Or we could walk," Frances suggested. She turned to Lord Winstead with hopeful eyes. "It's not very far to Winstead House, and Miss Wynter does love to make us take walks."

"Walking is healthful for the body and mind," Anne said primly.

"But far more enjoyable when one has company," Lord Winstead said.

Anne took a breath—the better to hold back a retort—and turned to the girls. "Let us begin," she said briskly, directing them to the top of the path. "Start over there and then make your way down. I shall wait right there on that bench."

"You're not coming?" Frances demanded. She gave Anne the sort of look normally reserved for those found guilty of high treason.

"I wouldn't want to get in your way," Anne demurred.

"Oh, but you would not *be* in the way, Miss Wynter," said Lord Winstead. "The path is very wide."

"Nevertheless."

"Nevertheless?" he echoed.

She gave a crisp nod.

"Hardly a rebuttal worthy of London's finest governess."

"A lovely compliment to be sure," she volleyed, "but unlikely to spur me to battle."

He stepped toward her, murmuring, "Coward."

"Hardly," she returned, managing to respond without even moving her lips. And then, with a bright smile: "Come along, girls, let's get started. I shall remain here for a moment to help you begin."

"I don't need help," Frances grumbled. "I just need to not have to *do* it."

Anne just smiled. She knew that Frances would be boasting of her steps and calculations later that evening.

"You, too, Lord Winstead." Anne gazed at him with her most benign expression. The girls were already moving forward, unfortunately at differing speeds, which meant that a cacophony of numbers filled the air.

"Oh, but I can't," he said. One of his hands fluttered up to rest over his heart.

"Why can't you?" Harriet asked, at the same moment that Anne said, "Of course you can."

"I feel dizzy," he said, and it was such an obvious clanker that Anne could not help but roll her eyes. "It's true," he insisted. "I have the . . . oh, what was it that befell poor Sarah . . . the vertigo."

"It was a stomach ailment," corrected Harriet, and she took a discreet step back.

"You didn't seem dizzy before," Frances said.

"Well, that was because I wasn't closing my eye."

That silenced all of them.

And then finally: "I beg your pardon?" From Anne, who really did want to know what closing his eye had to do with anything.

"I always close my eye when I count," he told her. With a completely straight face.

"You always— Wait a moment," Anne said suspiciously. "You close *one* of your eyes when you count?"

"Well, I could hardly close both."

"Why not?" Frances asked.

"I wouldn't be able to see," he said, as if the answer were plain as day.

"You don't need to be able to *see* to count," Frances replied.

"I do."

He was lying. Anne could not believe the girls

weren't howling in protest. But they weren't. In fact, Elizabeth looked utterly fascinated. "Which eye?" she asked.

He cleared his throat, and Anne was fairly certain she saw him wink each of his eyes, as if to remember which was the injured party. "The right one," he finally decided.

"Of course," Harriet said.

Anne looked at her. "What?"

"Well, he's right-handed, isn't he?" Harriet looked to her cousin. "Aren't you?"

"I am," he confirmed.

Anne looked from Lord Winstead to Harriet and back again. "And this is relevant because . . . ?"

Lord Winstead gave her a tiny shrug, saved from having to answer by Harriet, who said, "It just *is*."

"I'm sure I could take on the challenge next week," Lord Winstead said, "once my eye has healed. I don't know why it did not occur to me that I would lose my sense of balance with only the swollen eye to look through."

Anne's eyes—both of them—narrowed. "I thought one's balance was affected by one's hearing."

Frances gasped. "Don't tell me he's going *deaf*?"

"He's not going deaf," Anne retorted. "Although *I* might, if you yell like that again. Now, get going, the three of you, and carry on with your work. I'm going to sit down."

"As am I," Lord Winstead said jauntily. "But I shall be with you three in spirit."

The girls went back to their counting, and Anne

strode over to the bench. Lord Winstead was right behind her, and as they sat she said, "I can't believe they believed that nonsense about your eye."

"Oh, they didn't believe it," he said nonchalantly. "I told them earlier I'd give them a pound each if they endeavored to give us a few moments alone."

"What?" Anne screeched.

He doubled over laughing. "Of course I didn't. Good heavens, do you think me a complete dunce? No, don't answer that."

She shook her head, annoyed with herself for having been such an easy mark. Still, she couldn't be angry; his laughter was far too good-natured.

"I'm surprised no one has come over to greet you," she said. The park was not any more crowded than usual for this time of day, but they were hardly the only people out for a stroll. Anne knew that Lord Winstead had been an extremely popular gentleman when he'd lived in London; it was hard to believe that no one had noticed his presence in Hyde Park.

"I don't think it was common knowledge that I planned to return," he said. "People see what they expect to see, and no one in the park expects to see me." He gave her a rueful half grin and glanced up and to the left, as if motioning to his swollen eye. "Especially not in this condition."

"And not with me," she added.

"Who *are* you, I wonder?"

She turned, sharply.

"That's quite a reaction for so basic a question," he murmured.

"I am Anne Wynter," she said evenly. "Governess to your cousins."

"Anne," he said softly, and she realized he was savoring her name like a prize. He tilted his head to the side. "Is it Wynter with an *i* or a *y*?"

"*Y*. Why?" And then she couldn't help but chuckle at what she'd just said.

"No reason," he replied. "Just my natural curiosity." He was silent for a bit longer, then said, "It doesn't suit you."

"I beg your pardon?"

"Your name. Wynter. It does not suit you. Even with the *y*."

"We are rarely given the choice of our names," she pointed out.

"True, but still, I have often found it interesting how well some of us are suited to them."

She could not hide an impish smile. "What, then, does it mean to be a Smythe-Smith?"

He sighed, with perhaps *too* much drama. "I suppose we were doomed to perform the same musicale over and over and over . . ."

He looked so despondent she had to laugh. "Whatever do you mean by that?"

"It's a bit repetitive, don't you think?"

"Smythe-Smith? I think there is something rather friendly about it."

"Hardly. One would think if a Smythe married a Smith, they might be able to settle their differences and pick a name rather than saddling the rest of us with both."

Anne chuckled. "How long ago was the name hyphenated?"

"Several hundred years." He turned, and for a moment she forgot his scrapes and his bruises. She saw only him, watching her as if she were the only woman in the world.

She coughed, using it to mask her tiny motion away from him on the bench. He was dangerous, this man. Even when they were sitting in a public park, talking about nothing of great importance, she felt him.

Something within her had been awakened, and she desperately needed to shut it back away.

"I've heard conflicting stories," he said, seemingly oblivious to her turmoil. "The Smythes had the money and the Smiths had the position. Or the romantic version: The Smythes had the money *and* the position but the Smiths had the beautiful daughter."

"With hair of spun gold and eyes of cerulean blue? It sounds rather like an Arthurian legend."

"Hardly. The beautiful daughter turned out to be a shrew." He tilted his head to her with a dry grin. "Who did not age well."

Anne laughed, despite herself. "Why did the family not cast off the name, then, and go back to being Smythes?"

"I have no idea. Perhaps they signed a contract. Or someone thought we sounded more dignified with an extra syllable. At any rate, I don't even know if the story is true."

She laughed again, gazing out over the park to watch the girls. Harriet and Elizabeth were bickering over something, probably nothing more than a blade of grass, and Frances was powering on, taking giant steps that were going to ruin her results. Anne knew she should go over to correct her, but it was so pleasant to sit on the bench with the earl.

"Do you like being a governess?" he asked.

"Do I like it?" She looked at him with furrowed brow. "What an odd question."

"I can't think of anything less odd, considering your profession."

Which showed just how much he knew about having a job. "No one asks a governess if she likes being one," she said. "No one asks that of anyone."

She'd thought that would be the end of it, but when she glanced back at his face, he was watching her with a true and honest curiosity.

"Have you ever asked a footman if he likes being one?" she pointed out. "Or a maid?"

"A governess is hardly a footman or a maid."

"We are closer than you think. Paid a wage, living in someone else's house, always one misstep away from being tossed in the street." And while he was pondering that, she turned the tables and asked, "Do *you* like being an earl?"

He thought for a moment. "I have no idea." At her look of surprise, he added, "I haven't had much chance to know what it means. I held the title for barely a year before I left England, and I'm ashamed to say I didn't do much with it during that time. If the earldom is thriving, it is due to my father's excellent stewardship, and his foresight in appointing several capable managers."

Still, she persisted. "But you still *were* the earl. It did not matter what land you stood upon. When you made an acquaintance you said, 'I am Winstead,' not 'I am Mr. Winstead.'"

He looked at her frankly. "I made very few acquaintances while I was abroad."

"Oh." It was a remarkably odd statement, and she did not know how to respond. He didn't say anything more, and she did not think she could bear the touch of melancholy that had misted over them, so she said, "I *do* like being a governess. To them, at least," she clarified, smiling and waving at the girls.

"I take it this is not your first position," he surmised.

"No. My third. And I have also served as a companion." She wasn't sure why she was telling him all this. It was more of herself than she usually shared. But it wasn't anything he could not discover by quizzing his aunt. All of her previous positions had been disclosed when Anne had applied to teach the Pleinsworth daughters, even the one that had not ended well. Anne strove for honesty whenever possible, probably because it so often *wasn't* possible. And she was most grateful that Lady Pleinsworth had not thought less of her for having departed a position where every day had ended with her having to barricade her door against her students' father.

Lord Winstead regarded her with an oddly penetrating stare, then finally said, "I still don't think you're a Wynter," he said.

How odd that he seemed so stuck on the idea. Still, she shrugged. "There is not much for me to do about it. Unless I marry." Which, as they both knew, was an unlikely prospect. Governesses rarely had the opportunity to meet eligible gentlemen of their own station. And Anne did not want to marry, in any case. It was difficult to imagine giving any man complete control over her life and her body.

"Look at that lady, for example," he said, motioning with his head toward a woman who was disdainfully dodging Frances and Elizabeth as they leapt across the path. "She looks like a Wynter. Icy blond, cold of character."

"How can you possibly judge her character?"

"Some dissembling on my part," he admitted. "I used to know her."

Anne didn't even want to think about what that meant.

"I think you're an autumn," he mused.

"I would rather be spring," she said softly. To herself, really.

He did not ask her why. She didn't even think about his silence until later, when she was in her small room, remembering the details of the day. It was the sort of statement that begged for explanation, but he hadn't asked. He'd known not to.

She wished he *had* asked. She wouldn't have liked him so well if he had.

And she had a feeling that liking Daniel Smythe-

Smith, the equal parts famous and infamous Earl of Winstead, could lead only to downfall.

As DANIEL WALKED home that evening, after having stopped by Marcus's house to convey his formal congratulations, he realized that he could not recall the last time he had so enjoyed an afternoon.

He supposed this was not such a difficult achievement; he had spent the last three years of his life in exile, after all, frequently on the run from Lord Ramsgate's hired thugs. It was not an existence that lent itself to lazy outings and pleasant, aimless conversation.

But that was what his afternoon had turned out to be. While the girls counted their steps along Rotten Row, he and Miss Wynter had sat and chatted, talking about very little in particular. And all the time he could not stop thinking how very much he'd wanted to take her hand.

That was all. Just her hand.

He would bring it to his lips, and bow his head in tender salute. And he would have known that that simple, chivalrous kiss would be the beginning of something amazing.

That was why it would have been enough. Because it would be a promise.

Now that he was alone with his thoughts, his mind wandered to everything that promise might hold. The curve of her neck, the lush intimacy of her undone hair. He could not recall wanting a woman this way. It went beyond mere desire. His need for her went deeper than his body. He wanted to worship her, to—

The blow came out of nowhere, clipping him below his ear, sending him tumbling back against a lamppost.

"What the hell?" he grunted, looking up just in time to see two men lunging toward him.

"Aye, there's a good guv," one of them said, and as he moved, snakelike in the misty air, Daniel saw the glint of a knife, flashing in the lamplight.

Ramsgate.

These were his men. They had to be.

Damn it, Hugh had promised him it was safe to return. Had Daniel been a fool to believe him, so desperate to go home he'd not been able to bring himself to see the truth?

Daniel had learned how to fight dirty and mean in the last three years, and while the first of his attackers lay curled on the pavement from a kick to the groin, the other was forced to wrestle for control of the knife.

"Who sent you?" Daniel growled. They were face-to-face, almost nose to nose, their arms stretched high as they both strained for the weapon.

"I jest want yer coin," the ruffian said. He smiled, and his eyes held a glittery sheen of cruelty. "Give me yer money, and we'll all walk away."

He was lying. Daniel knew this as well as he knew how to draw breath. If he let go of the man's wrists, even for one moment, that knife would be plunged between his ribs. As it was, he had only moments before the man on the ground regained his equilibrium.

"Hey now! What's going on here?"

Daniel flicked his eyes across the street for just long enough to see two men running out from a public house. His attacker saw them, too, and with a jerk of his wrists, he flung the knife into the street. Twisting and shoving, he freed himself from Daniel's grasp and took off running, his friend scrambling behind him.

Daniel sprinted after them, determined to capture at least one. It would be the only way he would get any answers. But before he reached the corner, one of the men from the pub tackled him, mistaking him for one of the criminals.

"Damn it," Daniel grunted. But there was no use in cursing the man who'd knocked him to the street. He knew he might well be dead if not for his intervention.

If he wanted answers, he was going to have to find Hugh Prentice.

Now.

Chapter Five

Hugh lived in a small set of apartments in The Albany, an elegant building that catered to gentlemen of exceptional birth and modest means. Hugh certainly could have remained in his father's enormous manse, and in fact Lord Ramsgate had tried everything short of blackmail to force him to stay, but as Hugh had told Daniel on the long journey home from Italy, he no longer spoke to his father.

His father, unfortunately, still spoke to him.

Hugh was not home when Daniel arrived, but his valet was, and he showed Daniel to the sitting room, assuring him that Hugh was expected to return shortly.

For nearly an hour Daniel paced the room, going over every detail of the attack. It hadn't been the best lit of London streets, but it certainly wasn't considered one of the more dangerous. Then again, if a thief wanted to capture a heavy purse, he would need to venture beyond the rookeries of St. Giles and Old Nichol. Daniel would not have been the first gentleman to be robbed so close to Mayfair and St. James's.

It could have been a simple robbery. Couldn't it? They had said they wanted his money. It could have been the truth.

But Daniel had spent too long looking over his shoulder to accept the simple explanation for anything. And so when Hugh finally let himself into his rooms, Daniel was waiting for him.

"Winstead," Hugh said immediately. He did not appear to be surprised, but then again, Daniel didn't think he had ever seen Hugh appear surprised. He had always had the most remarkably expressionless face. It was one of the reasons he'd been so unbeatable at cards. That and his freakish aptitude for numbers.

"What are you doing here?" Hugh asked. He closed the door behind himself and limped in, leaning heavily on his cane. Daniel forced himself to watch his progress. When they had first met up again, back in Italy, it had been difficult for Daniel to watch Hugh's painful gait, knowing that he was the cause of it. Now he bore witness as a sort of penance, although after what had happened to him that very evening, he was not certain it was a penance he deserved.

"I was attacked," Daniel said curtly.

Hugh went still. Slowly, he turned, his eyes carefully sweeping from Daniel's face, to his feet, and back again. "Sit," he said abruptly, and he motioned to a chair.

Daniel's blood was rushing far too quickly to take a seat. "I would rather stand."

"Excuse me, then, if I sit," Hugh said with a self-deprecating twist of his lips. He made his way over to a chair, awkwardly, and then lowered himself down. When he finally took his weight off his bad leg, he sighed with audible relief.

This, he was not faking. He might be lying about other things, but not this. Daniel had seen Hugh's leg. It was twisted and puckered, its very existence an improbable feat of medicine. That he could put any weight on it at all was a miracle.

"Do you mind if I have drink?" Hugh inquired. He rested his cane on a table and then began to knead the muscles in his leg. He did not bother to hide his pain from his face. "It's over there," he winced, jerking his head toward a cabinet.

Daniel crossed the room and extracted a bottle of brandy. "Two fingers?" he asked.

"Three. Please. It's been a long day."

Daniel poured the drink and brought it over. He had not touched alcohol since that fateful drunken night, but then again, he did not have a shattered leg that needed numbing.

"Thank you," Hugh said, his voice somewhere between a groan and a whisper. He took a long swallow, and then another, closing his eyes as the fire rolled down his throat. "There," he said, once he'd regained his composure. He set the glass down and looked up. "I was told that your injuries came at the hands of Lord Chatteris."

"That was something else," Daniel said dismissively. "I was attacked by two men as I was walking home this evening."

Hugh straightened, his eyes sharpening. "Did they say anything?"

"They demanded money."

"But did they know your name?"

Daniel shook his head. "They did not say it."

Hugh was silent for a long moment, then said, "It's possible they were ordinary footpads."

Daniel crossed his arms and stared at him.

"I told you that I extracted a promise from my father," Hugh said quietly. "He will not touch you."

Daniel wanted to believe him. In fact, he did believe him. Hugh had never been a liar. Nor did he possess a vengeful nature. But was it possible Hugh had been duped?

"How do I know your father can be trusted?" Daniel asked. "He has spent the last three years in the pursuit of my death."

"And I have spent the last three years convincing him that this"—Hugh curled his lip and waved his hand over his ruined leg—"was as much my fault as yours."

"He would never believe that."

"No," Hugh agreed. "He is a stubborn ass. He always has been."

It was not the first time Daniel had heard Hugh refer to his father in such terms, but still, he was taken aback. There was something about the plainness of Hugh's tone that was unnerving.

"How can I know that I will be safe?" Daniel demanded. "I returned to England on the strength of your word, on your belief that your father would honor his promise. If something happens to me, or if, God help you, any member of my family, I will hunt you down to the ends of the earth."

Hugh did not need to point out that if Daniel was killed, there would be no hunting to be done.

"My father signed a contract," Hugh said. "You have seen it."

Daniel even possessed a copy. So did Hugh and Lord Ramsgate, and Hugh's solicitor, who was under strict instructions to keep it under lock and key. But still . . .

"He would not be the first man to disregard a signed document," Daniel said in a low voice.

"Indeed." Hugh's face was pinched, and there was a long-standing look to the shadows under his eyes. "But he will not disregard this one. I have made sure of it."

Daniel thought of his family, of his sister and mother, and his rollicking, giggling Pleinsworth cousins, whom he was just beginning to know again. And he thought of Miss Wynter, her face springing to the forefront of his mind. If something happened to him before he had the chance to know her . . .

If something happened to *her* . . .

"I need to know how you can be so certain," Daniel said, his voice dropping into a furious hush.

"Well . . ." Hugh brought his glass to his lips and took something deeper than a sip. "If you must know, I told him that if anything happens to you, I would kill myself."

If Daniel had been holding anything, anything at all, it would have crashed to the ground. It was a remarkable thing that *he* did not crash to the ground.

"My father knows me well enough to know that I do not say such a thing lightly," Hugh said, lightly.

Daniel couldn't speak.

"So if you would . . ." Hugh took another drink, this time barely touching his lips to the liquid. "I would appreciate if you would endeavor not to get yourself killed in an unhappy accident. I'm sure to blame it on my father, and honestly, I'd rather not see myself off unnecessarily."

"You're mad," Daniel whispered.

Hugh shrugged. "Sometimes I think so. My father would certainly agree."

"Why would you do such a thing?" Daniel could not imagine anyone else—not even Marcus, who was truly a brother to him—making the same sort of threat.

Hugh was silent for a very long while, the unfocused stare of his eyes broken only by the occasional blink. Finally, just when Daniel was sure that he would never answer, he turned and said, "I was stupid when I called you a cheat. I was drunk. And I believe you were drunk, too, and I did not believe you had the ability to beat me."

"I didn't," Daniel said. "All I had was luck."

"Yes," Hugh agreed. "But I don't believe in luck. I never have. I believe in skill, and even more in judgment, but I had no judgment that night. Not with cards, and not with people."

Hugh looked at his glass, which was empty. Daniel thought about offering to refill it, then decided that Hugh would ask if that was what he wanted.

"It was my fault that you had to leave the country," Hugh said, setting his glass on the table next to him. "I could not live with myself any longer, knowing that I had ruined your life."

"But I have also ruined yours," Daniel said quietly.

Hugh smiled, but it only touched one side of his mouth, and neither of his eyes. "It's just a leg."

But Daniel didn't believe him. He didn't think Hugh believed himself, either.

"I will see to my father," Hugh said, bringing a briskness to his tone that signaled their interview was coming to an end. "I do not believe he would be foolish enough to have been responsible for what happened to you this evening, but just in case, I shall remind him of my threat."

"You will inform me of the outcome of the meeting?"

"Of course."

Daniel made his way to the door, and as he turned to say good-bye, he saw that Hugh was struggling to rise to his feet. His tongue touched the top of his mouth, ready to say, *Don't,* but he bit back the word. Every man needed his pride.

Hugh reached out and grasped his cane, then made his achingly slow progress across the room to see Daniel out. "Thank you for coming this evening," Hugh said. He held out his hand, and Daniel took it.

"I am proud to call you my friend," Daniel said. He left then, but not before he saw Hugh turn swiftly away, his eyes wet with tears.

THE FOLLOWING AFTERNOON, after spending the morning in Hyde Park doing three remeasurements of Rotten Row, Anne sat at a writing desk in the Pleinsworth sitting room, tickling her chin with the feather of her quill as she considered which items to put on her to-do list. It was her afternoon free, and she'd been looking forward all week to running errands and shopping. Not that she ever had much to purchase, but she rather enjoyed poking about in shops. It was lovely to have a few moments during which she had responsibility for no one but herself.

Her preparations, however, were interrupted by the arrival of Lady Pleinsworth, who came sailing into the room in a swish of pale green muslin. "We leave tomorrow!" she announced.

Anne looked up, thoroughly confused, then stood. "I beg your pardon?"

"We cannot remain in London," Lady Pleinsworth said. "Rumors are flying."

They were? About what?

"Margaret told me that she has heard talk that Sarah was not actually ill on the night of the musicale and was instead trying to spoil the concert."

Anne did not know who Margaret was, but it could not be denied that the lady was well informed.

"As if Sarah would *do* such a thing," Lady Pleinsworth continued. "She is such a superior musician. And a dutiful daughter. She looks forward to the musicale all year."

There was no comment Anne could make about that, but fortunately for her, Lady Pleinsworth did not seem to require a response.

"There is only one way to combat these vicious lies," she continued, "and that is to leave town."

"To leave town?" Anne echoed. It seemed extreme. The season was just getting underway, and she'd thought that their main objective was to find a husband for Lady Sarah. Which they were unlikely to do back in Dorset, where the Pleinsworths had lived for seven generations.

"Indeed." Lady Pleinsworth let out a brisk sigh. "I know that Sarah *looks* as if her health has improved, and perhaps it has. But as far as the rest of the world is concerned, she must be at death's door."

Anne blinked, trying to follow the countess's logic. "Wouldn't that require the services of a physician?"

Lady Pleinsworth waved this off. "No, just healthful country air. Everyone knows one can't properly convalesce in the city."

Anne nodded, secretly relieved. She preferred life in the country. She had no connections in the southwest of England, and she liked it that way. Plus there was the complication of her infatuation with Lord Winstead. It behooved her to nip that squarely in the bud, and two hundred miles of countryside between the two of them seemed the best way to do it. Setting down her pen, she asked Lady Pleinsworth, "How long will we be in Dorset?"

"Oh, we're not going to Dorset. And thank heavens for that. It's such a grueling journey. We'd have to stay at least a fortnight for anyone to think Sarah had got the least bit of rest and respite."

"Then wh—"

"We're going to Whipple Hill," Lady Pleinsworth announced. "It is only near Windsor. It won't even require a full day to get there."

Whipple Hill? Why did that sound familiar?

"Lord Winstead suggested it."

Anne suddenly began to cough.

Lady Pleinsworth regarded her with some concern. "Are you quite well, Miss Wynter?"

"Just . . . ehrm . . . some . . . ehrm ehrm . . . dust in my throat. I think."

"Well, do sit down, if you think it will help. There is no need to stand on ceremony with me, at least not at the moment."

Anne nodded gratefully and retook her seat. Lord Winstead. She should have known.

"It is an ideal solution for us all," Lady Pleinsworth continued. "Lord Winstead wants to leave London, too. The notoriety, you know. Word is getting out that he has returned, and he will be deluged with callers. Who can blame the man for desiring a peaceful reunion with his family?"

"Then he will be accompanying us?" Anne asked carefully.

"Of course. It is his property. It would seem odd if we traveled there without him, even if I *am* his favorite aunt. I believe his sister and mother will be coming as well, although I am not certain." Lady Pleinsworth paused for breath, looking quite satisfied with the recent turn of events. "Nanny Flanders will supervise the packing for the girls, since it is your afternoon free. But if you would look everything over when you return, I would be most appreciative. Nanny is a dear, but she is getting on in years."

"Of course," Anne murmured. She adored Nanny, but she'd long since gone a bit deaf. Anne had always admired Lady Pleinsworth for keeping her on, but then again, she had been nurse to Lady Pleinsworth as a child, *and* Lady Pleinsworth's mother.

"We will be gone for a week," Lady Pleinsworth continued. "Please make sure you pack enough lessons to keep the girls busy."

A week? At the home of Lord Winstead? With Lord Winstead in residence?

Anne's heart sank and soared at the same time.

"Are you certain you are all right?" Lady Pleinsworth asked. "You're looking terribly pale. I do hope you have not caught Sarah's complaint."

"No, no," Anne assured her. "That would have been impossible."

Lady Pleinsworth looked at her.

"What I mean to say is, I haven't been in contact

with Lady Sarah," Anne said hastily. "I'm perfectly well. I need only a bit of fresh air. It is as you said. It cures everything."

If Lady Pleinsworth found that stream of babble to be out of character, she did not say so. "Well, then, it is good timing that you have the afternoon to yourself. Do you plan to go out?"

"I do, thank you." Anne rose to her feet and bustled over to the door. "I had best be on my way. I have many errands to attend to." She bobbed a quick curtsy, then dashed back up to her room to collect her things—a light shawl, in case the air grew cool, her reticule with a bit of pin money, and —she opened her bottom drawer and slid her hand under her meager stack of clothing—there it was. Carefully sealed and ready to be posted. Anne had enclosed a half crown in her last letter, so she was confident that Charlotte would be able to pay the postage when this one arrived. The only trick was making sure that no one else realized who had actually sent the letter.

Anne swallowed, surprised by the lump in her throat. One would think she'd be used to it by now, having to sign a false name in her letters to her sister, but it was the only way. Doubly false, actually. She didn't even sign them Anne Wynter, which she supposed was as much her name as Annelise Shawcross had ever been.

Carefully, she placed the letter in her reticule and headed down the stairs. She wondered if the rest of her family had ever seen her missives, and if so, who they thought Mary Philpott was. Charlotte would have had to have come up with a good story for that.

It was a fine spring day, with just enough breeze to make her wish her bonnet was more securely fastened. She headed down past Berkeley Square toward Piccadilly, where there was a receiving house just off the main road where she liked to drop her letters. It wasn't the closest spot to Pleinsworth House, but the area was busier, and she preferred the deeper cloak of anonymity it offered. Besides, she liked to walk, and it was always a treat to do so at her own pace.

Piccadilly was as crowded as ever, and she turned east, passing by several shops before lifting the hem of her skirt a few inches in order to cross the street. A half dozen carriages rolled by, but none quickly, and she easily picked her way across the cobbles, stepped onto the pavement, and—

Oh, dear God.

Was it . . . ? No, it couldn't be. He never came down to London. Or at least he didn't. That was to say, he hadn't, and—

Anne's heart pounded in her chest, and for a moment she felt the edges of her sight begin to blacken and curl. She forced air into her lungs. *Think.* She had to think.

The same coppery blond hair, the same devastatingly handsome profile. His looks had always been unique; it was difficult to imagine he had an unknown twin in the capital, gadding about on Piccadilly.

Anne felt tears, hot and furious, burning behind

her eyes. This was not fair. She had done everything that had been expected of her. She had cut off ties with everything and everyone she had known. She had changed her name, and gone into service, and promised that she would never, ever speak of what had happened in Northumberland so very long ago.

But George Chervil had not kept his part of the bargain. And if that was indeed him, standing outside Burnell's Haberdashery . . .

She could not stand there like a target and wait to find out. With a choked cry of frustration, she turned on her heel and ran . . . into the very first shop she came across.

Chapter Six

Eight years earlier ...

TONIGHT, ANNELISE THOUGHT with growing excitement. Tonight would be the night.

It would be a bit of a scandal, her becoming engaged before either of her older sisters, but it would not be entirely unexpected. Charlotte had never shown great interest in their local society, and Marabeth always looked so pinched and angry—it was hard to imagine anyone wanting to marry her.

Marabeth would have a fit, though, and their parents would surely console her, but for once they would not force their youngest daughter to give up a prize for the sake of the eldest. When Annelise married George Chervil, the Shawcrosses would become forever connected with the most important family in their corner of Northumberland. Even Marabeth would eventually realize that Annelise's coup was in her best interest.

A rising tide did indeed lift all boats, even prickly ones named Marabeth.

"You look rather like a cat in cream," Charlotte said, watching Annelise as she examined herself in her mirror, testing one set of earbobs against the other. They were paste, of course; the only proper jewels in the Shawcross family belonged to their mother, and all she had besides her wedding ring was a small broach, with three tiny diamonds and one large topaz. It wasn't even very pretty.

"I think George is going to ask me to marry him," Annelise whispered. She never could keep secrets from her sister. At least not until recently. Charlotte knew most of the details of Annelise's monthlong secret courtship, not *all* of them.

"Never say it!" Charlotte gasped with delight and clasped both of her sister's hands in hers. "I am so happy for you!"

"I know, I know." Annelise could not keep herself from grinning. Her cheeks would hurt by the end of the night, she was sure. But she was so happy. George was everything she had ever wanted in a husband. He was everything *any* girl had ever wanted—handsome, athletic, dashing. Not to mention incredibly well-connected. As Mrs. George Chervil, Annelise would live in the finest house for miles. Her invitations would be coveted, her friendship desired. Maybe they would even go to London for the season. Annelise knew that such travels were dear, but George would one day be a baronet. At some point he would need to take his proper place in society, wouldn't he?

"Has he been dropping hints?" Charlotte wanted to know. "Given you gifts?"

Annelise tilted her head to the side. She liked the way she looked when the light hit her pale skin just so. "He has not done anything so obvious. But there is such history behind the Midsummer Ball. Did you know his parents became engaged at the very same event? And now that George has turned twenty-five . . ." She turned to her sister with wide, excited eyes. "I overheard his father saying it was high time he married."

"Oh, Annie," Charlotte sighed. "It's so romantic." The Chervil family's Midsummer Ball was *the* event of the year, every year. If ever there was a moment when their village's most eligible bachelor would announce his engagement, this would be it.

"Which ones?" Annelise asked, holding up the two sets of earbobs.

"Oh, the blue, definitely," Charlotte said before grinning. "Because I must have the green to match my eyes."

Annelise laughed and hugged her. "I am so happy right now," she said. She squeezed her eyes tight, as if she couldn't possibly keep her feelings contained. Her happiness felt like a living thing, bouncing around inside of her. She had known George for years, and like every girl she knew, had secretly wished he would pay her special notice. And then he had! That spring she had caught him looking at her differently, and by the dawn of summer, he'd been secretly courting her. Opening her eyes, she looked at her sister and beamed. "I didn't think it was possible to be so happy."

"And it will only get better," Charlotte predicted. They stood, hands clasped, and walked to the door. "Once George proposes, your happiness will know no bounds."

Annelise giggled as they danced out the door. Her future was waiting, and she could not wait to reach it.

ANNELISE SAW GEORGE the instant she arrived. He was the sort of man one couldn't miss—brilliantly handsome with a smile that melted a girl from the inside out. Every girl was in love with him. Every girl had always been in love with him.

Annelise smiled her secret smile as she floated into the ballroom. The other girls might be in love with him, but *she* was the only who had been loved in return.

He'd told her so.

But after an hour of watching him greet his family's guests, she was growing impatient. She had danced with three other gentlemen—two of them quite eligible—and George hadn't once tried to cut in. Not that she'd done it to make him jealous—well, perhaps a little. But she always accepted invitations to dance, from anyone.

She knew she was beautiful. It would have been impossible to grow up with so many people saying so, every single day, and not know it. Annelise was some kind of throwback, people said, her glossy dark locks the result of an ancient Welsh invader. Her father's hair had been dark, too, back when he'd had hair, but everyone said it hadn't been like hers, with the shine and bounce and ever-so-gentle curl.

Marabeth had always been jealous. Marabeth, who actually looked quite like Annelise, but just not . . . as much. Her skin wasn't quite as pale, her eyes not quite as blue. Marabeth was forever painting Annelise as a spoilt little shrew, and maybe it was for that reason that Annelise decided, on her very first foray into local society, that she would dance with every man who asked. No one would accuse her of reaching above her station; she would be the kindhearted beauty, the girl everyone loved to love.

Now, of course, every man did ask, because what man didn't want to dance with the most beautiful girl at the ball? Especially with no risk of rejection.

This must be why George was showing no signs of jealousy, Annelise decided. He knew she had a kind heart. He knew that her dances with the other gentlemen meant nothing to her. No one could ever touch her heart the way he had.

"Why hasn't he asked me to dance?" she whispered to Charlotte. "I will perish from the anticipation, you know that I will."

"It's his parents' ball," Charlotte said soothingly. "He has responsibilities as a host."

"I know. I know. I just . . . *I love him so much!*"

Annelise coughed, feeling her cheeks grow hot with mortification. That had come out louder than she'd intended, but luckily no one seemed to have noticed.

"Come," Charlotte said with the brisk determination of one who has just seized upon a plan. "Let us take a turn around the room. We shall walk so close to Mr. Chervil that he will expire from wanting to reach out and take your hand."

Annelise laughed and linked her arm through Charlotte's. "You are the very best of sisters," she said, quite seriously.

Charlotte just patted her hand. "Smile now," she whispered. "He can see you."

Annelise looked up, and indeed, he was staring at her, his green-gray eyes smoldering with longing.

"Oh, my goodness," Charlotte said. "Just look at how he watches you."

"It makes me shiver," Annelise admitted.

"We shall walk closer," Charlotte decided, and they did, until there was no way they could not be noticed by George and his parents.

"Good evening," his father boomed jovially. "If it isn't the lovely Miss Shawcross. And another lovely Miss Shawcross." He gave them each a tiny bow from his head, and they curtsied in return.

"Sir Charles," Annelise murmured, eager for him to see her as a polite and dutiful young lady who would make him an excellent daughter-in-law. She turned to George's mother with the same deference. "Lady Chervil."

"Where is the other *other* lovely Miss Shaw-cross?" Sir Charles asked.

"I have not seen Marabeth in some time," Charlotte replied, just as George said, "I believe she is over there, by the doors to the garden."

Which gave Annelise the perfect opening to curtsy to him and say, "Mr. Chervil." He took her hand and kissed it, and she did not think it was her imagination that he lingered longer than he needed to.

"You are as enchanting as ever, Miss Shawcross." He released her hand, then straightened. "I am be-witched."

Annelise tried to speak, but she was overcome. She felt hot, and tremulous, and her lungs felt funny, as if there was not enough air in the world to fill them.

"Lady Chervil," Charlotte said, "I am so enam-ored of these decorations. Tell me, how did you and Sir Charles find just the right color of yellow to sig-nify summer?"

It was the most inane of questions, but Annelise adored her for it. George's parents immediately launched into conversation with Charlotte, and she and George were able to turn ever so slightly away from them.

"I haven't seen you all night," Annelise said breathlessly. Just being near him made her shiver with anticipation. When they had seen each other three nights earlier he had kissed her with such passion. It had burned in her memory, leaving her eager for more.

What he had done after the kiss hadn't been quite as enjoyable, but it had still been exciting. To know that she affected him so deeply, that she could make him lose control . . .

It was intoxicating. She had never known such power.

"I have been very busy with my parents," George said, but his eyes told her that he would rather be with her.

"I miss you," she said daringly. Her behavior was scandalous, but she *felt* scandalous, as if she could take the reins of her life and chart her own destiny. What a grand thing it was to be young and in love. The world would be theirs. They had only to reach out and grasp it.

George's eyes flared with desire, and he glanced furtively over his shoulder. "My mother's sitting room. Do you know where it is?"

Annelise nodded.

"Meet me there in a quarter of an hour. Don't be seen."

He went off to ask another girl to dance—the better to deflect any speculation about their hushed conversation. Annelise found Charlotte, who had finally finished her discussion of all things yellow, green, and gold. "I'm meeting him in ten minutes," she whispered. "Can you make sure that no one wonders where I am?"

Charlotte nodded, gave her hand a squeeze of support, then motioned with her head toward the door. No one was watching. It was the perfect time to leave.

It took longer to reach Lady Chervil's sitting room than Annelise had expected. It was clear across the building—probably why George had chosen it. And she'd had to take a circuitous route to avoid other partygoers who had also chosen to make their celebrations private. By the time she slipped into the darkened chamber, George was already there, waiting for her.

He was on her before she could even speak, kissing her madly, his hands reaching around to her bottom and squeezing with proprietary intimacy. "Oh, Annie," he groaned, "you're amazing. Coming here right in the middle of the party. So naughty."

"George," she murmured. His kisses were lovely, and it was thrilling that he desired her with such desperation, but she was not sure she liked being called naughty. That wasn't what she was, was it?

"George?" she said again, this time a question.

But he didn't answer. He was breathing hard, trying to lift her skirts even as he steered her to a nearby divan.

"George!" It was difficult, because she, too, was excited, but she wedged her hands between them and pushed him away.

"What?" he demanded, eyeing her with suspicion. And something else. Anger?

"I didn't come here for this," she said.

He barked with laughter. "What did you think

was going to happen?" He stepped toward her again, his eyes fierce and predatory. "I've been hard for you for days."

She blushed furiously, because she knew now what it meant. And while it was exciting that he wanted her so desperately, there was something discomfiting in it, too. She wasn't sure what, or why, but she was no longer so sure she wanted to be here with him, in such a dark and secluded room.

He grabbed her hand and tugged her toward him with enough of a jerk that she stumbled against him. "Let's have a spot of it, Annie," he murmured. "You know you want to."

"No, I— I just—" She tried to pull away, but he would not let her go. "It's the Midsummer Ball. I thought . . ." Her voice trailed off. She couldn't say it. She couldn't say it because one look at his face told her that he had never intended to ask her to marry him. He had kissed her, then seduced her, taking the one thing that should have been saved for her husband, and he thought he could take it again?

"Oh, my God," he said, looking as if he might laugh. "You thought I would marry you." And then he did laugh, and Annelise was sure that something inside of her died.

"You're beautiful," he said mockingly, "I'll grant you that. And I had a *fine* time between your thighs, but come now, Annie. You have no money to speak of, and your family certainly will not enhance my own."

She wanted to say something. She wanted to hit

him. But she could only stand there in dawning horror, unable to believe the words that were dripping from his lips.

"Besides," he said with a cruel smile, "I already have a fiancée."

Annelise's knees threatened to buckle beneath her, and she grabbed the side of his mother's desk for support. "Who?" she managed to whisper.

"Fiona Beckwith," he told her. "The daughter of Lord Hanley. I asked her last night."

"Did she accept?" Annelise whispered.

He laughed. Loudly. "Of course she accepted. And her father—the *viscount*—declared himself delighted. She is his youngest, but his favorite, and I have no doubt that he will provide for us handsomely."

Annelise swallowed. It was getting hard to breathe. She needed to get out of this room, out of this house.

"She's quite fetching, too," George said, ambling closer to her. He smiled, and it turned her stomach to see that it was the same smile he'd used when he'd seduced her before. He was a handsome bastard, and he knew it. "But I doubt," he murmured, letting one of his fingers tickle down the length of her cheek, "that she will be as wicked a romp as *you* were."

"No," she tried to say, but his mouth was on hers again, and his hands were everywhere. She tried to struggle, but that seemed only to amuse him. "Oh, you like it rough, do you?" he said with a laugh. He pinched her then, hard, but Annelise welcomed the pain. It woke her from whatever shock-filled stupor she'd descended into, and from the center of her being, she roared, thrusting him away from her.

"Get away from me!" she cried, but he only laughed. In desperation she grabbed the only weapon she could find, an antique letter opener, lying unsheathed on Lady Chervil's desk. Waving it in the air, she warned, "Don't come near me. I'm warning you!"

"Oh, Annie," he said condescendingly, and he stepped forward just as she waved wildly through the air.

"You bitch!" he cried, clutching his cheek. "You cut me."

"Oh, my God. Oh, my God. I didn't mean to." The weapon fell from her hands and she scooted back, all the way to the wall, almost as if she were trying to get away from herself. "I didn't mean to," she said again.

But maybe she had.

"I will kill you," he hissed. Blood was seeping through his fingers, staining the crisp snowy whiteness of his shirt. "Do you hear me?" he screamed. "I will see you in hell!"

Annelise shoved her way past him and ran.

THREE DAYS LATER Annelise stood before her father, and George's father, and listened to them agree on oh-so-many points.

She was a trollop.

She could have ruined George's life.

She might very well still ruin her sisters' lives.

If she turned out to be pregnant it was her own bloody fault and she'd better not think George had any obligation to marry her.

As if he should have to marry the girl who had scarred him for life.

Annelise still felt sick about that. Not for defending herself. No one seemed to agree with her on that, though. They all seemed to feel that if she'd given herself to him once, he was right to believe she'd do it again.

But she could still feel the awful jolt of it, the wet, meaty resistance when the blade had plunged into his flesh. She had not been expecting it. She'd only meant to wave the thing in the air, to scare him away.

"It is settled," her father bit off, "and you should get down on your knees to thank Sir Charles that he has been so generous."

"You will leave this town," Sir Charles said sharply, "and you will never return. You will have no contact with my son or any member of my family. You will have no contact with your family. It will be as if you never existed. Do you understand?"

She shook her head in slow disbelief. She did not understand. She could never understand this. Sir Charles, maybe, but her own family? Disowning her completely?

"We have found you a position," her father said, his voice curt and low with disgust. "Your mother's cousin's wife's sister needs a companion."

Who? Annelise shook her head, desperately trying to follow. Who was he talking about?

"She lives on the Isle of Man."

"What? No!" Anne stumbled forward, trying to take her father's hands. "It's so far. I don't want to go."

"Silence!" he roared, and the back of his hand came hard across her cheek. Annelise stumbled back, the shock of his attack far more acute than the pain. Her father had struck her. He had *struck* her. In all her sixteen years, he had never laid a hand to her, and now . . .

"You are already ruined in the eyes of all who know you," he hissed mercilessly. "If you do not do as we say, you will bring further shame upon your family and destroy whatever chances your sisters still have at making any sort of marriages."

Annelise thought of Charlotte, whom she adored more than anyone else in the world. And Marabeth, to whom she had never been close . . . But still, she was her sister. Nothing could have been more important.

"I will go," she whispered. She touched her cheek. It still burned from her father's blow.

"You shall leave in two days," he told her. "We have—"

"*Where is she?*"

Annelise gasped as George burst into the room. His eyes were wild, and his skin was covered with a sheen of sweat. He was breathing hard; he must have raced through the house when he heard that she was there. One side of his face was covered with bandages, but the edges had started to wilt and droop. Annelise was terrified they would simply fall away. She did not want to see what lay beneath.

"I will kill you," he roared, lunging at her.

She jumped back, instinctively running to her father for protection. And he must have had some shred of love for her left in his heart, because he stood in front of her, holding up one arm to block George as he surged forward until Sir Charles pulled his son back.

"You will pay for this," George railed. "Look at what you have done to me. Look at it!" He ripped the bandages from his face, and Annelise flinched at the sight of his wound, angry and red, a long, diagonal slash from cheekbone to chin.

It would not heal cleanly. Even she could see that.

"Stop," Sir Charles ordered. "Get a hold of yourself."

But George would not listen. "You will hang for this. Do you hear me? I will summon the magistrate and—"

"Shut *up*," his father snapped. "You will do no such thing. If you call her up before the magistrate, the story will get out and the Hanley girl will cry off faster than you can say please."

"Oh," George snarled, waving his hand before his face in a gesture of grand disgust, "and you don't think the story is going to get out when people see *this*?"

"There will be rumors. Especially when this one

leaves town." Sir Charles shot another scathing glance at Annelise. "But they will only be rumors. Bring in a magistrate and you might as well put the whole sordid mess in the paper."

For several moments Annelise thought that George might not back down. But then he finally yanked his glare away, snapping his head so fast that his wound began to bleed again. He touched his cheek, then looked down at the blood on his fingers. "You will pay for this," he said, walking slowly toward Annelise. "Maybe not today, but you will pay."

He touched his fingers to her cheek, slowly drawing a slash of blood in a diagonal, from cheekbone to chin. "I will find you," he said, and in that moment he almost sounded happy. "And it will be a fine day when I do."

Chapter Seven

Daniel did not consider himself a dandy, or even a Corinthian, but it had to be said—there was nothing like a well-made pair of boots.

The afternoon post had brought a missive from Hugh:

Winstead—

As promised, I visited my father this morning. It is my opinion that he was genuinely surprised, both to see me (we do not speak), and also when he was informed of your misfortune yesterday eve. In short, I do not believe that he bears responsibility for your attack.

I concluded the interview with a reiteration of my threat. It is always good to be reminded of the consequences of one's actions, but perhaps more pertinent was my delight at watching the blood drain from his face.

Yours and etc.,
H. Prentice (alive as long as you are)

And so, feeling as assured of his safety as he supposed he ever would, Daniel headed out to Hoby's of St. James's, where his foot and leg were measured with a precision that would have impressed Galileo himself.

"Do not move," Mr. Hoby demanded.

"I'm not moving."

"Indeed you are."

Daniel looked down at his stockinged foot, which was not moving.

Mr. Hoby's face pinched with disdain. "His grace the Duke of Wellington can stand for hours without moving so much as a muscle."

"He breathes, though?" Daniel murmured.

Mr. Hoby did not bother to look up. "We are not amused."

Daniel could not help but wonder if "we" referred to Mr. Hoby and the duke or if the famed bootmaker's self-regard had finally expanded to the extent that he was forced to speak of himself in the plural.

"We need you to hold still," Mr. Hoby growled.

The latter, then. An annoying habit, no matter how lofty the personage, but Daniel was inclined to put up with it, given the blissful perfection of Mr. Hoby's boots.

"I shall endeavor to do your bidding," Daniel said in his jolliest voice.

Mr. Hoby displayed no signs of amusement, instead barking for one of his assistants to hand him a pencil with which to trace Lord Winstead's foot.

Daniel held himself completely still (outdoing even the Duke of Wellington, whom he was quite sure *did* breathe while being measured), but before Mr. Hoby could finish his tracings, the door to the shop burst open, hitting the wall behind it with enough force to rattle the glass. Daniel jumped, Mr. Hoby cursed, Mr. Hoby's assistant cringed, and when Daniel looked down, the outline of his foot sported a baby toe that jutted forth like a reptilian claw.

Impressive.

The noise of the door slamming open would have attracted enough attention, but then it became clear that it was a *woman* who had come into the bootmaker's establishment, a woman who appeared to be in distress, a woman who—

"*Miss Wynter?*"

It could be no one else, not with those raven locks peeking out from her bonnet, or the incredibly long sweep of eyelashes. But more than that . . . It was strange, but Daniel rather thought that he had recognized her by the way she moved.

She jumped a foot, probably more, so startled by his voice that she stumbled into the display shelves behind her, the ensuing cascade of footwear halted only by the quick thinking of Mr. Hoby's beleaguered assistant, who leapt past her to save the day.

"Miss Wynter," Daniel said again, striding over to her side, "come now, what is the matter? You look as if you've seen a ghost."

She shook her head, but the movement was too jerky, and much too fast. "It's nothing," she said. "I . . . ah . . . There was . . ." She blinked and looked about, as if only just then realizing that she had run into a gentleman's shop. "Oh," she said, more breathing the word than anything else. "I'm so sorry. I-I appear to have come into the wrong storefront. Ehrm . . . If you'll all excuse me, I will just . . ." She peered out the shop window before putting her hand on the doorknob. "I'll be going now," she finally finished.

She did turn the doorknob then, but she did not actually pull open the door. The shop went silent, and everyone seemed to be waiting for her to leave, or speak again, or do *some*thing. But she just stood there, not so much frozen as paralyzed.

Carefully, Daniel took her arm and led her away from the window. "May I be of assistance?"

She turned, and he realized it was the first time she looked directly at him since she'd come in. But the connection was fleeting; she quickly returned her attention to the shop window, even as her body seemed to instinctively cringe away from it.

"We will have to continue another time," he called out to Mr. Hoby. "I shall be seeing Miss Wynter home in—"

"There was a rat," she blurted out. Quite loudly.

"A *rat?*" One of the other customers nearly shrieked it. Daniel could not recall his name, but he was a most fastidious dresser, complete with a brocaded pink waistcoat and matching buckles on his shoes.

"Outside the shop," Miss Wynter said, extending her arm toward the front door. Her index finger wagged and shook, as if the specter of the rodent was so grotesque that she could not bring herself to identify it directly.

Daniel found this curious, but no one else seemed to notice that her story had changed. How was it that she had gone into the wrong shop if she'd been trying to escape a rat?

"It ran over my shoe," she added, and this was enough to make the pink-buckled man sway on his feet.

"Allow me to convey you home," Daniel said, and then more loudly, since everyone was watching them anyway: "The poor lady has had a fright." He deemed that to be explanation enough, especially when he added that she was in the employ of his aunt. He quickly donned the boots he'd come in with, then tried to lead Miss Wynter out of the shop. But her feet seemed to drag, and when they reached the door, he leaned down and said, quietly, so that no one could hear, "Is everything quite all right?"

She swallowed, her lovely face drawn and taut. "Have you a carriage?"

He nodded. "It is just down the street."

"Is it closed?"

What an odd question. It was not raining; it was not even the least bit cloudy. "It can be."

"Could you have it brought forth? I am not certain I can walk."

She did still look shaky on her feet. Daniel nodded again, then sent one of Hoby's assistants out to fetch his carriage. A few minutes later they were ensconced in his landau, the canopy pulled up tight. He gave her a few moments to compose herself, then quietly asked, "What really happened?"

She looked up, and her eyes—such a remarkably dark shade of blue—held a touch of surprise.

"That must have been quite a rat," he murmured. "Almost the size of Australia, I should think."

He hadn't been trying to make her smile, but she did, anyway, the tiniest tilt of her lips. His own heart tilted, and it was difficult to understand how such a small change of expression on her part could cause such a large burst of emotion in his.

He had not liked seeing her so upset. He was only now realizing just how much.

He watched as she tried to decide what to do. She wasn't sure whether she could trust him—he could see that much in her face. She peered out the window, but only briefly, then settled back into her seat, still facing forward. Her lips trembled, and finally, in a voice so quiet and halting it nearly broke his heart, she said, "There is someone . . . I don't wish to see."

Nothing more. No explanation, no elaboration,

nothing but an eight-word sentence that brought forth a thousand new questions. He asked none of them, though. He *would,* just not yet. She wouldn't have answered him, anyway. He was astonished that she'd said as much as she had.

"Let us leave the area, then," he said, and she nodded gratefully. They headed east on Piccadilly— absolutely the wrong direction, but then again, precisely what Daniel had instructed the driver. Miss Wynter needed time to compose herself before she returned to Pleinsworth House.

And he was not quite ready to relinquish her company.

ANNE STARED OUT the window as the minutes rolled by. She wasn't sure where they were, and honestly, she didn't really care. Lord Winstead could be taking her to Dover and she wouldn't mind, just so long as they were far, far away from Piccadilly.

Piccadilly and the man who might have been George Chervil.

Sir George Chervil, she supposed he was now. Charlotte's letters did not arrive with the regularity Anne craved, but they were breezy and newsy and Anne's only link to her former life. George's father had died the year before, Charlotte had written, and George had inherited the baronetcy. The news had made Anne's blood run cold. She had despised the late Sir Charles, but she had also needed him. He had been the only thing keeping his son's vengeful nature in check. With Sir Charles gone, there was no one to talk sense into him. Even Charlotte had expressed concern; apparently George had paid a call on the Shawcrosses the day after his father's funeral. He had tried to paint it as a neighborly afternoon call, but Charlotte thought that he had asked far too many questions about Anne.

Annelise.

Sometimes she had to remind herself of the person she'd once been.

She'd known there was the possibility that George might be in London. When she'd taken the position with the Pleinsworths, it had been under the assumption that she would remain in Dorset year round. Lady Pleinsworth would take Sarah to town for the season, and the three younger girls would spend the summer in the country with their governess and nurse. And father, of course. Lord Pleinsworth never left the country. He was far more interested in his hounds than he'd ever been in people, which suited Anne just fine. If he wasn't absent, he was distracted, and it was almost as if she were working in an all-female household.

Which was *wonderful.*

But then Lady Pleinsworth had decided she couldn't do without all of her daughters, and while Lord Pleinsworth pondered his bassets and bloods, the household packed up and departed for London. Anne had spent the entire trip reassuring herself that even if George did come to town they would never cross paths. It was a big city. The largest in Europe. Maybe the world. George might have married the daughter of a viscount, but the Chervils did not move in the same lofty circles as the Pleinsworths or Smythe-Smiths. And even if they did find themselves at the same event, Anne certainly would not be in attendance. She was just the governess. The hopefully invisible governess.

Still, it was a danger. If Charlotte's gossip was true, George received a generous allowance from his wife's father. He had more than enough money to pay for a season in town. Maybe even enough to buy his way into a few of the top social circles.

He'd always said he liked the excitement of the city. She remembered that about him. She'd managed to forget many things, but that she remembered. That, along with a young girl's dream of promenading in Hyde Park on her handsome husband's arm.

She sighed, mourning the young girl but *not* her foolish dream. What an idiot she had been. What an abysmal judge of character.

"Is there anything I can do to make you more comfortable?" Lord Winstead asked quietly. He had not spoken for some time. She liked that about him. He was an affable man, easy in conversation, but he seemed to know when not to speak.

She shook her head, not quite looking at him. She wasn't trying to avoid him. Well, not *him* specifically. She would have avoided anyone at that moment. But then he moved. It was just a small thing, really, but she felt the seat cushion adjusting beneath them, and it was enough to remind her that he had rescued her this afternoon. He had seen her distress and saved her without so much as a question until they'd reached the carriage.

He deserved her thanks. It did not matter if her hands were still trembling or her mind was still racing with every dreadful possibility. Lord Winstead would never know just how much he had helped her, or even how much she appreciated it, but she could, at least, say thank you.

But when she turned to look at him, something else entirely popped out of her mouth. She'd meant to say, *Thank you*. But instead—

"Is that a new bruise?"

It was. She was sure of it. Right there on his cheek. A bit pinkish, not nearly as dark as the ones near his eye.

"You hurt yourself," she said. "What happened?"

He blinked, looking rather confused, and one of his hands came up to touch his face.

"The other side," she said, and even though she knew it was terribly risqué, she reached out with her fingers and gently touched his cheekbone. "It was not there yesterday."

"You noticed," he murmured, giving her a practiced smile.

"It's not a compliment," she told him, trying not to think about what it might mean that his face had become so familiar to her that she noticed a new splotch amidst the aftermath of his fight with Lord Chatteris. It was ridiculous, really. He *looked* ridiculous.

"Nonetheless, I can't help but be flattered that

you noticed the latest addition to my collection," he said.

She rolled her eyes. "Because personal injuries are such a dignified thing to collect."

"Are all governesses so sarcastic?"

From anyone else she would have taken it as a set-down, a reminder to remember her place. But that wasn't what he was about. And he was smiling as he said it.

She gave him a pointed look. "You're avoiding the question."

She thought he might have looked a little embarrassed. It was difficult to say; any blush that might have touched his cheeks was obscured by the current topic of conversation, namely, the bruises.

He shrugged. "Two ruffians attempted to make off with my purse last night."

"Oh, no!" she cried, completely surprising herself with the strength of her reaction. "What happened? Are you all right?"

"It was not as bad as it could have been," he demurred. "Marcus did more damage the night of the musicale."

"But common criminals! You could have been killed."

He leaned toward her. Just a little. "Would you have missed me?"

She felt her cheeks grow warm, and it took her a few moments to muster an appropriately stern expression. "You would have been missed by many people," she said firmly.

Including her.

"Where were you walking?" she asked. *Details,* she reminded herself. Details were important. Details were crisp and dry and had nothing to do with emotions or missing anyone or worrying or caring or any sort of –ing except knowing the facts. "Was it in Mayfair? I would not have thought it so dangerous."

"It was not Mayfair," he told her. "But not far from it. I was walking home from Chatteris House. It was late. I was not paying attention."

Anne did not know where the Earl of Chatteris lived, but it could not have been too far from Winstead House. All of the noble families lived in relative proximity to one another. And even if Lord Chatteris lived on the edge of the fashionable areas, Lord Winstead would hardly have needed to walk through slums to get home.

"I did not realize the city had grown so dangerous," she said. She swallowed, wondering if the attack upon Lord Winstead could have had anything to do with her spying George Chervil on Piccadilly. No, how could it? She and Lord Winstead had been seen in public together only once—the previous day at Hyde Park—and it would have been clear to any onlooker that she'd been there as governess to his young cousins.

"I suppose I should thank you for insisting upon seeing me home the other night," she said.

He turned, and the intensity in his eyes took her breath away. "I would not allow you to walk two steps alone at night, much less a half mile."

Her lips parted, and she thought that she must have meant to speak, but all she could do was stare.

Her eyes locked onto his, and it was remarkable, because she didn't notice the color of them, that amazingly bright light blue. She saw beyond that, to the depths of . . . something. Or maybe it wasn't that at all. Maybe it was she who had been exposed. Maybe he saw all of her secrets, her fears.

Her desires.

She breathed then—finally—and yanked her gaze away from his. What *was* that? Or more to the point, who was *she*? Because she did not know the woman who had stared at him as if gazing into her own future. She was not fanciful. She did not believe in fate. And she had *never* believed that eyes were the windows to the soul. Not after the way George Chervil had once looked at her.

She swallowed, taking a moment to regain her equilibrium. "You say that as if the sentiment is particular to me," she said, pleased with the relative normalcy of her voice, "but I know that you would insist upon doing the same for any lady."

He gave her a smile so flirtatious she had to wonder if she had imagined the intensity in his eyes just a few moments before. "Most ladies would pretend to be flattered."

"I think this is where I am meant to say that I am not most ladies," she said dryly.

"It certainly would flow well, were we on the stage."

"I shall have to inform Harriet," Anne said with a laugh. "She fancies herself a playwright."

"Does she now?"

Anne nodded. "I believe she has begun a new

opus. It sounds terribly depressing. Something about Henry VIII."

He winced. "That *is* grim."

"She is trying to convince me to take the role of Anne Boleyn."

He smothered a laugh. "There is no way my aunt is paying you enough."

Anne declined to comment on that, instead saying, "I do thank you for your concern the other night. But as for being flattered, I am far more impressed by a gentleman who values the safety and security of *all* women."

He took a moment to reflect on that, then nodded, his head jerking a little to the side as he did so. He was uncomfortable, Anne realized with surprise. He was not used to being complimented for such things.

She smiled to herself. There was something rather endearing about watching him shift in his seat. She supposed he was used to being praised for his charm or his good looks.

But for his good behavior? She had a feeling it was long overdue.

"Does it hurt?" she asked.

"My cheek?" He shook his head, then contradicted himself. "Well, a little."

"But the thieves look worse than you do?" she said with a smile.

"Oh, much worse," he said. "Much, much worse."

"Is that the point of fighting? To make sure one's opponent emerges in a worse state than oneself?"

"Do you know, I think it might be. Foolish, wouldn't you think?" He looked at her with a strange, ponderous expression. "It's what got me sent out of the country."

She did not know all of the details of his duel, but— "What?" she asked. Because really, even young men could not be so foolish.

"Well, not exactly," he allowed, "but it's the same sort of inanity. Someone called me a cheat. And I nearly killed him for it." He turned to her, his eyes piercing. "Why? Why would I do that?"

She didn't answer.

"Not that I *tried* to kill him." He sat back in his seat, the motion oddly forceful and sudden. "It was an accident." He was silent for a moment, and Anne watched his face. He did not look at her when he added, "I thought you should know."

She did know. He could never be the sort of man who would kill so trivially. But she could tell he did not wish to say any more about it. So instead she asked, "Where are we going?"

He did not answer immediately. He blinked, then glanced out the window, then admitted, "I do not know. I told the coachman to drive aimlessly about until given further direction. I thought perhaps you needed a few extra minutes before returning to Pleinsworth House."

She nodded. "It is my afternoon free. I am not expected anytime soon."

"Have you any errands you need to see completed?"

"No, I— Yes!" she exclaimed. Good heavens, how had she forgotten? "Yes, I do."

His head tilted toward her. "I should be happy to convey you to wherever you need to go."

She clutched her reticule, finding comfort in the quiet crinkling sound of the paper inside. "It is nothing, just a letter that must be posted."

"Shall I frank it? I never did manage to take my seat in the House of Lords, but I assume I possess franking privileges. My father certainly used his."

"No," she said quickly, even though this would have saved her a trip to a receiving house. Not to mention the expense for Charlotte. But if her parents saw the letter, franked by the Earl of Winstead . . .

Their curiosity would know no bounds.

"That is very kind of you," Anne said, "but I could not possibly accept your generosity."

"It's not my generosity. You may thank the Royal Mail."

"Still, I could not abuse your franking privilege in such a way. If you would just see me to a receiving house . . ." She looked out the window to determine their precise whereabouts. "I believe there is one on Tottenham Court Road. Or if not there, then . . . Oh, I had not realized we were so far to the east. We should go to High Holborn instead. Just before Kingsway."

There was a pause.

"You have quite a comprehensive knowledge of London receiving houses," he said.

"Oh. Well. Not really." She gave herself a swift mental kick and wracked her brain for an appropriate excuse. "It is only that I am fascinated by the postal system. It's really quite marvelous."

He looked at her curiously, and she couldn't tell if he believed her. Luckily for her, it was the truth, even if she'd said it to cover a lie. She *did* find the Royal Mail rather interesting. It was amazing how quickly one could get a message across the country. Three days from London to Northumberland. It seemed a miracle, really.

"I should like to follow a letter one day," she said, "just to see where it goes."

"To the address on its front, I would imagine," he said.

She pressed her lips together to acknowledge his little gibe, then said, "But *how*? That is the miracle."

He smiled a bit. "I must confess, I had not thought of the postal system in such biblical terms, but I am always happy to be educated."

"It is difficult to imagine a letter traveling any faster than it does today," she said happily, "unless we learn how to fly."

"There are always pigeons," he said.

She laughed. "Can you imagine an entire flock, lifting off to the sky to deliver our mail?"

"It is a terrifying prospect. Especially for those walking beneath."

That brought another giggle. Anne could not recall the last time she had felt so merry.

"To High Holborn then," he said, "since I would never allow you to entrust your missive to the pigeons of London." He leaned forward to open the flap in the landau's top, gave the driver instructions, then sat back again. "Is there anything else with which I might help you, Miss Wynter? I am entirely at your disposal."

"No, thank you. If you would just return me to Pleinsworth House . . ."

"So early in the afternoon? On your day off?"

"There is much to be done this evening," she told him. "We go to— Oh, but of course you know. We go tomorrow to Berkshire, to . . ."

"Whipple Hill," he supplied.

"Yes. At your suggestion, I believe."

"It did seem more sensible than your traveling all the way to Dorset."

"But did you—" She cut herself off, then looked away. "Never mind."

"Are you asking if I had already intended to go?" He waited a moment, then said, "I did not."

The tip of her tongue darted out to moisten her lips, but still, she did not look at him. It would be far too dangerous. She should not wish for things that were out of her reach. She *could* not. She'd tried that once, and she'd been paying for it ever since.

And Lord Winstead was quite possibly the most impossible dream of all. If she allowed herself to want him, it would destroy her.

But oh, how she wanted to want him.

"Miss Wynter?" His voice filtered over her like a warm breeze.

"That is—" She cleared her throat, trying to find her voice, the one that actually sounded like herself.

"That is very kind of you to adjust your schedule for your aunt."

"I did not do it for my aunt," he said softly. "But I expect you know that."

"Why?" she asked softly. She knew she would not have to explain the query; he would know what she meant.

Not why did he do it. Why *her*?

But he didn't answer. At least not right away. And then, finally, just when she thought she might have to look up and into his face, he said, "I don't know."

She did look then. His answer had been so frank and unexpected that she couldn't *not* look. She turned her face to his, and when she did, she was gripped by the strangest, most intense longing to simply reach out and touch her hand to his. To somehow *connect*.

But she didn't. She couldn't. And she knew that, even if he did not.

Chapter Eight

THE FOLLOWING EVENING, Anne stepped down from the Pleinsworths' traveling coach and looked up, taking in her first glance at Whipple Hill. It was a lovely house, solid and stately, situated amidst gently rolling hills that sloped down to a large, tree-lined pond. There was something very homey about it, Anne thought, which struck her as interesting since it was the ancestral estate of the Earls of Winstead. Not that she was terribly familiar with the great homes of the aristocracy, but those that she had seen had always been terribly ornate and imperious.

The sun had already set, but the orange glow of twilight still hung in the air, lending just a touch of warmth to the rapidly approaching night. Anne was eager to find her room and perhaps have a bowl of hot soup for supper, but the night before their departure Nanny Flanders had come down with a stomach ailment. With Nanny remaining behind in London, Anne had been pressed into double duty, serving as nurse and governess, which meant that she would be required to get the girls settled into their room before she could tend to any of her own needs. Lady Pleinsworth had promised her an extra afternoon off while they were in the country, but she had not been specific as to when, and Anne feared that it would slip her mind completely.

"Come along, girls," she said briskly. Harriet had run ahead to one of the other carriages—the one with Sarah and Lady Pleinsworth—and Elizabeth had run back to the other. Although what she was talking about with the ladies' maids, Anne could not begin to guess.

"I'm right here," Frances said gamely.

"So you are," Anne replied. "Gold star for you."

"It's really too bad that you don't have *actual* gold stars. I shouldn't have to pinch up my pin money each week."

"If I had actual gold stars," Anne replied with a quirk of her brow, "I shouldn't have to be your governess."

"Touché," Frances said admiringly.

Anne gave her a wink. There was something rather satisfying about earning the regard of a ten-year-old. "Where are your sisters?" she muttered, then called, "Harriet! Elizabeth!"

Harriet came bounding back. "Mama says I may eat with the adults while we are here."

"Ooooh, Elizabeth is not going to be happy about that," Frances predicted.

"Not happy about what?" Elizabeth asked. "And you would not believe what Peggy just told me."

Peggy was Sarah's maid. Anne quite liked her, although she was a terrible gossip.

"What did she say?" Frances asked. "And Harriet will be eating with the adults while we're here."

Elizabeth gasped in righteous outrage. "That is patently unfair. And Peggy said that Sarah said that Daniel said that Miss Wynter is to eat with the family as well."

"*That* won't happen," Anne said firmly. It would be highly out of the ordinary—a governess generally only joined the family when she was needed to bolster the numbers—but beyond that, she had work to do. She popped her hand lightly on Frances's head. "I shall be eating with you."

The unexpected blessing of Nanny Flanders having taken sick. Anne could not imagine what Lord Winstead had been thinking, requesting that she join the family for supper. If ever there was a move designed to put her in an awkward position, that was it. The lord of the manor asking to dine with the governess? He might as well just come out and say he was trying to get her into his bed.

Which she had a feeling he was. It wouldn't be the first time she'd had to fend off unwanted advances from her employers.

But it would be the first time a part of her had wanted to give in.

"Good evening!" It was Lord Winstead, come out onto the portico to greet them.

"Daniel!" Frances shrieked. She did a 180 degree turn, kicking up dust all over her sisters, and ran toward him, practically knocking him down as she launched herself into his arms.

"Frances!" Lady Pleinsworth scolded. "You are far too old to be jumping on your cousin."

"I don't mind," Lord Winstead said with a laugh. He tousled Frances's hair, which earned him a wide grin.

Frances twisted her head backwards to ask her mother, "If I'm too old to jump on Daniel, does that mean I'm old enough to eat with the adults?"

"Not even close to it," Lady Pleinsworth replied pertly.

"But Harriet—"

"—is five years your elder."

"We shall have a grand time in the nursery," Anne announced, walking over to pluck her charge off Lord Winstead. He turned to face her, his eyes flaring with a familiarity that made her skin turn warm. She could tell he was about to say something about her joining the family for supper, so she quickly added, in a voice that everyone could hear, "Normally I take my supper in my room, but with Nanny Flanders sick, I am more than happy to take her place with Elizabeth and Frances in the nursery."

"Once again, you are our savior, Miss Wynter,"

chimed Lady Pleinsworth. "I don't know what we would do without you."

"First the musicale and now this," Lord Winstead said approvingly.

Anne glanced at him, trying to discern his motive for saying such a thing, but he had already turned his attention back to Frances.

"Perhaps we shall stage a concert while we are here," Elizabeth suggested. "It would be great fun."

It was hard to tell in the twilight, but Anne thought she might have seen Lord Winstead blanch. "I did not bring your viola," she said quickly. "Nor Harriet's violin."

"What about—"

"And not your contrabassoon, either," Anne said to Frances before she could even ask.

"Oh, but this is Whipple Hill," Lady Pleinsworth said. "No Smythe-Smith home would be complete without a generous assortment of musical instruments."

"Even a contrabassoon?" Frances asked hopefully.

Lord Winstead looked dubious, but he said, "I suppose you can look."

"I shall! Miss Wynter, will you help me?"

"Of course," Anne murmured. It seemed as good an enterprise as any to keep her out of the way of the family.

"With Sarah feeling so much better, you won't have to play the pianoforte this time," Elizabeth pointed out.

It was a good thing Lady Sarah had already entered the house, Anne thought, because she would have had to stage an elaborate relapse right then and there.

"Let us all come inside," Lord Winstead said. "There is no need to change from your traveling clothes. Mrs. Barnaby has seen to an informal supper, of which we may all partake, Elizabeth and Frances included."

And you, too, Miss Wynter.

He didn't say it. He didn't even look at her, but Anne felt the words nonetheless.

"If you will be dining *en famille*," Anne said to Lady Pleinsworth, "I should be most grateful to retire to my room. I find myself weary from the journey."

"Of course, my dear. You will need to reserve your energy for this week. I'm afraid we shall be working you to the bone. Poor Nanny."

"Don't you mean poor Miss Wynter?" Frances asked.

Anne smiled at her charge. Indeed.

"Never fear, Miss Wynter," Elizabeth said. "We shall go easy on you."

"Oh you shall, shall you?"

Elizabeth assumed an innocent mien. "I am willing to forgo all mathematics for the duration."

Lord Winstead chuckled, then turned to Anne. "Shall I have someone show you to your room?"

"Thank you, my lord."

"Come with me. I shall see to it." He turned to

his aunt and cousins. "The rest of you, go along to the breakfast room. Mrs. Barnaby had the footmen set up supper there, since we are so informal this evening."

Anne had no choice but to follow him through the main hall and then to a long portrait gallery. She appeared to be at the early side of it, she thought, judging from the Elizabethan ruff on the rather portly man staring down at her. She looked about for a maid, or a footman, or whoever it was he planned to have show her to her room, but they were quite alone.

Except for two dozen Winsteads of years gone by.

She stood and clasped her hands primly in front of her. "I'm sure you wish to join your family. Perhaps a maid . . ."

"What kind of host would I be?" he asked smoothly. "Pawning you off like a piece of baggage."

"I beg your pardon?" Anne murmured with some alarm. Surely he could not mean . . .

He smiled. Like a wolf. "I shall see you to your room myself."

DANIEL DID NOT know what manner of devil had come over him, but Miss Wynter had looked so unbearably fetching as she squinted up at the third Earl of Winstead (too many turkey legs shared with Henry VIII, that much was clear). He'd planned to summon a maid to show her to her room, truly he had, but apparently he could not resist the delicate wrinkle of her nose.

"Lord Winstead," she began, "surely you recognize the impropriety of such a . . . such a . . ."

"Oh, don't worry," he said, happy to save her from her articulation difficulties. "Your virtue is safe with me."

"But not my reputation!"

She did have a point there.

"I shall be quick as a . . ." He paused. "Well, whatever it is that is quick and not terribly unattractive."

She stared at him as if he'd sprouted horns. Unattractive horns.

He smiled gamely. "I shall be down to supper so quickly no one will even realize I went with you."

"That is not the point."

"Isn't it? You said you were concerned for your reputation."

"I am, but—"

"So quick," he interrupted, putting an end to whatever manner of protest she'd been working toward. "I'd hardly have time to ravish you even if that *were* my intention."

She gasped. "Lord Winstead!"

Wrong thing to say. But so terribly entertaining.

"I jest," he said to her.

She stared at him.

"The saying of it is the jest," he quickly explained. "Not the sentiment."

Still, she said nothing. And then: "I think you have gone mad."

"It is certainly a possibility," he said agreeably. He motioned to the corridor that led to the west stairs.

"Here, come this way." He waited for a moment, then added, "It's not as if you have a choice."

She stiffened, and he realized that he had said something terribly wrong. Wrong because of something that had happened in her past, some other time when she had had no choices.

But perhaps also wrong simply because it was wrong, no matter what her history. He did not pinch the maids or corner young girls at parties. He had always tried to treat women with respect. There was no justification for offering Miss Wynter anything less.

"I beg your pardon," he said, bowing his head in esteem. "I have behaved badly."

Her lips parted, and she blinked several times in rapid succession. She did not know whether to believe him, and he realized in stunned silence that her indecision was heartbreaking.

"My apology is genuine," he said.

"Of course," she said quickly, and he thought she meant it. He hoped she did. She would have said the same even if she hadn't, just to be polite.

"I would explain, though," he told her, "that I said you had no choice not because of your position in the employ of my aunt but rather because you simply do not know your way about the house."

"Of course," she said again.

But he felt compelled to say more, because . . . because . . . Because he could not bear the thought of her thinking badly of him. "Any visitor would have been in the same position," he said, hoping he did not sound defensive.

She started to say something, then stopped herself, probably because it had been another "*Of course.*" He waited patiently—she was still standing over by the painting of the third earl—content just to watch her until she finally said, "Thank you."

He nodded. It was a gracious movement, elegant and urbane, the same sort of acknowledgment he'd done thousands of times. But inside he was nearly swept away by a cascading rush of relief. It was humbling. Or, more to the point, unnerving.

"You are not the sort of man to take advantage," she said, and in that moment he *knew*.

Someone had hurt her. Anne Wynter knew what it meant to be at the mercy of someone stronger and more powerful.

Daniel felt something within him harden with fury. Or maybe sorrow. Or regret.

He didn't know what he felt. For the first time in his life, his thoughts were a jumble, tossing and turning and writing over each other like an endlessly edited story. The only certainty was that it was taking every ounce of his strength not to close the difference between them and pull her against him. His body remembered her, her scent, her curves, even the precise temperature of her skin against his.

He wanted her. He wanted her completely.

But his family was waiting for him at supper, and his ancestors were staring down at him from their portrait frames, and *she*—the woman in question—was watching him with a wariness that broke his heart.

"If you will wait right here," he said quietly, "I will fetch a maid to show you to your room."

"Thank you," she said, and she bobbed a small curtsy.

He started to walk to the far end of the gallery, but after a few steps he stopped. When he turned around, she was standing precisely where he'd left her.

"Is something amiss?" she asked.

"I just want you to know—" he said abruptly.

What? What did he want her to know? He didn't even know why he'd spoken.

He was a fool. But he knew that already. He'd been a fool since the moment he'd met her.

"Lord Winstead?" she asked, after a full minute had passed without his having finished his statement.

"It's nothing," he muttered, and he turned again, fully expecting his feet to carry him out of the gallery. But they didn't. He stood breathlessly still, his back to her as his mind screamed at him to just . . . move. Take a step. *Go!*

But instead he turned, some traitorous part of him still desperate for one last look at her.

"As you wish," she said quietly.

And then, before he had a chance to consider his actions, he found himself striding back toward her. "Precisely," he said.

"I'm sorry?" Her eyes clouded with confusion. Confusion twinned with unease.

"As I wish," he repeated. "That's what you said."

"Lord Winstead, I don't think—"

He came to a halt three feet away from her.

Beyond the length of his arms. He trusted himself, but not completely.

"You shouldn't do this," she whispered.

But he was too far gone. "I *wish* to kiss you. That is what I wanted you to know. Because if I'm not going to do it, and it appears that I am not, because it isn't what you want, at least not right now . . . but if I'm not going to do it, you need to know that I wanted it." He paused, staring at her mouth, at her lips, full and trembling. "I still want it."

He heard a rush of air gasp across her lips, but when he looked into her eyes, their blue so midnight they might as well have been black, he knew that she wanted him. He had shocked her, that much was obvious, but still, she wanted him.

He wasn't going to kiss her now; he had already realized it was not the right time. But he had to let her know. She had to *know* just what it was he wanted.

What she wanted, too, if only she allowed herself to see it.

"This kiss," he said, his voice burning with tightly held desire. "This kiss . . . I wish for it with a fervor that shakes my soul. I have no idea why I wish it, only that I felt it the moment I saw you at the piano, and it has only intensified in the days since."

She swallowed, and the candlelight danced across her delicate neck. But she didn't say anything. That was all right; he had not expected her to.

"I want the kiss," he said huskily, "and then I want more. I want things you cannot even know about."

They stood in silence, eyes locked.

"But most of all," he whispered, "I want to kiss you."

And then, in a voice so soft it was barely more than breath, she said, "I want it, too."

Chapter Nine

I WANT IT, TOO.

She was mad.

There could be no other explanation. She had spent the last two days telling herself all the reasons why she could not possibly allow herself to want this man, and now, at the first moment when they were truly alone and secluded, she said *that*?

Her hand flew up to cover her mouth, and she had no idea if it was from shock or because her fingertips had more sense than the rest of her and were trying to prevent her from making a huge, huge mistake.

"Anne," he whispered, staring at her with searing intimacy.

Not Miss Wynter. *Anne.* He was taking liberties; she had not given him permission to use her given name. But she could not summon the outrage she knew she should feel. Because when he called her Anne, it was the first time she felt as if the name was truly hers. For eight years she had called herself Anne Wynter, but to the rest of the world she was always Miss Wynter. There had been no one in her life to call her Anne. Not a single person.

She wasn't sure she'd even realized it until this very moment.

She'd always thought she wanted to be Annelise again, to return to a life where her biggest concern was which dress to wear each morning, but now, when she heard Lord Winstead whisper her name, she realized that she liked the woman she'd become. She might not have liked the events that had brought her to this point, or the still present fear that George Chervil might someday find her and try to destroy her, but she liked *herself*.

It was an amazing thought.

"Can you kiss me just once?" she whispered. Because she *did* want it. She wanted a taste of perfection, even if she knew she could pursue it no further. "Can you kiss me once, and then never do so again?"

His eyes clouded, and for a moment she thought he might not speak. He was holding himself so tightly that his jaw trembled, and the only noise was the labored sound of his breath.

Disappointment trickled through her. She didn't know what she had been thinking, to ask such a thing. One kiss, and then nothing else? One kiss, when she, too, knew that she wanted so much more? She was—

"I don't know," he said abruptly.

Her eyes, which she had allowed to drift down to their feet, flew back to his face. He was still watching her with unwavering intensity, staring as if she might be his salvation. His face was not healed, with cuts and scrapes on his skin, and blue-black bruising around his eye, but in that moment he was the most beautiful thing she had ever seen.

"I don't think once will be enough," he said.

His words were thrilling. What woman wouldn't want to be so desired? But the careful part of her, the sensible part, realized that she was treading down a dangerous path. She had done this once before, allowed herself to fall for a man who would never marry her. The only difference was that this time she understood this. Lord Winstead was an earl—recently disgraced, it was true—but still an earl, and with his looks and charm, society would soon reopen their arms.

And she was . . . what? A governess? A false governess whose life history began in 1816 when she'd stepped off the ferry, seasick and petrified, and placed her feet on the rocky soil of the Isle of Man.

Anne Wynter had been born that day, and Annelise Shawcross . . .

She had disappeared. Gone in a puff like the spray of the ocean all around her.

But really, it didn't matter who she was. Anne Wynter . . . Annelise Shawcross . . . Neither one of them was a suitable match for Daniel Smythe-Smith, Earl of Winstead, Viscount Streathermore, and Baron Touchton of Stoke.

He had more names than she did. It was almost funny.

But not really. His were all true. He got to keep them all. And they were a badge of his position, of every reason why she should not be here with him, tipping her face toward his.

But still, she wanted this moment. She wanted to kiss him, to feel his arms around her, to lose herself in his embrace, to lose herself in the very night that surrounded them. Soft and mysterious, aching with promise . . .

What was it about a night like this?

He reached out and took her hand, and she let him. His fingers wrapped through hers, and even though he did not pull her toward him, she felt the tug, hot and pulsing, drawing her closer. Her body knew what to do. It knew what it wanted.

It would have been so easy to deny it if it hadn't been what her heart wanted, too.

"I cannot make that promise," he said softly, "but I will tell you this. Even if I don't kiss you now, if I turn and walk away and go eat supper and pretend none of this ever happened, I can't promise that I will never kiss you again." He lifted her hand to his mouth. She'd removed her gloves in the carriage, and her bare skin prickled and danced with desire where his lips touched it.

She swallowed. She did not know what to say.

"I can kiss you now," he said, "without the promise. Or we can do nothing, also without the promise. It is your choice."

If he had sounded overconfident, she would have found the strength to pull away. If his posture had held swagger, or if there had been anything in his voice that spoke of seduction, it would have been different.

But he wasn't making threats. He wasn't even making promises. He was simply telling her the truth.

And giving her a choice.

She took a breath. Tilted her face toward his.

And whispered, "Kiss me."

She would regret this tomorrow. Or maybe she wouldn't. But right now she did not care. The space between them melted away, and his arms, so strong and safe, wrapped around her. And when his lips touched hers, she thought she heard him say her name again.

"Anne."

It was a sigh. A plea. A benediction.

Without hesitation she reached out to touch him, her fingers sinking softly into his dark hair. Now that she had done it, had actually asked him to kiss her, she wanted it all. She wanted to take control of her life, or at least of this moment.

"Say my name," he murmured, his lips moving along her cheek to her earlobe. His voice was warm against her ear, seeping into her skin like a balm.

But she couldn't. It was too intimate. Why this

might be so, she had no idea, since she had already thrilled to the sound of her name on his lips, and more to the point, she was wrapped in his arms and desperately wanted to stay there forever.

But she wasn't quite ready to call him Daniel.

Instead she let out a little sigh, or maybe it was a little moan, and she let herself lean more heavily into him. His body was warm, and hers was so hot that she thought they might go up in flames.

His hands slid down her back, one settling at the small of it, the other reaching down to cup her bottom. She felt herself lifted, pressed hard against him, hard against the evidence of his need for her. And although she knew she should be shocked, or at the very least reminded that she should not be here with him, she could only shiver with delight.

It was so lovely to be so desired. To have someone want her so desperately. *Her.* Not some pretty little governess one could back into a corner and paw at. Not the companion of some lady whose nephew thought she ought to be grateful for the attention.

Not even some young girl who was really just an easy mark.

Lord Winstead wanted *her.* He'd wanted her before he'd even known who she was. That night at Winstead House, when he'd kissed her . . . For all he'd known she was the daughter of a duke, whom he'd be honor bound to marry just for being alone with her in a darkened hallway. And maybe that wasn't so meaningful, because it wasn't as if they'd shared more than a few sentences, but he still wanted her now, and she didn't think it was just because he thought he could take advantage of her.

But eventually sanity settled upon her, or maybe it was simply the specter of reality, and she forced herself to pull away from his kiss. "You need to get back," she said, wishing her voice was a bit steadier. "They will be waiting for you."

He nodded, and his eyes looked a little wild, as if he didn't quite know what had just happened within him.

Anne understood. She felt precisely the same way.

"Stay here," he finally said. "I will send a maid to show you to your room."

She nodded, watching as he headed across the gallery, his gait not quite as purposeful as she was used to seeing in him.

"But this—" he said, turning with one out-stretched arm. "This is not over." And then, in a voice that held desire, and determination, and more than a little bewilderment, he added, "It can't be over."

This time she did not nod. One of them had to be sensible. Over was the only thing it *could* be.

ENGLISH WEATHER DID not have a lot to recommend it, but when the sun and air got it right, there was no place more perfect, especially in the morning, when the light was still slanted and pink, and the dew-topped grass sparkled in the breeze.

Daniel was feeling particularly fine as he headed down to breakfast. The morning sun was streaming through every window, bathing the house in a celestial glow, the heavenly aroma of bacon wafted past his nose, and—not that there had been *much* of an ulterior motive to this—the previous night he had suggested that Elizabeth and Frances take their breakfast with the rest of the family rather than up in the nursery.

It was silly for them to eat apart in the mornings. It was extra work for everyone involved, and of course *he* did not want to be deprived of their company. He had only just returned to the country after three long years away. This, he told them, was the time to be with his family, especially his young cousins, who had changed so much in his absence.

Sarah might have given him a sarcastic look when he said that, and his aunt might have wondered aloud as to why, then, he was not with his own mother and sister. But he was excellent at ignoring his female relations when it suited him, and besides, he could hardly have responded what with the whooping and cheering coming from the two youngest Pleinsworths.

So it was settled. Elizabeth and Frances would not take their breakfast in the nursery and instead come down with the rest of the family. And if the girls were down, then Miss Wynter would also be there, and breakfast would be lovely, indeed.

With an admittedly goofy spring in his step, he made his way across the main hall to the breakfast room, pausing only to peek through the sitting room at the large window, which some enterprising footman had pulled open to let in the warm, spring air. What a day, what a day. Birds were chirping, the sky was blue, the grass was green (as always, but it was still an excellent thing), and he had kissed Miss Wynter.

He nearly bounced right off his feet, just thinking about it.

It had been splendid. Marvelous. A kiss to deny all previous kisses. Really, he didn't know what he'd been doing with all those other women, because whatever had happened when his lips had touched theirs, those had *not* been kisses.

Not like last night.

When he reached the breakfast room, he was delighted to see Miss Wynter standing by the sideboard. But any thought of flirtation was dashed when he also spied Frances, who was being directed to put more food on her plate.

"But I don't like kippers," Frances said.

"You don't have to eat them," Miss Wynter replied with great patience. "But you will not survive to dinner with only one piece of bacon on your plate. Have some eggs."

"I don't like them that way."

"Since when?" Miss Wynter asked, sounding rather suspicious. Or perhaps merely exasperated.

Frances wrinkled her nose and bent over the chafing dish. "They look very runny."

"Which can be rectified immediately," Daniel announced, deciding it was as good a time as any to make his presence known.

"Daniel!" Frances exclaimed, her eyes lighting with delight.

He stole a glance at Miss Wynter—he still was not quite thinking of her as Anne, except, it seemed, when he had her in his arms. Her reaction was not quite so effusive, but her cheeks did turn an extremely fetching shade of pink.

"I'll ask the cook to prepare you a fresh portion," he said to Frances, reaching out to tousle her hair.

"You'll do no such thing," Miss Wynter said sternly. "These eggs are perfectly acceptable. It would be a dreadful waste of food to prepare more."

He glanced down at Frances, giving her a sympathetic shrug. "There will be no crossing Miss Wynter, I'm afraid. Why don't you find something else to your liking?"

"I am not fond of kippers."

He glanced over at the offending dish and grimaced. "I'm not, either. I don't know anyone who is, quite frankly, except for my sister, and I'll tell you, she ends up smelling like fish for the rest of the day."

Frances gasped with gleeful horror.

Daniel looked over at Miss Wynter. "Do you like kippers?"

She stared back. "Very much."

"Pity." He sighed and turned back to Frances. "I shall have to advise Lord Chatteris about it now that he and Honoria are to be married. I can't imagine he will wish to be kissing someone with kippers on her breath."

Frances clapped a hand over her mouth and

giggled ecstatically. Miss Wynter gave him an extremely stern look and said, "This is hardly an appropriate conversation for children."

To which he simply *had* to say, "But it is for adults?"

She almost smiled. He could tell she wanted to. But she said, "No."

He gave a sad nod. "Pity."

"I shall have toast," Frances announced. "With heaps and heaps of jam."

"One heap only, please," Miss Wynter instructed.

"Nanny Flanders let's me have two heaps."

"I'm not Nanny Flanders."

"Hear, hear," Daniel remarked quietly.

Miss Wynter gave him A look.

"In front of the children. Really," he scolded, murmuring the words as he brushed by her so that Frances wouldn't hear. "Where is everyone else?" he asked loudly, taking a plate and heading straight for the bacon. Everything was better with bacon.

Life was better with bacon.

"Elizabeth and Harriet will be down shortly," Miss Wynter replied. "I don't know about Lady Pleinsworth and Lady Sarah. We are not anywhere near their rooms."

"Sarah hates getting up in the morning," Frances said, eyeing Miss Wynter as she scooped out her jam.

Miss Wynter eyed her back, and Frances stopped at one scoop, looking a bit deflated as she took her seat.

"Your aunt is also not an early riser," Miss Wynter said to Daniel, carefully filling her own plate. Bacon, eggs, toast, jam, a Cornish pasty . . . She was quite the fan of breakfast, he saw.

A big scoop of butter, a more moderate portion of orange marmalade, and then . . .

Not the kippers.

The kippers. At least three times as much as a normal human being should consume.

"Kippers?" he asked. "Must you?"

"I told you I liked them."

Or more to the point, he'd told her how well they served as armor against a kiss.

"They are practically the national food of the Isle of Man," she said, plopping one last slimy little fish on her plate for good measure.

"We have been studying the Isle of Man for geography," Frances said glumly. "The people are Manx. There are cats that are Manx. That's the only good thing about it. The word *Manx*."

Daniel could not even think of a comment.

"It ends in an *x*," Frances explained, not that that cleared things up any.

Daniel cleared his throat, deciding not to pursue the x-ish (x-ient? x-astic?) avenue of conversation, and followed Miss Wynter back to the table. "It's not a very large island," he commented. "I wouldn't have thought there was much to study."

"To the contrary," she remarked, taking a seat diagonal from Frances. "The island is very rich in history."

"And fish, apparently."

"It is," Miss Wynter admitted, jabbing a kipper with her fork, "the only thing I miss from my time there."

Daniel regarded her curiously as he sat next to her, taking the seat directly across from Frances. It was such an odd statement, coming from a woman so tight-lipped about her past.

But Frances interpreted the comment in an entirely different manner. Half-eaten toast triangle dangling from her fingertips, she froze, staring at her governess in utter amazement. "Then why," she finally demanded, "are you making *us* study it?"

Miss Wynter looked at her with impressive equanimity. "Well, I could hardly plan a lesson about the Isle of Wight." She turned to Daniel and said, "Honestly, I don't know the first thing about it."

"She has a very good point," he told Frances. "She can hardly teach what she does not know."

"But it is of no use," Frances protested. "At least the Isle of Wight is close. We might someday actually *go* there. The Isle of Man is in the middle of *nowhere*."

"The Irish Sea, actually," Daniel put in.

"One never knows where life will take you," Miss Wynter said quietly. "I can assure you that when I was your age, I was quite certain I would never step foot on the Isle of Man."

There was something about her voice that was arrestingly solemn, and neither Daniel nor Frances said a word. Finally, Miss Wynter gave a little shrug, turned back to her food, speared another kipper, and said, "I don't even know that I could have located it on a map."

There was another silence, this one more awkward than the last. Daniel decided it was time to address the aural chasm and said, "Well." Which, as usual, bought him enough time to think of something marginally more intelligent to say:

"I have peppermints in my office."

Miss Wynter turned. Then blinked. Then said, "I beg your pardon?"

"Brilliant!" Frances put in, the Isle of Man forgotten completely. "I love peppermints."

"And you, Miss Wynter?" he asked.

"She likes them," Frances said.

"Perhaps we may walk to the village," Daniel said, "to purchase some."

"I thought you said you had some," Frances reminded him.

"I do." He glanced over at Miss Wynter's kippers, his brows going up in alarm. "But I have a feeling that I don't have enough."

"Please," Miss Wynter said, spearing yet another little fishie with her fork and letting it tremble in the air. "Not on my account."

"Oh, I think it might be on everyone's account."

Frances looked from him to her governess and back, frowning mightily. "I do not understand what you are talking about," she announced.

Daniel smiled placidly at Miss Wynter, who chose not to respond.

"We are having our lessons outside today," Frances told him. "Would you like to accompany us?"

"Frances," Miss Wynter said quickly, "I'm sure his lordship—"

"Would *love* to accompany you," Daniel said with great flair. "I was just thinking what a marvelous day it is outside. So sunny and warm."

"Wasn't it sunny and warm in Italy?" Frances asked.

"It was, but it wasn't the same." He took a large bite of his bacon, which also hadn't been the same in Italy. Everything else one could eat had been better, but not the bacon.

"How?" Frances asked.

He thought about that for a moment. "The obvious answer would be that it was often simply too hot to enjoy oneself."

"And the less obvious answer?" Miss Wynter asked.

He smiled, absurdly happy that she had chosen to enter the conversation. "I'm afraid it's less obvious to me, too, but if I had to put it into words, I would say that it had something to do with feeling as if one belonged. Or, I suppose, not."

Frances nodded sagely.

"It could be a lovely day," Daniel continued. "Perfection, really, but it could never be the same as a lovely day in England. The smells were different, and the air was drier. The scenery was gorgeous, of course, especially down by the sea, but—"

"We're down by the sea," Frances interrupted.

"What are we, ten miles away here at Whipple Hill?"

"A good deal more than that," Daniel said, "but you could never compare the English Channel to the Tyrrhenian Sea. One is green-gray and wild, and the other ground-glass blue."

"I should love to see a ground-glass blue ocean," Miss Wynter said with a wistful sigh.

"It is spectacular," he admitted. "But it isn't home."

"Oh, but think how heavenly it would be," she continued, "to be on the water and not be violently ill."

He chuckled despite himself. "You are prone to seasickness, then?"

"Dreadfully so."

"I never get seasick," Frances said.

"You've never been on the water," Miss Wynter pointed out pertly.

"Ergo, I never get seasick," Frances replied triumphantly. "Or perhaps I should say that I have never *been* seasick."

"It would certainly be more precise."

"You are such a governess," Daniel said affectionately.

But her face took on a queer expression, as if perhaps she hadn't wanted to be reminded of this fact. It was a clear sign to change the subject, so he said, "I cannot even remember how we came to be discussing the Tyrrhenian Sea. I was—"

"It was because I was asking about Italy," Frances put in helpfully.

"—going to say," he said smoothly, since of course he'd known exactly how they'd come to be discussing the Tyrrhenian Sea, "that I am very much looking forward to joining you for your lesson *en plein air*."

"That means out of doors," Frances said to Miss Wynter.

"I know," she murmured.

"I know you know," Frances replied. "I just wanted to make sure you knew that *I* knew."

Elizabeth arrived then, and while Frances was ascertaining whether *she* knew the translation for *en plein air*, Daniel turned to Miss Wynter and said, "I trust I will not intrude this afternoon if I accompany you for lessons."

He knew very well that she could not possibly say anything other than "Of course not." (Which was precisely what she did say.) But it seemed as good a sentence as any to begin a conversation. He waited until she was through eating her eggs, then added, "I would be happy to assist in any way."

She touched her serviette delicately to her mouth, then said, "I am sure the girls would find it far more gratifying if you took part in the lessons."

"And you?" He smiled warmly.

"I would find it gratifying as well." Said with a hint of mischief.

"Then that is what I shall do," he replied grandly. Then he frowned. "You do not plan any dissection this afternoon, I trust?"

"We perform only vivisection in my classroom," she said, with a remarkably straight face.

He laughed, loudly enough that Elizabeth, Frances, and Harriet, who had also come down, turned in his direction. It was remarkable, because the three of them really did not resemble each other overmuch, but in that moment, with their faces molded into the exact same expressions of curiosity, they looked identical.

"Lord Winstead was inquiring about our lesson plan for the day," Miss Wynter explained.

There was a silence. Then they must have decided that a further pursuance lacked excitement, and they turned as one back to their food.

"What are we studying this afternoon?" Daniel asked.

"This afternoon?" Miss Wynter echoed. "I expect full attendance at half ten."

"This morning, then," he amended, duly chastened.

"Geography first—*not* the Isle of Man," she said loudly, when three young heads swiveled angrily in her direction. "Then some arithmetic, and finally we shall focus on literature."

"My favorite!" Harriet said enthusiastically, taking the seat next to Frances.

"I know," Miss Wynter replied, giving her an indulgent smile. "It is why we are saving it for last. It's the only way I can guarantee holding your attention through the entire day."

Harriet smiled sheepishly, then brightened quite suddenly. "May we read from one of my works?"

"You know that we are studying Shakespeare's histories," Miss Wynter said apologetically, "and—" She stopped short. Quite short.

"And what?" Frances asked.

Miss Wynter regarded Harriet. Then she regarded Daniel. And then, as he began to feel rather like a lamb to slaughter, she turned back to Harriet and asked, "Did you bring your plays with you?"

"Of course. I never go anywhere without them."

"You never know when you might have the opportunity to have one staged?" Elizabeth said, somewhat meanly.

"Well, there is that," Harriet replied, ignoring her sister's dig or (and Daniel thought this was more likely) simply not noticing it. "But the big fear," she continued, "is fire."

He *knew* he shouldn't inquire, but he just could not stop himself. "Fire?"

"At home," she confirmed. "What if Pleinsworth House burned to the ground while we are here in Berkshire? My life's work, lost."

Elizabeth snorted. "If Pleinsworth House burns to the ground, I assure you that we will have far bigger worries than the loss of your scribblings."

"I fear hail myself," Frances announced. "And locusts."

"Have you ever read one of your cousin's plays?" Miss Wynter asked innocently.

Daniel shook his head.

"They're rather like this conversation, actually," she said, and then, while he was absorbing *that*, she turned to her charges and announced, "Good news, everyone! Today, instead of *Julius Caesar,* we will study one of Harriet's plays."

"*Study*?" Elizabeth asked, all horror.

"Read from," Miss Wynter corrected. She turned to Harriet. "You may choose which one."

"Oh, my heavens, that will be difficult." Harriet set down her fork and placed a hand over her heart as she thought, her fingers spread like a lopsided starfish.

"*Not* the one with the frog," Frances said forcefully. "Because you know I will have to be the frog."

"You're a very good frog," Miss Wynter said supportively.

Daniel kept quiet, watching the exchange with interest. And dread.

"Nevertheless," Frances said with a sniff.

"Don't worry, Frances," Harriet said, giving her hand a pat, "we won't perform *The Marsh of the Frogs*. I wrote that years ago. My recent work is much more nuanced."

"How far along are you on the one about Henry VIII?" Miss Wynter asked.

"A yen to have your head lopped off?" Daniel murmured. "She did want to cast you as Anne Boleyn, didn't she?"

"It's not ready," Harriet said. "I have to revise the first act."

"I told her it needs a unicorn," said Frances.

Daniel kept his eyes on the girls but leaned toward Miss Wynter. "Am I going to have to be a unicorn?"

"If you're lucky."

He whipped his head around to face her. "What does *that* m—"

"Harriet!" she called out. "We really must choose a play."

"Very well," Harriet said, sitting up exceptionally tall in her seat. "I think we should perform . . ."

Chapter Ten

"*THE STRANGE, SAD Tragedy of Lord Finstead*???????"

Daniel's reaction could best be summed up in two words: *Oh* and *no*.

"The ending is really quite hopeful," Harriet told him.

His expression, which he was fairly certain hovered somewhere between *stunned* and *aghast,* added *dubious* to its repertoire. "You have the word *tragedy* in the title."

Harriet frowned. "I might have to change that."

"I don't think it's going to work very well as *The Strange, Sad Comedy,*" Frances said.

"No, no," Harriet mused, "I'd have to rework it completely."

"But *Fin*stead," Daniel persisted. "Really?"

Harriet looked up at him. "Do you think it sounds too fishy?"

Whatever mirth Miss Wynter had been holding onto burst out in a spray of eggs and bacon. "Oh!" she exclaimed, and really, it was difficult to summon any sympathy for her plight. "I'm sorry, oh, that was rude. But—" She might have meant to say more. Daniel couldn't tell; her laughter got hold of her again, cutting off all intelligible speech.

"It's a good thing you're wearing yellow," Elizabeth said to Frances.

Frances glanced down at her bodice, shrugged, then lightly brushed herself off with her serviette.

"Too bad the fabric doesn't have little sprigs of red flowers," Elizabeth added. "The bacon, you know." She turned to Daniel as if waiting for some sort of confirmation, but he wanted no part of any conversation that included partially digested airborne bacon, so he turned to Miss Wynter and said:

"Help me. Please?"

She gave him an abashed nod (but not nearly so abashed as she ought) and turned to Harriet. "I think that Lord Winstead refers to the rhyming qualities of the title."

Harriet blinked a few times. "It doesn't rhyme."

"Oh, for heaven's sake," Elizabeth burst out. "*Fin*stead *Win*stead?"

Harriet's gasp very nearly sucked the air from the room. "I never noticed!" she exclaimed.

"Obviously," her sister drawled.

"I must have been thinking about you when I wrote the play," Harriet said to Daniel. From her expression, he gathered he was meant to feel flattered, so he tried to smile.

"You have been much in their thoughts," Miss Wynter told him.

"We shall have to change the name," Harriet said with an exhausted sigh. "It's going to be a horrible lot of work. I shall have to recopy the entire play. Lord Finstead is in almost every scene, you know." She turned to Daniel. "He is the protagonist."

"I'd surmised," he said dryly.

"You will have to play his role."

He turned to Miss Wynter. "There's no getting out of it, is there?"

She looked utterly amused, the traitorous wench. "I'm afraid not."

"Is there a unicorn?" Frances asked. "I make an excellent unicorn."

"I think *I'd* rather be the unicorn," Daniel said glumly.

"Nonsense!" Miss Wynter chimed in. "You must play our hero."

To which Frances naturally replied, "Unicorns can be heroes."

"Enough with the unicorns!" Elizabeth burst out.

Frances stuck out her tongue.

"Harriet," Miss Wynter said. "As Lord Winstead has not yet read your play, perhaps you can tell him about his character."

Harriet turned to him with breathless delight. "Oh, you will love being Lord Finstead. He used to be very handsome."

Daniel cleared his throat. "Used to be?"

"There was a fire," Harriet explained, her brief sentence ending with the kind of sad sigh Daniel assumed was normally reserved for victims of actual fires.

"Wait a moment," he said, turning to Miss Wynter with growing alarm. "The fire doesn't occur on stage, does it?"

"Oh, no," Harriet answered for her. "Lord Finstead is already gravely disfigured when the play opens." And then, in a burst of prudence that was both reassuring and surprising, she added, "It would be far too dangerous to have a fire on stage."

"Well, that's—"

"Besides," Harriet cut in, "it would be hardly necessary to help you with your character. You're already . . ." She motioned to her own face with her hand, waving it in a bit of a circle.

He had no idea what she was doing.

"Your bruises," Frances said in a very loud whisper.

"Ah, yes," Daniel said. "Yes, of course. Sadly, I do know a bit about facial disfigurement at present."

"At least you won't need any makeup," Elizabeth said.

Daniel was thanking God for small favors, but then Harriet said, "Well, except for the wart."

Daniel's gratitude was swiftly retracted. "Harriet," he said, looking her in the eye as he would an adult, "I really must tell you, I have never been a thespian."

Harriet waved this off like a gnat. "That is what is so wonderful about my plays. Anyone can enjoy himself."

"I don't know," Frances said. "I did not like being that frog. My legs hurt the next day."

"Perhaps we *should* choose *The Marsh of the Frogs,*" Miss Wynter said innocently. "Bottle green is all the rage in men's clothing this year. Surely Lord Winstead will have something in his wardrobe in the color."

"I am *not* playing a frog." His eyes narrowed wickedly. "Unless you do, too."

"There is only one frog in the play," Harriet said blithely.

"But isn't the title *The Marsh of the Frogs*?" he asked, even though he should have known better. "Plural?" Good Lord, the entire conversation was making him dizzy.

"That's the irony," Harriet said, and Daniel managed to stop himself just before he asked her what she meant by that (because it fulfilled no definition of irony *he'd* ever heard).

His brain hurt.

"I think it would be best for Cousin Daniel to read the play for himself," Harriet said. She looked over at him. "I'll fetch the pages right after breakfast. You can read it while we do our geography and maths."

He had a feeling he'd rather do geography and maths. And he didn't even *like* geography. Or maths.

"I'll have to think up a new name for Lord Finstead," Harriet continued. "If I don't, everyone will assume he is really you, Daniel. Which of course he's not. Unless . . ." Her voice trailed off, quite possibly for dramatic effect.

"Unless what?" he asked, even though he was fairly certain he did not want to hear her answer.

"Well, you've never ridden a stallion backwards, have you?"

His mouth opened, but no sound came out. Surely he would be forgiven for such a deficit, because, really. A stallion? Backwards?

"Daniel?" Elizabeth prodded.

"No," he finally managed to say. "No, I have not."

Harriet shook her head regretfully. "I didn't think so."

And Daniel was left feeling as if he somehow did not measure up. Which was ludicrous. And galling. "I'm fairly certain," he said, "that there is not a man on this planet who can ride a stallion backwards."

"Well, that depends, I would think," said Miss Wynter.

Daniel couldn't believe she was encouraging this. "I can't imagine on what."

One of her hands did a little flip in the air until the palm was facing up, as if waiting for an answer to drop down from heaven. "Is the man sitting backwards on the horse, or is the horse actually moving in reverse?"

"Both," Harriet replied.

"Well, then I don't think it can be done," Miss

Wynter replied, and Daniel almost thought she was taking the conversation seriously. At the last moment she turned away, and he saw the telltale tightening at the corners of her mouth as she tried not to laugh. She was poking fun at him, the wretch.

Oh, but she had chosen the wrong opponent. He was a man with five sisters. She didn't stand a chance.

He turned to Harriet. "What role will Miss Wynter be playing?" he asked.

"Oh, I won't be taking a role," Miss Wynter cut in. "I never do."

"And why is that?"

"I supervise."

"I can supervise," Frances said.

"Oh, no, you can't," Elizabeth said, with the speed and vehemence of a true older sister.

"If anyone is going to supervise, it ought to be me," Harriet said. "I wrote the play."

Daniel rested one elbow on the table, then rested his chin in his hand and regarded Miss Wynter with carefully studied thoughtfulness, maintaining this position for just long enough to make her shift nervously in her seat. Finally, unable to take his perusal any longer, she burst out with, "What is it?"

"Oh, nothing, really," he sighed. "I was just thinking that I hadn't taken you for a coward."

The three Pleinsworth daughters let out identical gasps, and their eyes, wide as dinner plates, darted back and forth from Daniel to Miss Wynter, as if they were following a tennis match.

Which he supposed they were of a sort. And it was definitely Miss Wynter's turn to volley.

"It is not cowardice," she returned. "Lady Pleinsworth hired me to shepherd these three young girls to adulthood so that they may join the company of educated women." And while Daniel was trying to follow *that* overblown bit of nonsense, she added, "I am merely doing the job for which my services were engaged."

The three pairs of eyes lingered on Miss Wynter for one more second, then lobbed over to Daniel.

"A noble endeavor to be sure," he countered, "but surely their learning can only be improved by watching your fine example."

And the eyes were back on Miss Wynter.

"Ah," she said, and he was quite certain she was stalling for time, "but in my many years as a governess, I have learned that my talents do not lie in thespian pursuits. I would not wish to pollute their minds with such a sad talent as myself."

"Your thespian talents could hardly be worse than mine."

Her eyes narrowed. "That is perhaps true, but you are not their governess."

His eyes narrowed. "That is certainly true, but hardly relevant."

"*Au contraire,*" she said, with noticeable relish. "As their male cousin, you are not expected to set an example of ladylike behavior."

He leaned forward. "You're enjoying yourself, aren't you?"

She smiled. Maybe a little bit. "Very much so."

"I think this might be better than Harriet's play," Frances said, her eyes following her sisters' back to Daniel.

"I'm writing it down," Harriet said.

Daniel looked over at her. He couldn't help it. He knew for a fact that the only utensil she was holding was a fork.

"Well, I'm committing it to memory so that I might write it down at a future time," she admitted.

Daniel turned back to Miss Wynter. She looked terribly correct, sitting in her chair with her perfect posture. Her dark hair was pulled back into its requisite bun, every strand pinned meticulously into place. There was nothing about her that was remotely out of the ordinary, and yet . . .

She was radiant.

To his eye, at least. Probably to every male eye in England. If Harriet, Elizabeth, and Frances couldn't see it, it was because they were, well, girls. And young ones at that, who wouldn't know to view her as a rival. Unfettered by jealousy or prejudice, they saw her the way he rather thought she wanted to be seen—loyal, intelligent, with a fierce and clever wit.

And pretty, of course. It was the strangest thing, and he had no idea where the notion had come from, but he had a feeling that Miss Wynter liked being pretty as much as she hated being beautiful.

And he found her all the more fascinating for it.

"Tell me, Miss Wynter," he finally said, choosing

his words with measured deliberation, "have you ever *tried* to act in one of Harriet's plays?"

Her lips pressed together. She'd been cornered by a yes-or-no question, and she was not happy about it. "No," she finally replied.

"Don't you think it's time?"

"Not really, no."

He settled his eyes firmly on hers. "If I'm in the play, you're in the play."

"It would be helpful," Harriet said. "There are twenty characters, Miss Wynter, and without you, we'd each have to play five."

"If you join in," Frances added, "we'll only have to do four each."

"Which," Elizabeth concluded triumphantly, "is a twenty percent reduction!"

Daniel still had his chin resting in his hand, so he tilted his head ever so slightly to give the impression of increased consideration. "No compliments for the excellent application of their mathematical skills, Miss Wynter?"

She looked about ready to boil, not that he could blame her with everyone conspiring against her. But the governess within her was quite unable to resist pointing out, "I told you that you would find it useful to be able to do sums and tables in your heads."

Harriet's eyes grew bright with excitement. "Then that means you'll join us?"

Daniel wasn't certain how she'd reached that interpretation, but he wasn't one to let an opportunity pass by, so he immediately threw in his support with, "Well done, Miss Wynter. We all must occasionally venture outside our areas of comfort. I'm so terribly proud of you."

The look she gave him clearly said, *I will eviscerate you, you pompous wretch.* But of course she could never utter such a thing in front of the children, which meant that he could watch happily as she seethed.

Checkmate!

"Miss Wynter, I think you should be the evil queen," Harriet said.

"There's an evil queen?" Daniel echoed. With obvious delight.

"Of course," Harriet replied. "Every good play has an evil queen."

Frances actually raised her hand. "And a un—"

"Don't say it," Elizabeth growled.

Frances crossed her eyes, put her knife to her forehead in an approximation of a horn, and neighed.

"It is settled, then," Harriet said decisively. "Daniel shall be Lord Finstead"—she held up a restraining hand—"who won't be Lord Finstead but rather some other name which I will think of later; Miss Wynter shall be the evil queen, Elizabeth will be . . ." She narrowed her eyes and regarded her sister, who regarded her back with outright suspicion.

"Elizabeth will be the beautiful princess," Harriet finally announced, much to the amazement of Elizabeth.

"What about me?" Frances asked.

"The butler," Harriet replied without even a second of hesitation.

Frances's mouth immediately opened to protest.

"No, no," Harriet said. "It's the best role, I promise. You get to do everything."

"Except be a unicorn," Daniel murmured.

Frances tilted her head to the side with a resigned expression.

"The next play," Harriet finally gave in. "I shall find a way to include a unicorn in the one I'm working on right now."

Frances pumped both fists in the air. "Huzzah!"

"But only if you stop talking about unicorns right now."

"I second the motion," Elizabeth said, to no one in particular.

"Very well," Frances acceded. "No more unicorns. At least not where you can hear me."

Harriet and Elizabeth both looked as if they might argue, but Miss Wynter interceded, saying, "I think that's more than fair. You can hardly stop her from talking about them entirely."

"Then it's settled," Harriet said. "We shall work out the smaller roles later."

"What about you?" Elizabeth demanded.

"Oh, I'm going to be the goddess of the sun and moon."

"The tale gets stranger and stranger," Daniel said.

"Just wait until act seven," Miss Wynter told him.

"Seven?" His head snapped up. "There are seven acts?"

"Twelve," Harriet corrected, "but don't worry, you're in only eleven of them. Now then, Miss Wynter, when do you propose that we begin our rehearsals? And may we do so out of doors? There is a clearing by the gazebo that would be ideal."

Miss Wynter turned to Daniel for confirmation. He just shrugged and said, "Harriet is the playwright."

She nodded and turned back to the girls. "I was going to say that we may start after the rest of our lessons, but given that there are twelve acts to get through, I am granting a one-day holiday from geography and maths."

There was a rousing cheer from the girls, and even Daniel felt swept along in the general joy. "Well," he said to Miss Wynter, "it's not every day one gets to be strange *and* sad."

"Or evil."

He chuckled. "Or evil." Then he got a thought. A strange, sad thought. "I don't die at the end, do I?"

She shook her head.

"That's a relief, I must say. I make a terrible corpse."

She laughed at that, or rather, she held her lips together firmly while she tried not to laugh. The girls were chattering madly as they took their final bites of breakfast and fled the room, and then he was left sitting next to Miss Wynter, just the two of them and their plates of breakfast, the warm morning sun filtering upon them through the windows.

"I wonder," he said aloud, "do we get to be wicked?"

Her fork clattered against her plate. "I beg your pardon?"

"Sad, strange, and evil are all very well and good, but I'd like to be wicked. Wouldn't you?"

Her lips parted, and he heard the tiny airy rush of her gasp. The sound tickled his skin, made him want to kiss her.

But everything seemed to make him want to kiss her. He felt like a young man again, perpetually randy, except that this was far more specific. Back at university he'd flirted with every woman he'd met, stealing kisses or, more to the point, accepting them when they'd been offered freely.

This was different. He didn't want a woman. He wanted *her*. And he supposed that if he had to spend the afternoon being strange, sad, and disfigured just to be in her company, it would be well worth it.

Then he remembered the wart.

He turned to Miss Wynter and said firmly, "I am not getting a wart."

Really, a man had to draw the line somewhere.

Chapter Eleven

Six hours later, as Anne adjusted the black sash that was meant to denote her as the evil queen, she had to admit that she could not recall a more enjoyable afternoon.

Ludicrous, yes; completely without academic value, absolutely. But still, completely and utterly enjoyable.

She had had fun.

Fun. She couldn't remember the last time.

They had been rehearsing all day (not that they planned to actually perform *The Strange, Sad Tragedy of the Lord Who Was Not Finstead* in front of an audience), and she could not begin to count the number of times she had had to stop, doubled over with laughter.

"Thou shalt never smite my daughter!" she intoned, waving a stick through the air.

Elizabeth ducked.

"Oh!" Anne winced. "I'm so sorry. Are you all right?"

"I'm fine," Elizabeth assured her. "I—"

"Miss Wynter, you're breaking character again!" Harriet bemoaned.

"I almost hit Elizabeth," Anne explained.

"I don't care."

Elizabeth exhaled in a puff of indignation. "*I* care."

"Maybe you shouldn't use a stick," Frances said.

Harriet spared her sister a disdainful glance before turning back to the rest of them. "May we return to the script?" she said in a voice so prim it spun right into sarcasm.

"Of course," Anne said, looking down at her script. "Where were we? Oh, yes, don't smite my daughter and all that."

"*Miss Wynter.*"

"Oh, no, I wasn't saying the line. I was just finding it." She cleared her throat and waved her stick in the air, giving Elizabeth wide berth. "Thou shalt never smite my daughter!"

How she managed that without laughing she would never know.

"I don't want to smite her," Lord Winstead said, with enough drama to make a Drury Lane audience weep. "I want to marry her."

"Never."

"No, no, no, Miss Wynter!" Harriet exclaimed. "You don't sound upset at all."

"Well, I'm not," Anne admitted. "The daughter is a bit of a ninny. I should think the evil queen would be glad to get her off her hands."

Harriet sighed the sigh of the very-long-suffering. "Be that as it may, the evil *queen* doesn't think her daughter is a ninny."

"I think she's a ninny," Elizabeth chimed in.

"But you *are* the daughter," Harriet said.

"I know! I've been reading her lines all day. She's an idiot."

As they bickered, Lord Winstead moved closer to Anne and said, "I do feel a bit of a lecherous old man, trying to marry Elizabeth."

She chuckled.

"I don't suppose you'd consider swapping roles."

"With you?"

He scowled. "With Elizabeth."

"After you said I made a perfect evil queen? I think not."

He leaned a little closer. "Not to split hairs, but I believe I said you made a perfect*ly* evil queen."

"Oh, yes. That is so much better." Anne frowned. "Have you seen Frances?"

He tilted his head to the right. "I believe she's off rooting about in the bushes."

Anne followed his gaze uneasily. "Rooting?"

"She told me she was practicing for the next play."

Anne blinked at him, not following.

"For when she gets to be a unicorn."

"Oh, of course." She chuckled. "She is rather tenacious, that one."

Lord Winstead grinned, and Anne's stomach did a little flip. He had such a lovely smile. Wickedly mischievous, but with . . . oh, Anne had no idea how to describe it except that he was good man, an honorable man who knew right from wrong, and no matter how naughty his grins . . .

She knew he would not hurt her.

Even her own father had not proved so dependable.

"You look very serious of a sudden," Lord Winstead said.

Anne blinked herself out of her reverie. "Oh, it's nothing," she said quickly, hoping she wasn't blushing. Sometimes she had to remind herself that he could not peer straight into her thoughts. She looked over at Harriet and Elizabeth, who were still arguing, although by now they had moved off the topic of the intelligence (or lack thereof) of the beautiful princess and had started in on—

Good Lord, were they discussing wild boars?

"I think we need to take a break," she said.

"I'll tell you one thing," Lord Winstead said. "I am *not* playing the boar."

"I don't think you need to worry on that score," Anne said. "Frances will certainly snatch that one up."

He looked at her. She looked at him. And together they burst out laughing, so hard that even Harriet and Elizabeth stopped their sniping.

"What's so funny?" Harriet asked, followed by Elizabeth's extremely suspicious "Are you laughing at me?"

"We're laughing at everyone," Lord Winstead said, wiping tears from his eyes. "Even ourselves."

"I'm hungry," Frances announced, emerging from the bushes. There were a few leaves stuck to her dress and a small stick jutting out from the side of her head. Anne didn't think it was meant to be a unicorn's horn, but the effect was quite charming nonetheless.

"I'm hungry, too," Harriet said with a sigh.

"Why doesn't one of you run back to the house and ask the kitchen for a picnic hamper?" Anne suggested. "We could all use some sustenance."

"I'll go," Frances offered.

"I'll go with you," Harriet told her. "I do some of my best thinking while I'm walking."

Elizabeth looked at her sisters, then at the adults. "Well, I'm not going to stay here by myself," she said, the adults apparently not counting as proper company, and the three girls took off for the house, their pace quickly moving from brisk walk to out-and-out race.

Anne watched as they disappeared over the rise. She probably shouldn't be out here alone with Lord Winstead, but it was difficult to muster an objection. It was the middle of the day, and they were out of doors, and more to the point, she'd had so much fun that afternoon that she didn't think she could muster an objection to anything just then.

She had a smile on her face, and she was quite happy to keep it there.

"I would think you could remove your sash," Lord Winstead suggested. "No one needs to be evil all the time."

Anne laughed, her fingers sliding along the length of black ribbon. "I don't know. I find I'm rather enjoying being evil."

"As well you should. I must confess, I'm rather jealous of your evildoings. Poor Lord Finstead, or whatever his name turns out to be, could use a bit more malevolence. He's a rather hapless fellow."

"Ah, but he wins the princess in the end," Anne reminded him, "and the evil queen must live the rest of her life in an attic."

"Which begs the question," he said, turning toward her with furrowed brow. "Why *is* Lord Finstead's tale sad? The strange bit is abundantly clear, but if the evil queen ends up in the attic—"

"It's *his* attic," Anne interrupted.

"Oh." He looked like he was trying not to laugh. "Well, that changes everything."

And then they did laugh. The both of them. Together.

Again.

"Oh, I'm hungry, too," Anne said, once her mirth had melted down to a smile. "I hope the girls don't take too long."

And then she felt Lord Winstead's hand take hers. "I hope they take long enough," he murmured. He tugged her to him, and she let him, far too happy in the moment to remember all the ways he would surely break her heart.

"I told you I would kiss you again," he whispered.

"You told me you would try."

His lips touched hers. "I knew I would succeed."

He kissed her again, and she pulled away, but only an inch or so. "You're rather sure of yourself."

"Mmm-hmm." His lips found the corner of her mouth, then floated softly along her skin until she couldn't help herself and her head fell back to allow him access to the curve of her neck.

Her pelisse slipped away, baring more of her skin to the cool afternoon air, and he kissed her, right along the edge of her bodice, before coming back to her mouth. "Dear God, I want you so much," he said, his voice nothing more than a rasp. He held her more tightly, both of his hands cupping her bottom and pulling her forward . . . up . . . until she was seized by a mad urge to wrap her legs around him. It was what he wanted, and God help her, it was what she wanted, too.

Thank heavens for her skirt, which was possibly the only thing stopping her from behaving with utter shamelessness. But still, when one of his hands reached into her bodice, she didn't refuse. And when his palm gently grazed her nipple, all she did was moan.

This would have to stop. But not just yet.

"I dreamed about you last night," he whispered against her skin. "Do you want to know what it was?"

She shook her head, even though she did, desperately. But she knew her limits. She could go down this road only so far. If she heard his dreams, heard the words from his lips as they rained down softly against her, she would want it, everything he said.

And it hurt too much to want something she could never have.

"What did you dream about?" he asked.

"I don't dream," she replied.

He went still, then drew back so that he could look at her. His eyes—that amazingly bright light blue—were filled with curiosity. And maybe a touch of sadness.

"I don't dream," she said again. "I haven't for years." She said it with a shrug. It was such a normal thing for her now; it hadn't occurred to her until that moment how strange it might seem to others.

"But you did as a child?" he asked.

She nodded. She hadn't really thought about it before, or maybe she just hadn't wanted to think about it. But if she had dreamed since she left Northumberland eight years earlier, she had not remembered. Every morning before she opened her eyes, there was nothing but the black of the night. A perfectly empty space, filled with absolute emptiness. No hopes. No dreams.

But also no nightmares.

It seemed a small price to pay. She wasted enough of her waking hours worrying about George Chervil and his mad quest for revenge.

"You don't find that strange?" he asked.

"That I don't dream?" She knew what he'd meant, but for some reason she'd needed to state it out loud.

He nodded.

"No." Her voice came out flat. But certain. Maybe it was strange, but it was also safe.

He didn't say anything, but his eyes searched hers with penetrating intensity until she had to look away. He was seeing far too much of her. In less than a week this man had uncovered more of her than she'd revealed to anyone in the past eight years. It was unsettling.

It was dangerous.

Reluctantly she pulled herself from his embrace, stepping just far enough away so that he could not reach out for her. She bent to retrieve her pelisse from where it lay on the grass, and without speaking she refastened it around her shoulders. "The girls will be back soon," she said, even though she knew that they wouldn't. It would be at least another quarter of an hour before they returned, probably more.

"Let's take a stroll, then," he suggested, offering her his arm.

She eyed him suspiciously.

"Not everything I do is with lascivious intent," he said with a laugh. "I thought I might show you one of my favorite places here at Whipple Hill." As she placed her hand on his arm he added, "We're only a quarter mile or so from the lake."

"Is it stocked?" she asked. She couldn't remember

the last time she'd gone fishing, but oh, how she had enjoyed it as a child. She and Charlotte had been the bane of their mother, who had wanted them to pursue more feminine activities. Which they had, eventually. But even after Anne had become obsessed with frocks and gowns and keeping tally of every single time an eligible gentleman glanced at an eligible young lady . . .

She'd still loved to go fishing. She'd even been happy to do the gutting and cleaning. And of course the eating. One could not understate the satisfaction to be found in catching one's own food.

"It should be stocked," Lord Winstead said. "It always was before I left, and I would not think that my steward would have had cause to change the directive." Her eyes must have been shining with delight, for he smiled indulgently and asked, "Do you like to fish, then?"

"Oh, very much so," she said with a wistful sigh. "When I was a child . . ." But she did not finish her sentence. She'd forgotten that she did not speak of her childhood.

But if he was curious—and she was quite certain he must be—he did not show it. As they walked down the gentle slope toward a leafy stand of trees, he said only, "I loved to fish as a child, too. I came all the time with Marcus—Lord Chatteris," he added, since of course she was not on a first-name basis with the earl.

Anne took in the landscape around her. It was a glorious spring day, and there seemed a hundred different shades of green rippling along the leaves and grass. The world felt terribly new, and deceptively hopeful. "Did Lord Chatteris visit often as a child?" she asked, eager to keep the conversation on benign matters.

"Constantly," Lord Winstead replied. "Or at least every school holiday. By the time we were thirteen I don't know that I ever came home without him." They walked a bit more, then he reached out to pluck a low-hanging leaf. He looked at it, frowned, then finally set it aloft with a little flick of his fingers. It went spiraling through the air, and something about the fluttery motion must have been mesmerizing, because they both stopped walking to watch it make its way back down to the grass.

And then, as if the moment had never happened, Lord Winstead quietly picked up the conversation where it had been left off. "Marcus has no family to speak of. No siblings, and his mother died when he was quite young."

"What about his father?"

"Oh, he hardly spoke to him," Lord Winstead replied. But he said it with such nonchalance, as if there was nothing at all peculiar about a father and son who did not speak. It was rather unlike him, Anne thought. Not uncaring, precisely, but . . . Well, she didn't know what it was, except that it surprised her. And then she was surprised that she knew him well enough to notice such a thing.

Surprised and perhaps a little bit alarmed, because she *shouldn't* know him so well. It was not her place, and such a connection could lead only to heartbreak. She knew that, and so should he.

"Were they estranged?" she asked, still curious about Lord Chatteris. She had only met the earl once, and briefly at that, but it seemed they had something in common.

Lord Winstead shook his head. "No. I rather think the elder Lord Chatteris simply had nothing to say."

"To his own son?"

He shrugged. "It is not so uncommon, really. Half of my schoolmates probably couldn't have told you the color of their parents' eyes."

"Blue," Anne whispered, suddenly overcome by a huge, churning wave of homesickness. "And green." And her sisters' eyes were also blue and green, but she regained her composure before she blurted that out, too.

He tilted his head toward her, but he did not ask her any questions, for which she was desperately grateful. Instead he said, "My father had eyes exactly like mine."

"And your mother?" Anne had met his mother, but she had had no cause to take note of her eyes. And she did want to keep the conversation centered on him. Everything was easier that way.

Not to mention that it was a topic in which she seemed to have great interest.

"My mother's eyes are also blue," he said, "but a darker shade. Not as dark as yours—" He turned his head, looking at her quite intently. "But I have to say, I don't know that I've ever seen eyes quite like yours. They almost look violet." His head tilted the tiniest bit to the side. "But they don't. They're still blue."

Anne smiled and looked away. She'd always been proud of her eyes. It was the one vanity she still allowed herself. "From far away they look brown," she said.

"All the more reason to cherish the time one spends in close proximity," he murmured.

Her breath caught and she stole a glance at him, but he was no longer looking at her. Instead he was motioning ahead with his free arm, saying, "Can you see the lake? Just through those trees."

Anne craned her neck just enough to catch a silvery glint peeking between the tree trunks.

"In the winter you can see it quite well, but once the leaves come out, it's obscured."

"It's beautiful," Anne said sincerely. Even now, unable to see most of the water, it was idyllic. "Does it get warm enough to swim in?"

"Not on purpose, but every member of my family has managed to be submerged at one point or another."

Anne felt a laugh tickle her lips. "Oh, dear."

"Some of us more than once," Lord Winstead said sheepishly.

She looked over at him, and he looked so adorably boyish that she quite simply lost her breath. What would her life have been if she had met him instead of George Chervil when she was sixteen?

Or if not him (since she could never have married an earl, even as Annelise Shawcross), then someone just like him. Someone named Daniel Smythe, or Daniel Smith. But he would have been Daniel. *Her* Daniel.

He would have been heir to a baronetcy, or heir to nothing at all, just a common country squire with a snug and comfortable home, ten acres of land, and a pack of lazy hounds.

And she would have loved it. Every last mundane moment.

Had she really once craved excitement? At sixteen she'd thought she wanted to come to London and go to the theater, and the opera, and every party for which she was issued an invitation. A dashing young matron—that's what she had told Charlotte she wanted to be.

But that had been the folly of youth. Surely, even if she had married a man who would whisk her off to the capital and immerse her in the glittering life of the ton . . . Surely she would have tired of it all and wanted to return to Northumberland, where the clocks seemed to tick more slowly, and the air turned gray with fog instead of soot.

All the things she had learned, she had learned too late.

"Shall we go fishing this week?" he asked as they came to the shore of the lake.

"Oh, I should love that above all things." The words rushed from her lips in a happy flurry. "We'll have to bring the girls, of course."

"Of course," he murmured, the perfect gentle-man.

For some time they stood in silence. Anne could have remained there all day, staring out at the still, smooth water. Every now and then a fish would pop to the surface and break through, sending tiny rip-ples out like rings on a bull's-eye.

"If I were a boy," Daniel said, as transfixed by the water as she, "I would have to throw a rock. I would have to."

Daniel. When had she started to think of him as such?

"If I were a girl," she said, "I would have to take off my shoes and stockings."

He nodded, and then with a funny half smile, he admitted, "I would have probably pushed you in."

She kept her eyes on the water. "Oh, I would have taken you with me."

He chuckled, and then fell back into silence, happy just to watch the water, and the fish, and bits of dandelion fluff that stuck to the surface near the shore.

"This has been a perfect day," Anne said quietly.

"Almost," Daniel whispered, and then she was in his arms again. He kissed her, but it was different this time. Less urgent. Less fiery. The touch of their lips was achingly soft, and maybe it didn't make her feel crazed, like she wanted to press herself against him and take him within her. Maybe instead he made her feel weightless, as if she could take his hand and float away, just so long as he never stopped kissing her. Her entire body tingled, and she stood on her tiptoes, almost waiting for the moment she left the ground.

And then he broke the kiss, pulling back just far enough to rest his forehead against hers. "There," he said, cradling her face in his hands. "Now it's a perfect day."

Chapter Twelve

Almost precisely one day later, Daniel was sitting in Whipple Hill's wood-paneled library, wondering how it had come to pass that *this* day was so utterly less perfect than the one before.

After he had kissed Miss Wynter down by the lake, they had hiked back up to the clearing where poor Lord Finstead had been courting his beautiful but dim-witted princess, arriving only moments before Harriet, Elizabeth, and Frances did, accompanied by two footmen with picnic hampers. After a hearty meal, they had read from *The Strange, Sad Tragedy of Lord Finstead* for several more hours, until Daniel had begged for mercy, claiming that his sides hurt from so much laughter.

Even Harriet, who kept trying to remind them

that her masterwork was not a comedy, took no offense.

Back to the house they'd gone, only to discover that Daniel's mother and sister had arrived. And while everyone was greeting everyone else as if they had not seen each other just two days earlier, Miss Wynter slipped away and retired to her room.

He had not seen her since.

Not at supper, which she'd been required to take in the nursery with Elizabeth and Frances, and not at breakfast, which . . . Well, he didn't know why she hadn't come down to breakfast. All he knew was that it was well past noon and he was still uncomfortably full from having lingered at the table for two hours, hoping for a glimpse of her.

He'd been on his second complete breakfast by the time Sarah had seen fit to inform him that Lady Pleinsworth had given Miss Wynter much of the day off. It was a bonus, apparently, for all the extra work she had been performing. First the musicale, and now her double duty as governess and nanny. Miss Wynter had mentioned that she wanted to go to the village, Sarah had told him, and with the sun once again peeking through the clouds, it seemed an ideal day for her outing.

And so Daniel had set out to do all those things the lord of a manor was supposed to do when he wasn't wildly infatuated with the governess. He met with the butler. He looked over the account books from the last three years, belatedly remembering that he did not particularly like adding sums, and he'd never been good at it, anyway.

There ought to have been a thousand things to do, and he was sure there were, but every time he sat down to complete a task, his mind wandered to *her*. Her smile. Her mouth when it was laughing, her eyes when they were sad.

Anne.

He liked her name. It suited her, simple and direct. Loyal to the bone. Those who did not know her well might think that her beauty required something more dramatic—perhaps Esmerelda, or Melissande.

But *he* knew her. He did not know her past, and he did not know her secrets, but he knew *her*. And she was an Anne through and through.

An Anne who was currently someplace he was not.

Good heavens, this was ridiculous. He was a grown man, and here he was moping about his (albeit large) house, all because he missed the company of the governess. He could not sit still, he could not even seem to sit straight. He even had to change chairs in the south salon because he was facing a mirror, and when he spied his reflection, he looked so hangdog and pathetic he could not tolerate it.

Finally he went off to find someone who might be up for a game of cards. Honoria liked to play; Sarah, too. And if misery did not love company, at least it could be distracted by it. But when he arrived in the blue drawing room, all of his female relations (even the children), were huddled around a table, deep in discussions about Honoria's upcoming wedding.

Daniel began his very quiet retreat to the door.

"Oh, Daniel," his mother exclaimed, catching him before he could make his escape, "do come join us. We're trying to decide if Honoria should be married in lavender-blue or blue-lavender."

He opened his mouth to ask the difference, then decided against it. "Blue-lavender," he said firmly, not having a clue as to what he was talking about.

"Do you think so?" his mother responded, frowning. "I really think lavender-blue would be better."

The obvious question would have been why she'd asked his opinion in the first place, but once again, he decided that the wise man did not make such queries. Instead he gave the ladies a polite bow and informed them that he was going to go off and catalogue the recent additions to the library.

"The library?" Honoria asked. "Really?"

"I like to read," he said.

"So do I, but what has that to do with cataloguing?"

He leaned down and murmured in her ear, "Is this where I am supposed to say aloud that I am trying to escape a gaggle of women?"

She smiled, waited until he straightened, and replied, "I believe this is where you say that it has been far too long since you have read a book in English."

"Indeed." And off he went.

But after five minutes in the library, he could not bear it any longer. He was not a man who liked to mope, and so finally, after he realized that he had been resting his forehead on the table for at least a minute, he sat up, considered all the reasons why he might need to head down to the village (this took about half a second), and decided to head on out.

He was the Earl of Winstead. This was his home, and he'd been gone for three years. He had a moral duty to visit the village. These were his people.

He reminded himself never to utter those words aloud, lest Honoria and Sarah expire from laughter, and he donned his coat and walked out to the stables. The weather was not quite so fine as the day before, with more clouds above than sky. Daniel did not think it would rain, at least not in the immediate future, so he had his curricle readied for the two-mile journey. A coach was far too ostentatious for a trip to the village, and there seemed no reason not to drive himself. Besides, he rather liked the touch of the wind on his face.

And he'd missed driving his curricle. It was a fast little carriage, not as dashing as a phaeton, but also not as unstable. And he'd had it for only two months when he'd been forced to leave the country. Needless to say, smart little curricles had not been thick on the ground for exiled young Englishmen on the run.

When he reached the village, he handed off his reins to a boy at the posting inn and set off to make his calls. He would need to visit every establishment, lest someone feel slighted, so he started at the bottom of the high street at the chandler and worked his way up. News of his appearance in town spread quickly, and by the time Daniel entered Percy's Fine Hats and Bonnets (only his third call of the day), Mr. and Mrs. Percy were waiting at the front of their store with identically wide smiles on their faces.

"My lord," Mrs. Percy said, dropping into as deep a curtsy as her largish frame would allow. "May I be one of the first to welcome you home? We are both so honored to see you again."

She cleared her throat, and her husband said, "Indeed."

Daniel gave both of them a gracious nod, surreptitiously glancing about the establishment for other customers. Or rather, one other customer. Specifically. "Thank you, Mrs. Percy, Mr. Percy," he said. "I am delighted to be home."

Mrs. Percy nodded enthusiastically. "We never believed any of the things they said about you. Not a thing."

Which led Daniel to wonder what sorts of things had been said. As far as he knew, every tale that had been spread about him had been true. He *had* dueled with Hugh Prentice, and he had shot him in the leg. As for his fleeing the country, Daniel didn't know what sort of embellishment that story might have acquired; he rather thought that Lord Ramsgate's ranting vows of revenge would have been titillating enough.

But if Daniel hadn't wanted to debate the merits of blue-lavender and lavender-blue with his mother, he *definitely* did not wish to discuss himself with Mrs. Percy.

The Sad, Strange Tale of Lord Winstead. That's what it would be.

So he simply said, "Thank you," and moved quickly to a display of hats, hoping that his interest in their merchandise might overshadow Mrs. Percy's interest in his life.

Which it did. She immediately launched into a list of the qualities of their most recent top hat design, which, she assured him, could be made to fit his head precisely.

Mr. Percy said, "Indeed."

"Would you care to try one on, my lord?" Mrs. Percy asked. "I think you'll find that the curve of the brim is most flattering."

He did need a new hat, so he reached out to take it from her hands, but before he could place it onto his head, the door to the shop opened, tugging onto a small bell that tinkled merrily through the air. Daniel turned, but he didn't need to see her before he knew.

Anne.

The air changed when she walked into a room.

"Miss Wynter," he said, "what a lovely surprise."

She looked startled, but only for a moment, and while Mrs. Percy regarded her with obvious curiosity, she bobbed a curtsy and said, "Lord Winstead."

"Miss Wynter is governess to my young cousins," he said to Mrs. Percy. "They are visiting for a short spell."

Mrs. Percy expressed her pleasure in making the acquaintance, Mr. Percy said, "Indeed," and Anne was whisked off to the ladies' side of the shop, where Mrs. Percy had a dark blue bonnet with striped ribbons that would suit her *perfectly*. Daniel ambled along after them, still holding the black topper in his hands.

"Oh, your lordship," Mrs. Percy exclaimed, once she realized that he had followed, "won't you tell Miss Wynter how lovely she looks?"

He preferred her without a bonnet, with the sun glinting on her hair, but when she looked up at him, the sooty sweep of her lashes framing the dark, dark blue of her eyes, he didn't think there was a man in Christendom who would have disagreed with him when he said, "Most lovely, indeed."

"There, you see," Mrs. Percy said to Anne with an encouraging smile. "You look like a vision."

"I do like it," Anne said wistfully. "Very much. But it's terribly dear." She untied the ribbons with reluctant fingers, pulled it from her head, then looked down at it with obvious longing.

"Such workmanship would cost you twice as much in London," Mrs. Percy reminded her.

"I know," Anne said with a rueful smile, "but governesses aren't paid twice as much in London. So I rarely have much left over for bonnets, even those as lovely as yours."

Daniel suddenly felt like a bit of a cad, standing there with the top hat in his hand, a top hat they all knew he could have bought and sold a thousand times without even feeling a pinch in his pocket. "Excuse me," he said, clearing his throat awkwardly. He popped back over to the men's side of the shop, handed the hat to Mr. Percy, who said, "Indeed," and then returned to the ladies, who were still gazing down at the blue bonnet.

"Here you are," Miss Wynter said, finally handing it back to Mrs. Percy. "I shall certainly tell Lady Pleinsworth how lovely your bonnets are. I am sure that she will wish to take her daughters shopping while she is visiting."

"Daughters?" Mrs. Percy echoed, brightening at the prospect.

"Four of them," Daniel told her amiably. "And my mother and sister are at Whipple Hill, as well."

While Mrs. Percy was fanning herself, flushed from the excitement of having seven aristocratic ladies in residence so close to her hat shop, Daniel took the opportunity to offer his arm to Anne.

"May I escort you on your next errand?" he asked her, knowing full well how awkward it would be for her to refuse in front of Mrs. Percy.

"I'm almost done," she told him. "I've only to buy a bit of sealing wax."

"Luckily for you, I know exactly where that can be purchased."

"The stationer's, I would imagine."

Good gracious, she was making this difficult. "Yes, but I know where the stationer's *is*," he said.

She motioned with her finger someplace vaguely to the west. "Across the street, I think, and up the hill."

He shifted his position so that Mr. and Mrs. Percy

could not easily watch their conversation. Under his breath, he said, "Will you stop being so difficult and let me escort you to buy your sealing wax?"

Her mouth was pressed shut, which meant that the little snort of laughter he heard must have come through her nose. All the same, she still looked quite dignified as she said, "Well, if you put it that way, I don't see how I could possibly refuse."

He thought of several replies, but he had a feeling none would be as witty from his lips as they were in his head, so instead he nodded in acknowledgment and held out his arm, which she took with a smile.

Once they stepped outside, however, Anne turned to him with narrowed eyes and asked, quite bluntly, "Are you following me?"

He coughed. "Well, I wouldn't say *following,* exactly."

"Not exactly?" Her lips were doing a very good job of not smiling, but her eyes were not.

"Well," he said, adopting his most innocent expression, "I *was* in the hat shop before you came in. Some might even say that you were following me."

"Some might," she agreed. "But not me. Or you."

"No," he said, biting back a grin. "Definitely not."

They began walking uphill toward the stationer's shop, and even though she had not pressed the matter any further, he was enjoying the conversation far too much to let it go, so he said, "If you must know, I had been made aware of your possible presence in the village."

"Clearly, I must know," she murmured.

"And as I was also required to complete a few errands—"

"You?" she interrupted. "Required?"

He decided to ignore that. "*And* as it looked as if it might rain, I thought it my duty as a gentleman to make my trip into the village today, lest you get caught in inclement weather without proper conveyance home."

She was quiet for just long enough to level a dubious stare in his direction, then said (not asked, *said*), "Really."

"No," he admitted with a grin, "I was mostly just looking for you. But I do need to visit with all the shopkeepers eventually, and I—" He stopped, looked up. "It's raining."

Anne held out her hand, and sure enough, a fat drop landed near her fingertips. "Well, I suppose that shouldn't be a surprise. The clouds have been gathering all day."

"Shall we see about your sealing wax and be off, then? I came in my curricle and am more than happy to see you home."

"Your curricle?" she asked, eyebrows up.

"You'll still get wet," he allowed, "but you'll look very stylish while doing so." At her answering grin, he added, "And you'll get back to Whipple Hill faster."

By the time they took care of her sealing wax, choosing a deep, dark blue the exact color of the bonnet she'd left behind, the rain was coming down lightly but steadily. Daniel offered to wait with her in the village until it let up, but she told him she was expected back by teatime, and besides, who was to say that it would let up? The clouds were covering the sky like a thick blanket; it could very well rain until next Tuesday. "And it's not raining *that* hard," she said, frowning out the stationer's window.

True enough, but when they reached Percy's Fine Hats and Bonnets, he stopped and asked her, "Do you recall if they sold umbrellas?"

"I think they did."

He held up a finger, signaling for her to wait, and was back out with an umbrella in no more time than it took for him to direct them to send the bill to Whipple Hill and Mr. Percy to say, "Indeed."

"My lady," Daniel said, with enough gallantry to make her smile. He pushed the umbrella open and held it above her as they made their way down to the posting inn.

"You should hold it over yourself as well," she said, carefully stepping over puddles. The hem of her dress was getting wet, even as she tried to lift it off the ground with her hands.

"I am," he lied. But he didn't mind getting wet. His hat would resist the rain far better than her bonnet, in any case.

The posting inn wasn't much farther, but when they arrived, the rain was coming down with a bit more vigor, so Daniel suggested once again that they wait for the rain to let up. "The food is rather good here," he told her. "No kippers this time of day, but I'm sure we can find something to your liking."

She chuckled, and to his great surprise, she said, "I am a bit hungry."

He glanced at the sky. "I don't think you'll be home by teatime."

"It's all right. I can't imagine anyone would expect me to walk home in this."

"I shall be completely honest," he told her. "They were deep in discussions about the upcoming wedding. I sincerely doubt anyone has even noticed you're gone."

She smiled as they headed inside to the dining room. "That is how it should be. Your sister should have the wedding of her dreams."

And what of *your* dreams?

The question traveled to the tip of his tongue, but he held it back. It would make her uncomfortable and ruin the lovely, easy camaraderie that had settled upon them.

And he doubted she would answer.

He was growing to treasure each tiny drop of her past that slipped by her lips. The colors of her parents' eyes, the fact that she had a sister, and both loved to fish . . . These were the little things she revealed, and whether she did so by accident or on purpose, he couldn't be sure.

But he wanted more. When he looked in her eyes, he wanted to understand everything, every moment that had brought her to *this* moment. He didn't want to call it obsession—that seemed far too dark for what he felt.

A mad infatuation, that's what it was. A strange

and giddy flight of fancy. Surely he wasn't the first man to have been so quickly enchanted by a beautiful woman.

But as they settled into their seats in the inn's busy dining room, he looked at her across the table and it wasn't her beauty he saw. It was her heart. And her soul. And he had a sinking feeling that his life was never going to be the same.

Chapter Thirteen

"Oh, my," Anne said, allowing herself a little shiver as she sat down. She'd been wearing her coat, but the cuffs did not fit tightly, and the rain had slid down her sleeves. She was now drenched to her elbows and freezing to boot. "It's difficult to imagine that it's nearly May."

"Tea?" Daniel asked, signaling to the innkeeper.

"Please. Or anything that is hot." She pulled off her gloves, pausing to frown at a little hole that was growing at the tip of her right forefinger. That wouldn't do. She needed all the dignity she could muster in that finger. Heaven knew she shook it at the girls often enough.

"Is something amiss?" Daniel inquired.

"What?" She looked up and blinked. Oh, he must have seen her glaring at her glove. "It's just my glove." She held it up. "A small hole in the seam. I shall have to mend it this evening." She gave it a closer inspection before setting it down on the table beside her. There was only so much mending a glove could take, and she suspected hers were nearing the end of their tether.

Daniel asked the innkeeper for two mugs of tea, then turned back to her. "At the risk of revealing myself to be completely ignorant of the realities of life in service, I must say that I find it difficult to believe that my aunt does not pay you enough to purchase a new pair of gloves."

Anne was quite sure that he was, indeed, completely ignorant of the realities of life in service, but she did appreciate that he at least acknowledged the deficit. She also suspected that he was completely ignorant of the *cost* of a pair of gloves, or just about anything else, for that matter. She had been shopping with the upper classes often enough to know that they never bothered to inquire the price of anything. If they liked it, they bought it and had the bill sent to their homes, where someone else would take care of making sure it was paid.

"She does," she said to him. "Pay me enough, that is. But there is virtue in thrift, wouldn't you say?"

"Not if it means your fingers are freezing."

She smiled, perhaps a little patronizingly. "It will hardly come to that. These gloves have at least one or two more mendings left in them."

He scowled. "How many times have you mended them already?"

"Oh, goodness, I don't know. Five? Six?"

His expression turned to one of mild outrage. "That is entirely unacceptable. I will inform Aunt Charlotte that she must provide you with an adequate wardrobe."

"You will do no such thing," she said with haste. Good heavens, was he mad? One more show of undue interest from him, and Anne would be out on the street. It was bad enough that she was sitting with him in front of the entire village at the posting inn, but at least she had the excuse of the inclement weather. She could hardly be faulted for having taken refuge from the rain.

"I assure you," she said, motioning to the gloves, "these are in better condition than most people's." Her eyes fell to the table, where his gloves, made of gloriously luxurious lined leather, sat in an untended heap. She cleared her throat. "Present company excluded."

He shifted very slightly in his seat.

"Of course it is quite possible that your gloves have been mended and remended as well," she added without thinking. "The only difference is that your valet whisks them from your sight before you even notice they require attention."

He did not say anything, and she instantly felt ashamed of her comment. Reverse snobbery was not nearly so bad as the real thing, but still, she ought to be better than that. "I beg your pardon," she said.

He stared at her for a moment longer, then asked, "Why are we talking about gloves?"

"I have absolutely no idea." But that wasn't quite true. He might have been the one to bring it up, but she had not needed to go on about it. She'd wanted to remind him of the difference in their stations, she realized. Or maybe she'd wanted to remind herself.

"Enough of that," she said briskly, giving the overdiscussed handwear a pat. She looked up at him again, about to say something completely benign about the weather, but he was smiling at her in a way that made his eyes crinkle, and—

"I think you're healing," she heard herself say. She hadn't realized how much swelling there had been along with the bruise that wrapped around his eye, but now that it was gone, his smile was different. Perhaps even more joyful.

He touched his face. "My cheek?"

"No, your eye. It's still a bit discolored, but it doesn't look swollen any longer." She gave him a regretful sort of look. "Your cheek looks much the same."

"Really?"

"Well, actually worse, I'm sorry to say, but that's to be expected. These things usually look worse before they look better."

His brows rose. "And how is it that you have come to be such an expert on scrapes and bruises?"

"I'm a governess," she said. Because really, that ought to be explanation enough.

"Yes, but you teach three girls—"

She laughed at this, cutting him off rather neatly. "Do you think that girls never get into mischief?"

"Oh, I know that they do." He tapped one hand against his heart. "Five sisters. Did you know that? Five."

"Is that meant to invoke pity?"

"It certainly *should*," he said. "But still, I don't recall them ever coming to blows."

"Half the time Frances thinks she's a unicorn," Anne said plainly. "Trust me when I tell you that she acquires more than her fair share of bumps and bruises. And besides that, I've taught little boys, too. Someone must give them instruction before they go off to school."

"I suppose," he said with a little shrug of concession. Then, with a cheeky quirk of his brows, he leaned forward and murmured, "Would it be improper of me to admit that I am inordinately flattered by your attention to the details of my face?"

Anne snorted out a laugh. "Improper *and* ludicrous."

"It is true that I have never felt quite so colorful," he said, with a clearly feigned sigh.

"You are a veritable rainbow," she agreed. "I see red and . . . well, no orange and yellow, but certainly green and blue and violet."

"You forgot indigo."

"I did not," she said, with her very best governess voice. "I have always found it to be a foolish addition to the spectrum. Have you ever actually *seen* a rainbow?"

"Once or twice," he replied, looking rather amused by her rant.

"It's difficult enough to note the difference between the blue and violet, much less find the indigo in between."

He paused for a moment, then, lips twitching with humor, said, "You've given this a lot of thought."

Anne pressed her own lips together, trying not to smile in return. "Indeed," she finally said, then burst out laughing. It was the most ridiculous conversation, and so perfectly lovely at the same time.

Daniel laughed with her, and they both sat back as a maid came by with two steaming mugs of tea. Anne instantly put her hands around hers and sighed with pleasure as the warmth seeped through her skin.

Daniel took a sip, shivered as the hot liquid went down his throat, then sipped again. "I think I look very dashing," he said, "all mottled and bruised. Perhaps I should start making up stories of how I was injured. Fighting with Marcus lacks all excitement."

"Don't forget the footpads," she reminded him.

"And that," he replied in a dry voice, "lacks all dignity."

She smiled at that. It was a rare man who could poke fun at himself.

"What do you think?" he asked, turning as if to preen. "Shall I say I wrestled with a wild boar? Or perhaps fought off pirates with a machete?"

"Well, that depends," she returned. "Did you have the machete or did the pirates?"

"Oh, the pirates, I should think. It's far more impressive if I held them off with my bare hands." He waved them about as if practicing some ancient Oriental technique.

"Stop," she said, laughing. "Everyone is looking at you."

He shrugged. "They would look, regardless. I haven't been here in three years."

"Yes, but they'll think you a madman."

"Ah, but I'm allowed to be eccentric." He gave her a dashing half smile and let his eyebrows bob up and then down. "It's one of the perks of the title."

"Not the money and the power?"

"Well, those, too," he admitted, "but right now I'm most enjoying the eccentricity. The bruises help the cause, don't you think?"

She rolled her eyes, taking another sip of her tea.

"Perhaps a scar," he mused, turning to present her with his cheek. "What do you think? Right along here. I could—"

But Anne did not hear the rest of his words. She only saw his hand, slicing through air from his temple to his chin. A long, furious diagonal, just like—

She saw it—George's face as he ripped the bandages from his skin in his father's study.

And she felt it, the awful plunge of the knife when it had gone through his skin.

She turned away quickly, trying to breathe. But she couldn't. It was like a vise around her lungs, a great weight sitting on her chest. She was choking and drowning at the same time, desperate for air.

Oh, dear God, why was this happening now? It had been years since she'd felt this kind of spontaneous terror. She'd thought she was past it.

"Anne," Daniel said urgently, reaching across the table to take her hand. "What can be wrong?"

It was as if his touch snapped some sort of constricting band, because her entire body suddenly spasmed with a deep, convulsive breath. The black edges that had been squeezing down on her vision shimmered and dissolved, and very slowly, she felt her body returning to normal.

"Anne," he said again, but she didn't look at him. She did not want to see the concern on his face. He had been joking, she knew that perfectly well. How on earth would she explain such an overreaction?

"The tea," she said, hoping he did not remember that she had already put down her mug when he'd made his comment. "I think—" She coughed, and she was not faking it. "I think it went down the wrong way."

He watched her face intently. "Are you certain?"

"Or maybe it was too hot," she said, her shoulders quivering in a nervous little shrug. "But I'm almost recovered now, I assure you." She smiled, or at least tried to. "It's terribly embarrassing, really."

"Can I help you in any way?"

"No, of course not." She fanned herself. "My goodness, I'm suddenly quite warm. Are you?"

He shook his head, his eyes never leaving her face.

"The tea," she said, trying to sound bright and cheery. "As I said, it's quite hot."

"It is."

She swallowed. He saw through her act, she was sure of it. He did not know what the truth was, just that she was not saying it. And for the first time since she'd left home eight years earlier, she felt a pang of remorse over her silence. She had no obligation to share her secrets with this man, and yet, here she was, feeling evasive and guilty.

"Do you think the weather has improved?" she asked, turning to face the window. It was hard to tell; the glass was old and wavy, and the inn's large overhang shielded it from the direct onslaught of the rain.

"Not yet, no," he replied.

She turned back, murmuring, "No, of course not." She fixed a smile on her face. "I should finish my tea, in any case."

He looked at her curiously. "You're no longer too warm?"

She blinked, taking a moment to remember that she had been fanning herself just a few moments earlier. "No," she said. "Funny, that." She smiled again and brought her mug to her lips. But she was saved from having to figure out how to set the conversation back on its previous, easygoing course by a loud crashing noise just outside the dining room.

"What can that be?" Anne asked, but Daniel was already on his feet.

"Stay here," he ordered, and strode quickly to the door. He looked tense, and Anne saw something familiar in his stance. Something she'd seen in herself, time and again. It was almost as if he was expecting trouble. But that made no sense. She'd heard that the man who had driven him out of the country had dropped his quest for revenge.

But she supposed that old habits died very hard. If George Chervil suddenly choked on a chicken bone or moved to the East Indies, how long would it take her to stop looking over her shoulder?

"It was nothing," Daniel said, coming back to the table. "Just a drunkard who managed to wreak havoc from the inn to the stables and back." He picked up his mug of tea, took a long swig, then added, "But the rain is thinning out. It's still drizzling, but I think we should leave soon."

"Of course," Anne said, coming to her feet.

"I've already asked them to bring the carriage around," he said, escorting her to the door.

She gave him a nod as she stepped outside. The fresh air was bracing, and she did not mind the cold. There was a cleansing quality to the chilly mist, and it made her feel more like herself.

And right then, in that very moment, that wasn't such a bad person to be.

DANIEL STILL HAD no idea what had happened to Anne back in the dining room. He supposed it could have been exactly what she'd said, that she'd choked on a bit of her tea. He'd done so before, and it was certainly enough to set a body coughing, especially when the tea was steaming hot.

But she'd looked terribly pale, and her eyes—in

that split second before she'd turned away—had looked hunted. Terrified.

It brought to mind that time he'd seen her in London, when she'd stumbled into Hoby's, scared out of her wits. She'd said she'd seen someone. Or rather, she'd said there was someone she did not want to see.

But that was London. This was Berkshire, and more to the point, they had been sitting in an inn full of villagers he'd known since birth. There hadn't been a soul in that room who would have had cause to harm so much as a hair on her head.

Maybe it *was* the tea. Maybe he'd imagined everything else. Anne certainly seemed back to normal now, smiling at him as he helped her up into the curricle. The half canopy had been raised against the rain, but even if the weather held, they would both be thoroughly chilled by the time they reached Whipple Hill.

Hot baths for the both of them. He'd order them the moment they arrived.

Although sadly, not to be shared.

"I've never ridden in a curricle," Anne said, smiling as she tightened the ribbons on her bonnet.

"No?" He did not know why this surprised him. Certainly a governess would have no cause to ride in one, but everything about her spoke of a gentle birth. At some point in her life she must have been an eligible young lady; he could not imagine she hadn't had scores of gentlemen begging for her company in their curricles and phaetons.

"Well, I've been in a gig," she said. "My former employer had one, and I had to learn to drive it. She was quite elderly, and no one trusted her with the reins."

"Was this on the Isle of Man?" he asked, keeping his voice deliberately light. It was so rare that she offered pieces of her past. He was afraid she would bottle herself back up if he questioned too intensely.

But she did not seem put off by his query. "It was," she confirmed. "I'd only driven a cart before that. My father would not have kept a carriage that seated only two people. He was never a man for impracticalities."

"Do you ride?" he asked.

"No," she said simply.

Another clue. If her parents had been titled, she would have been placed in a sidesaddle before she could read.

"How long did you live there?" he asked conversationally. "On the Isle of Man."

She did not answer right away, and he thought she might not do so at all, but then, in a soft voice, laced with memory, she said, "Three years. Three years and four months."

Keeping his eyes scrupulously on the road, he said, "You don't sound as if you have fond memories."

"No." She was quiet again, for at least ten seconds, then she said, "It was not dreadful. It was just . . . I don't know. I was young. And it was not home."

Home. Something she almost never mentioned. Something he knew he should not ask about, so instead he said, "You were a lady's companion?"

She nodded. He just barely saw it out of the corner of his eye; she seemed to have forgotten that he was watching the horses and not her. "It was not an onerous position," she said. "She liked to be read to, so I did quite a lot of that. Needlework. I wrote all of her correspondence, as well. Her hands shook quite a bit."

"You left when she died, I presume."

"Yes. I was quite fortunate in that she had a great-niece near Birmingham who was in need of a governess. I think she knew that her time was near, and she made the arrangements for a new position before she passed." Anne was quiet for a moment, then he felt her straighten beside him, almost as if she were shaking off the foggy mantle of memory. "And I've been a governess ever since."

"It seems to suit you."

"Most of the time, yes."

"I should think—" He cut himself off sharply. Something was amiss with the horses.

"What is it?" Anne asked.

He shook his head. He couldn't talk right now. He needed to focus. The team was pulling to the right, which made no sense. Something snapped, and the horses took off at breakneck speed, pulling the curricle along with them until—

"Dear God above," Daniel breathed. As he watched in horror, still struggling to control the team, the harness came separated from the shaft and the horses took off to the left.

Without the carriage.

Anne let out a little cry of surprised terror as the curricle sped down the hill, tilting wildly on its two wheels. "Lean forward!" Daniel yelled. If they could keep the carriage balanced, they could ride out the hill until they slowed down. But the canopy weighted it down at the back, and bumps and ruts in the oft-traveled road made it nearly impossible to hold their positions leaning forward.

And then Daniel remembered the turn. Halfway down the hill the road curved sharply to the left. If they continued straight on, they'd be tossed down the hill, into a thick wood.

"Listen to me," he said to Anne urgently. "When we reach the bottom of the hill, lean left. With everything you have, lean left."

She gave a frantic nod. Her eyes were terrified, but she was not hysterical. She would do what she needed to do. As soon as—

"Now!" he yelled.

They both threw themselves to the left, Anne landing half atop him. The curricle lifted onto one wheel, its wooden spokes protesting with a horrible shriek at the extra burden. "Forward!" Daniel yelled, and they heaved themselves forward, causing the carriage to turn left, narrowly missing the edge of the road.

But as they turned, their left wheel—the only one in contact with the ground—caught on something, and the curricle pitched forward, bouncing into the air before landing back on its wheel with a sickening crack. Daniel held on for dear life, and he thought Anne was doing the same, but as he watched in helpless terror, the curricle spit her out, and the wheel— Oh, dear God, the wheel! If it ran over her—

Daniel did not stop to think. He hurled himself to the right, toppling the curricle before it could strike Anne, who was somewhere on the ground, somewhere to the left.

The curricle smacked against the earth, skidding for several yards before coming to a halt in the mud. For a moment Daniel could not move. He'd been punched before, he'd fallen off horses; hell, he'd even been shot. But never had his breath been so completely ripped from his body as when the curricle hit the ground.

Anne. He had to get to her. But he had to breathe first, and his lungs felt as if they'd gone into a spasm. Finally, still gasping for air, he crawled out of the overturned carriage. "Anne!" he tried to bellow, but it was all he could do to wheeze her name. His hands squelched into the mud, and then his knees, and then, using the splintered side of the curricle for support, he managed to stagger to his feet.

"Anne!" he called again, this time with more volume. "Miss Wynter!"

There was no response. No sound at all, save for the rain, slapping against the sodden ground.

Still barely able to stand, Daniel searched frantically from his spot next to the curricle, turning in circles as he held on for support, looking for any sign of Anne. What had she been wearing? Brown. She'd been in brown, a medium shade of it, perfect for blending in with the mud.

She must be behind him. The curricle had rolled and skidded for some distance after she'd been thrown out. Daniel tried to make his way to the back of the carriage, his boots finding little traction in the deepening mud. He slid, losing his balance, and he pitched forward, his hands flailing for anything that might keep him upright. At the last moment, they closed around a thin strip of leather.

The harness.

Daniel looked down at the leather in his hands. It was the trace, meant to connect the horse to the carriage shaft. But it had been cut. Only the very end looked frayed, as if it had been left dangling by a thread, ready to snap at the slightest pressure.

Ramsgate.

His body filled with rage, and Daniel finally found the energy to move beyond the broken curricle and search for Anne. By God, if anything had happened to her . . . If she was seriously injured . . .

He would kill Lord Ramsgate. He would eviscerate him with his bare hands.

"Anne!" he yelled, spinning madly in the mud as he searched for her. And then—was that a boot? He rushed forward, stumbling through the rain until he saw her clearly, crumpled on the ground, half on the road, half in the wood.

"Dear God," Daniel whispered, and he ran forward, terror grabbing at his heart. "Anne," he said frantically, reaching her side and feeling for a pulse. "Answer me. God help me, answer me now."

She did not respond, but the steady pulse at her wrist was enough to give him hope. They were only about half a mile from Whipple Hill. He could carry her that far. He was shaking, and bruised, and probably bleeding, but he could do this.

Carefully, he lifted her into his arms and began the treacherous walk home. The mud made each step a balancing act, and he could barely see through his hair, plastered over his eyes by the rain. But he kept going, his exhausted body finding strength through terror.

And fury.

Ramsgate would pay for this. Ramsgate would pay, and maybe Hugh would pay, too, and by God, the whole world would pay if Anne's eyes never opened again.

One foot in front of the other. That's what he did, until Whipple Hill came into view. And then he was on the drive, and in the circle, and finally, just when his muscles were screaming and quivering, and his knees threatened to buckle, he made it up the three steps to the grand front entrance and kicked the door, hard.

And again.

And again.

And again and again and again until he heard footsteps hurrying toward him.

The door opened, and there was the butler, who let out a loud "My lord!" And then, as three footmen rushed forward to relieve Daniel of his burden, he sank to the floor, spent and terrified.

"Take care of her," he gasped. "Get her warm."

"Right away, my lord," the butler assured him, "but you—"

"No!" Daniel ordered. "Take care of her first."

"Of course, my lord." The butler rushed over to the terrified footman who was holding Anne, oblivious to the rivers of water rushing down his sleeves. "Go!" he ordered. "Go! Take her upstairs, and you" —he jerked his head toward a maid who had come into the hall to gawk—"begin heating water for a bath. Now!"

Daniel closed his eyes, reassured by the flurry of activity unfolding around him. He had done what he needed to do. He had done all he could do.

For now.

Chapter Fourteen

WHEN ANNE FINALLY came to, her mind slowly shifting from unrelenting black to swirling clouds of gray, the first thing she felt were hands, poking and prodding, trying to remove her clothing.

She wanted to scream. She tried to, but her voice would not obey. She was shivering uncontrollably, her muscles were aching and exhausted, and she wasn't sure she could open her mouth, much less make a sound.

She'd been cornered before, by overconfident young men who viewed the governess as fair game, by a master of a house who figured he was paying her salary, anyway. Even by George Chervil, who had set her life down this road in the first place.

But she had always been able to defend herself. She'd had her strength, and her wits, and with

George even a weapon. Now she had none of those things. She could not even open her eyes.

"No," she moaned, squirming and shifting on what seemed to be a cold, wooden floor.

"Shhh," came an unfamiliar voice. It was a woman, though, which Anne found reassuring. "Let us help you, Miss Wynter."

They knew her name. Anne could not decide if that was a good thing or not.

"Poor dear," the woman said. "Your skin is like ice. We're going to put you in a hot bath."

A bath. A bath sounded like heaven. She was so cold—she couldn't remember ever being so cold before. Everything felt heavy . . . her arms, legs, even her heart.

"Here we are, love," came the woman's voice again. "Just let me get at these buttons."

Anne struggled once more to open her eyes. It felt as if someone had placed weights on her lids, or submerged her in some sort of sticky goo she couldn't quite escape.

"You're safe now," the woman said. Her voice was kind, and she seemed to want to help.

"Where am I?" Anne whispered, still trying to force her eyes open.

"You're back at Whipple Hill. Lord Winstead carried you back through the rain."

"Lord Winstead . . . He—" She gasped, and her eyes finally opened to reveal a bathroom, far more elegant and ornate than the one to which she was currently assigned up in the nursery. There were two maids with her, one adding water to a steaming bath, the other attempting to remove her sodden clothing.

"Is he all right?" Anne asked frantically. "Lord Winstead?" Flashes of memory rushed at her. The rain. The horses breaking free. The horrifying sound of splintering wood. And then the curricle, hurtling forward on just one wheel. And then . . . nothing. Anne could not recall a thing. They must have crashed—why couldn't she remember it?

Dear God, what had happened to them?

"His lordship is well," the maid assured her. "Exhausted as a body can be, but it's nothing a bit of rest won't cure." Her eyes shone with pride as she adjusted Anne's position so that she could peel her sleeves from her arms. "He's a hero, he is. A true hero."

Anne rubbed her face with her hand. "I can't remember what happened. A few bits and pieces, but that's all."

"His lordship told us you were thrown from the carriage," the maid said, getting to work on the other sleeve. "Lady Winstead said you likely hit your head."

"Lady Winstead?" When had she seen Lady Winstead?

"His lordship's mother," the maid explained, misinterpreting Anne's query. "She knows a bit about injuries and healing, she does. She examined you right there on the floor of the front hall."

"Oh, dear God." Anne didn't know why this was so mortifying, but it was.

"Her ladyship said you've a lump, right about here." The maid touched her own head, a couple of inches above her left ear.

Anne's hand, still rubbing her temple, moved upward through her hair. She found the bump instantly, bulging and tender. "Ow," she said, pulling her fingers away. She looked at her hand. There was no blood. Or maybe there had been, and the rain had washed it away.

"Lady Winstead said she thought you'd want some privacy," the maid continued, sliding Anne's dress from her body. "We're to get you warmed and washed and then put into bed. She sent for a doctor."

"Oh, I'm sure I don't need a doctor," Anne said quickly. She still felt awful—sore, and cold, and with a lumpy explanation for her raging headache. But they were temporary sorts of ailments, the kind one instinctively knew needed nothing but a soft bed and hot soup.

But the maid just shrugged. "She already sent for one, so I don't think you've got much choice."

Anne nodded.

"Everyone is right worried about you. Little Lady Frances was crying, and—"

"Frances?" Anne interrupted. "But she never cries."

"She was this time."

"Oh, please," Anne begged, heartbroken with worry. "Please have someone let her know that I'm all right."

"A footman will be up with more hot water soon. We'll have him tell Lady—"

"A footman?" Anne gasped, her hands instinctively covering her nudity. She was still in her chemise, but wet, it was practically transparent.

"Don't worry," the maid said with a chuckle. "He leaves it at the door. It's just so Peggy doesn't have to carry it up the stairs."

Peggy, who was pouring yet another bucket of water into the tub, turned and smiled.

"Thank you," Anne said quietly. "Thank you both."

"I'm Bess," the first maid told her. "Do you think you can stand up? Just for a minute? This slip has got to come off over your head."

Anne nodded, and with help from Bess she rose to her feet, holding onto the side of the large porcelain tub for support. Once the chemise had been removed, Bess helped Anne into the tub, and she sank down gratefully into the water. It was too hot, but she didn't mind. It felt so good to be something other than numb.

She soaked in the bath until the water faded to lukewarm, then Bess helped her into her wool nightgown, which Bess had brought down from Anne's room in the nursery.

"Here you are," Bess said, leading Anne across the plush carpet to a beautiful canopied bed.

"What room is this?" Anne asked, taking in the elegant surroundings. Scrollwork swirled along the ceilings, and the walls were covered in damask of the most delicate silvery blue. It was by far the grandest room she'd ever slept in.

"The blue guest bedroom," Bess said, fluffing her pillows. "It's one of the finest at Whipple Hill. Right on the same hallway as the family."

As the family? Anne looked up in surprise.

Bess shrugged. "His lordship insisted upon it."

"Oh," Anne said with a gulp, wondering what the rest of his family thought about that.

Bess watched as Anne settled in under the heavy quilts, then asked, "Shall I tell everyone that you're able to receive visitors? I know they'll want to see you."

"Not Lord Winstead?" Anne asked in horror. Surely they would not allow him to enter her bedroom. Well, not *her* bedroom, but still, a bedroom. With her in it.

"Oh, no," Bess reassured her. "He's off in his own bed, asleep, I hope. I don't think we'll see him for at least a day. The poor man is exhausted. I reckon you weigh quite a bit more wet than you do dry." Bess chuckled at her own joke, then left the room.

Less than a minute later, Lady Pleinsworth entered. "Oh, my poor, poor girl," she exclaimed. "You gave us such a fright. But my heavens, you look vastly better than you did an hour ago."

"Thank you," Anne said, not quite comfortable with such effusiveness on the part of her employer. Lady Pleinsworth had always been kind, but she had never attempted to make Anne feel like a member of the family. Nor had Anne expected her to. It was the odd lot of the governess—not quite a servant but most definitely not of the family. Her first employer—the old woman on the Isle of Man—had warned her about it. Forever stuck between upstairs and down, a governess was, and she'd best get used to it quickly.

"You should have seen yourself when his lordship brought you in," Lady Pleinsworth said as she settled into a chair by the bed. "Poor Frances thought you were dead."

"Oh, no, is she still upset? Has someone—"

"She's fine," Lady Pleinsworth said with a brisk wave of her hand. "She insists, however, upon seeing you for herself."

"That would be most agreeable," Anne said, trying to stifle a yawn. "I would enjoy her company."

"You'll need to rest first," Lady Pleinsworth said firmly.

Anne nodded, sinking a little further into her pillows.

"I'm sure you'll want to know how Lord Winstead is," Lady Pleinsworth continued.

Anne nodded again. She did want to know, desperately, but she'd been forcing herself not to ask.

Lady Pleinsworth leaned forward, and there was something in her expression Anne could not quite read. "You should know that he very nearly collapsed after carrying you home."

"I'm sorry," Anne whispered.

But if Lady Pleinsworth heard her, she gave no

indication. "Actually, I suppose one would have to say he *did* collapse. Two footmen had to help him up and practically carry him to his room. I vow I have never seen the like."

Anne felt tears stinging her eyes. "Oh, I'm sorry. I'm so, so sorry."

Lady Pleinsworth looked at her with a queer expression, almost as if she'd forgotten who she'd been talking to. "There's no need for that. It's not your fault."

"I know, but . . ." Anne shook her head. She didn't know what she knew. She didn't know anything any longer.

"Still," Lady Pleinsworth said with a wave of her hand, "you should be grateful. He carried you for over half a mile, you know. And he was injured himself."

"I am grateful," Anne said quietly. "Very much so."

"The reins snapped," Lady Pleinsworth told her. "I must say I am appalled. It is unconscionable that equipage in such poor repair would be allowed out of the stables. Someone will lose their position over this, I am sure."

The reins, Anne thought. That made sense. It had all happened so suddenly.

"At any rate, given the severity of the accident, we must be thankful that neither of you was more seriously injured," Lady Pleinsworth continued. "Although I'm told that we do want to watch you closely with that lump on your head."

Anne touched it again, wincing.

"Does it hurt?"

"A bit," Anne admitted.

Lady Pleinsworth seemed not to know what to do with that information. She shifted slightly in her seat, then squared her shoulders, then finally said, "Well."

Anne tried to smile. It was ridiculous, but she almost felt as if *she* was supposed to try to make Lady Pleinsworth feel better. It was probably from all those years in service, always wanting to please her employers.

"The doctor will be here soon," Lady Pleinsworth finally continued, "but in the meantime, I will make sure that someone tells Lord Winstead that you have awakened. He was most worried about you."

"Thank—" Anne started to say, but apparently Lady Pleinsworth was not done.

"It is curious, though," she said, pressing her lips together. "How did you come to be in his carriage in the first place? The last I saw him, he was here at Whipple Hill."

Anne swallowed. This was not the sort of conversation that one wanted to treat with anything but the utmost of care. "I saw him in the village," she said. "It started to rain, and he offered to drive me back to Whipple Hill." She waited for a moment, but Lady Pleinsworth did not speak, so she added, "I was most appreciative."

Lady Pleinsworth took a moment to consider her answer, then said, "Yes, well, he is very generous that way. Although as it turns out, you'd have done better to walk." She stood briskly and patted the bed. "You must rest now. But do not sleep. I've been told you're not to sleep until the doctor arrives to examine you." She frowned. "I believe I *will* send Frances in. At the very least, she'll keep you awake."

Anne smiled. "Perhaps she might read to me. She hasn't practiced reading aloud in quite some time, and I should like to see her work on her diction."

"Ever the teacher, I see," Lady Pleinsworth said. "But that's what we want in a governess, isn't it?"

Anne nodded, not quite certain if she had been complimented or told to remember her place.

Lady Pleinsworth walked to the door, then turned. "Oh, and as to that, don't worry about the girls. Lady Sarah and Lady Honoria will be sharing your duties while you are recuperating. I'm sure between the two of them they can work out a lesson plan."

"Maths," Anne said with a yawn. "They need to do maths."

"Maths it is, then." Lady Pleinsworth opened the door and stepped into the hallway. "Do try to get some rest. But don't sleep."

Anne nodded and closed her eyes, even though she knew she shouldn't. She did not think she would sleep, though. Her body was exhausted, but her mind was racing. Everyone told her that Daniel was all right, but she was still worried, and she would be until she saw him for herself. There was nothing she could do about it now, though, not when she could barely walk.

And then Frances bounded in, hopped onto the bed beside Anne, and proceeded to chatter her ear off. It was, Anne realized later, exactly what she needed.

THE REST OF the day passed peacefully enough. Frances stayed until the doctor arrived, who said that he wanted Anne to keep awake until nightfall. Then Elizabeth came, bearing a tray of cakes and sweets, and finally Harriet, who carried with her a small sheaf of paper—her current opus, *Henry VIII and the Unicorn of Doom.*

"I'm not certain Frances is going to be appeased by an evil unicorn," Anne told her.

Harriet looked up with one arched brow. "She did not specify that it must be a *good* unicorn."

Anne grimaced. "You're going to have a battle on your hands, that's all I'm going to say on the matter."

Harriet shrugged, then said, "I'm going to begin in act two. Act one is a complete disaster. I've had to rip it completely apart."

"Because of the unicorn?"

"No," Harriet said with a grimace. "I got the order of the wives wrong. It's divorced, beheaded, died, divorced, beheaded, widowed."

"How cheerful."

Harriet gave her a bit of a look, then said, "I switched one of the divorces with a beheading."

"May I give you a bit of advice?" Anne asked.

Harriet looked up.

"Don't ever let anyone hear you say that out of context."

Harriet laughed aloud at that, then gave her papers a little shake to indicate that she was ready to begin. "Act two," she read with a flourish. "And don't worry, you shouldn't be too confused, especially now that we've reviewed all the wifely demises."

But before Harriet reached act three, Lady Pleinsworth entered the room, her expression urgent and grave. "I must speak with Miss Wynter," she said to Harriet. "Please leave us."

"But we haven't even—"

"*Now,* Harriet."

Harriet gave Anne a *what-can-this-be* look, which Anne did not acknowledge, not with Lady Pleinsworth standing over her, looking like a thundercloud.

Harriet gathered her papers and left. Lady Pleinsworth walked to the door, listened to make sure that Harriet had not lingered to eavesdrop, then turned to Anne and said, "The reins were cut."

Anne gasped. "What?"

"The reins. On Lord Winstead's curricle. They had been cut."

"No. That's impossible. Why would—" But she knew why. And she knew who.

George Chervil.

Anne felt herself blanch. How had he found her here? And how could he have known—

The posting inn. She and Lord Winstead had been inside at least half an hour. Anyone who had been watching her would have realized that she would be riding home in his curricle.

Anne had long since accepted that time would not dampen George Chervil's fire for revenge, but she'd never thought he would be so reckless as to threaten the life of another person, especially someone of Daniel's position. He was the Earl of Winstead, for heaven's sake. The death of a governess would most likely go uninvestigated, but an earl?

George was insane. Or at least more so than he'd been before. There could be no other explanation.

"The horses came back several hours ago," Lady Pleinsworth continued. "The grooms were sent out to retrieve the curricle, and that's when they saw it. It was a clear act of sabotage. Worn leather does not snap in an even, straight line."

"No," Anne said, trying to take it all in.

"I don't suppose you have some nefarious enemy in your past you've neglected to tell us about," Lady Pleinsworth said.

Anne's throat went dry. She was going to have to lie. There was no other—

But Lady Pleinsworth must have been engaging in a bit of gallows humor, because she did not wait for a reply. "It's Ramsgate," she said. "God *damn* it, the man has lost all reason."

Anne could only stare, not sure if she was relieved that she'd been spared the sin of lying or shocked that Lady Pleinsworth had so furiously taken the Lord's name in vain.

And maybe Lady Pleinsworth was right. Maybe

this had nothing to do with Anne, and the villain was indeed the Marquess of Ramsgate. He'd chased Daniel out of the country three years earlier; surely it was within his character to try to have him murdered now. And he certainly would not care if he took the life of a governess in the process.

"He promised Daniel he would leave him alone," Lady Pleinsworth raged, pacing the room. "That's the only reason he came back, you know. He thought he would be safe. Lord Hugh went all the way to Italy to tell him that his father had promised to put an end to all this nonsense." She let out a frustrated noise, her hands fisted tightly at her sides. "It has been three years. Three years he was in exile. Isn't that enough? Daniel didn't even kill his son. It was just a wound."

Anne kept quiet, not sure that she was supposed to be taking part in this conversation.

But then Lady Pleinsworth turned and looked at her directly. "I assume you know the story."

"Most of it, I believe."

"Yes, of course. The girls would have told you everything." She crossed her arms, then uncrossed them, and it occurred to Anne that she had never seen her employer so distraught. Lady Pleinsworth gave her head a shake, then said, "I don't know how Virginia is going to bear it. It nearly killed her before when he left the country."

Virginia must be Lady Winstead, Daniel's mother. Anne had not known her given name.

"Well," Lady Pleinsworth said, then abruptly added, "I suppose you can sleep now. The sun's gone down."

"Thank you," Anne said. "Please give—" But she stopped there.

"Did you say something?" Lady Pleinsworth inquired.

Anne shook her head. It would have been inappropriate to ask Lady Pleinsworth to give her regards to Lord Winstead. Or if not that, then unwise.

Lady Pleinsworth took a step toward the door, then paused. "Miss Wynter," she said.

"Yes?"

Lady Pleinsworth turned slowly around. "There is one thing."

Anne waited. It was not like her employer to leave such silences in the middle of conversation. It did not bode well.

"It has not escaped my notice that my nephew . . ." Again, she paused, possibly searching for the correct combination of words.

"Please," Anne blurted out, certain that her continued employment was hanging by a thread. "Lady Pleinsworth, I assure you—"

"Don't interrupt," Lady Pleinsworth said, although not unkindly. She held up a hand, instructing Anne to wait as she gathered her thoughts. Finally, just when Anne was sure she could not bear it any longer, she said, "Lord Winstead seems quite taken with you."

Anne hoped Lady Pleinsworth did not expect a reply.

"I am assured of your good judgment, am I not?" Lady Pleinsworth added.

"Of course, my lady."

"There are times when a woman must exhibit

a sensibility that men lack. I believe this is one of those times."

She paused and looked at Anne directly, indicating that this time she *did* expect a reply. So Anne said, "Yes, my lady," and prayed that was enough.

"The truth is, Miss Wynter, I know very little about you."

Anne's eyes widened.

"Your references are impeccable, and of course your behavior since joining our household has been above reproach. You are quite the finest governess I have ever employed."

"Thank you, my lady."

"But I don't know anything about your family. I don't know who your father was, or your mother, or what sort of connections you might possess. You have been well brought up, that much is clear, but beyond that . . ." She held up her hands. And then she looked directly into Anne's eyes. "My nephew must marry someone with a clear and unstained status."

"I realize that," Anne said quietly.

"She will almost certainly come from a noble family."

Anne swallowed, trying not to let any emotion show on her face.

"It is not strictly necessary, of course. It is possible he might marry a girl from the gentry. But she would have to be most exceptional." Lady Pleinsworth took a step toward her, and her head tilted slightly to the side, as if she were trying to see right down inside of her. "I like you, Miss Wynter," she said slowly, "but I do not know you. Do you understand?"

Anne nodded.

Lady Pleinsworth walked to the door and placed her hand on the knob. "I suspect," she said quietly, "that you do not want me to know you."

And then she departed, leaving Anne alone with her flickering candle and tortuous thoughts.

There was no misconstruing the meaning of Lady Pleinsworth's comments. She had been warning her to stay away from Lord Winstead, or rather, to make sure that *he* stayed away from *her*. But it had been bittersweet. She'd left a sad little door open, hinting that Anne *might* be considered a suitable match if more were known of her background.

But of course that was impossible.

Could you imagine? Telling Lady Pleinsworth the truth about her background?

Well, the thing is, I'm not a virgin.

And my name is not really Anne Wynter.

Oh, and I stabbed a man and now he's madly hunting me until I'm dead.

A desperate, horrified giggle popped out of Anne's throat. What a resumé that was.

"I'm a prize," she said into the darkness, and then she laughed some more. Or maybe she cried. After a while, it was hard to tell which was which.

Chapter Fifteen

The following morning, before any female member of his family could put a stop to what Daniel knew was improper behavior, he strode down the hall and rapped sharply on the door to the blue guest bedroom. He was already dressed for traveling; he planned to leave for London within the hour.

There was no sound from within the chamber, so Daniel knocked again. This time he heard a bit of rustling, followed by a groggy "Enter."

He did, shutting the door behind him just in time to hear Anne gasp, "My lord!"

"I need to speak with you," he said succinctly.

She nodded, scrambling to pull her covers up to her chin, which he frankly thought was ridiculous, given the thoroughly unappealing sack she appeared to have put on in lieu of a nightgown.

"What are you doing here?" she asked, blinking furiously.

Without preamble, he said, "I'm leaving for London this morning."

She didn't say anything.

"I'm sure you know by now that the harness was cut."

She nodded.

"It was Lord Ramsgate," he said. "One of his men. Probably the one I went out to investigate. The one I told you was a drunkard."

"You said he wreaked havoc from the stables to the inn," she whispered.

"Indeed," he said, every muscle in his body straining to keep himself perfectly still as he spoke. If he moved, if he let down his guard for even one moment, he did not know what would happen. He might scream. He might beat the walls. All he knew was that something furious was building within him, and every time he thought it was done, that his rage could not possibly expand further, something inside seemed to pop and crackle. His skin grew too tight, and the anger, the fury—it fought to break free.

Hotter. Blacker. Squeezing at his very soul.

"Lord Winstead?" she said quietly, and he could not imagine what sliver of rage had shown on his face, because her eyes had grown wide and alarmed. And then, in the barest of whispers: "Daniel?"

It was the first time she had said his name.

He swallowed, clenching his teeth together as he

fought for control. "This would not be the first time he has tried to kill me," he finally said. "But it is the first time he has very nearly killed someone else in the attempt."

He watched her closely. She was still clutching the covers under her chin, her fingers wrapped over the edge. Her mouth moved, as if she wanted to say something. He waited.

She did not speak.

He remained still, his body straight, his hands clasped behind his back. There was something so unbearably formal about the tableau, despite the fact that Anne was in bed, her hair mussed with sleep, a single thick braid resting on her right shoulder.

They did not usually speak with such stiffness. Perhaps they should have done, perhaps that would have saved him from such infatuation, which would have saved her from being in his company on the day Ramsgate had chosen to make his move.

It would have been better for her if they had never met, clearly.

"What will you do?" she finally asked.

"When I find him?"

She gave a small nod.

"I don't know. If he's lucky I won't strangle him on sight. He was probably behind the attack in London, too. The one we all thought was just bad luck, a couple of petty thieves out for a heavy purse."

"It might have been," she said. "You can't know. People are robbed all the time in London. It's—"

"Are you defending him?" he asked incredulously.

"No! Of course not. It's just that . . . Well . . ." She swallowed, the convulsive movement rippling down her throat. When she spoke again her voice was quite small. "You don't have all of the information."

For a moment he just stared at her, not trusting himself to speak. "I spent the last three years running from his men in Europe," he finally said. "Did you know that? No? Well, I did. And I'm sick of it. If he wanted revenge on me, he has surely wrought it. Three years of my life, stolen. Do you have any idea what that's like? To have three years of your life ripped from you?"

Her lips parted, and for a moment he thought she might actually say yes. She looked dazed, almost hypnotized, and then finally she said, "I'm sorry. Go on."

"I will speak to his son first. I can trust Lord Hugh. Or at least I always thought I could." Daniel closed his eyes for a moment and simply breathed, trying to keep hold of an equilibrium that would not stay still. "I don't know whom I can trust any longer."

"You can—" She stopped. Swallowed. Had she been about to say that he could trust her? He looked at her closely, but she had turned away, her eyes focused on the nearby window. The curtains were drawn, but she was still staring at it as if there were something to see. "I wish you the safest of journeys," she whispered.

"You're angry with me," he said.

Her head whipped around to face him. "No. No, of course not. I would never—"

"You would not have been injured had you not been in my curricle," he cut in. He would never forgive himself for the injuries he had caused her. He needed her to know that. "It is my fault that you—"

"No!" she cried out, and she jumped from the bed, rushing toward him but then stopping abruptly. "No, that's not true. I— I just— No," she said, so firmly that her chin bobbed in sharp punctuation. "It's not true."

He stared at her. She was almost within his reach. If he leaned forward, if he stretched out his arm, he could take hold of her sleeve. He could pull her to him, and together they would melt, he into her, she into him, until they would not know where one ended and the other began.

"It's not your fault," she said with quiet force.

"I am the one upon whom Lord Ramsgate wishes revenge," he reminded her softly.

"We are not—" She looked away, but not before she wiped one of her eyes with the back of her hand. "We are not responsible for the actions of others," she said. Her voice shook with emotion, and her gaze did not meet his. "Especially not those of a madman," she finished.

"No," he said, his voice a strange staccato in the soft morning air. "But we do bear responsibility for those around us. Harriet, Elizabeth, and Frances— would you not have me keep them safe?"

"No," she said, her brow coming together in distress. "That's not what I meant. You know it wasn't—"

"I am responsible for every person on this land," he cut in. "For you, too, while you are here. And as long as I know that someone wishes me ill, it is my charge and obligation to make sure that I do not carry a single other person into my danger."

She stared at him with wide, unblinking eyes, and Daniel wondered what she saw. *Who* she saw. The words coming from his mouth were unfamiliar. He sounded like his father, and his grandfather before him. Was this what it meant to have inherited an ancient title, to have been entrusted with the lives and livelihoods of all who resided on his land? He had been made the earl so young, and then been forced to leave England but a year later.

This was what it meant, he finally realized. This was what it all meant.

"I will not see you hurt," he said, his voice so low it almost shook.

She closed her eyes, but then the skin at her temples wrinkled and tensed, almost as if she was in pain.

"Anne," he said, stepping forward.

But she shook her head, almost violently, and an awful choking sob burst from her throat.

It nearly tore him in two.

"What is it?" he said, crossing the distance between them. He put his hands on her upper arms, maybe to support her . . . maybe to support himself. And then he had to stop, to simply breathe. The urge to hold her closer was overwhelming. When he'd come into her room this morning he had told himself he would not touch her, he would not come close enough to feel the way the air moved across her skin. But this—he could not bear it.

"No," she said, her body twisting, but not enough to make him think she meant it. "Please. Go. Just go."

"Not until you tell—"

"I can't," she cried out, and then she did shake him off, stepping back until they were once again separated by the chill air of the morning. "I can't tell you what you want to hear. I can't be with you, and I can't even see you again. Do you understand?"

He did not answer. Because he did understand what she was saying. But he did not agree with it.

She swallowed and her hands came to cover her face, rubbing and stretching across her skin with such anguish that he almost reached out to stop her. "I can't be with you," she said, the words coming out with such suddenness and force that he wondered just whom she was trying to convince. "I am not . . . the person . . ."

She looked away.

"I am not a suitable woman for you," she said to the window. "I am not of your station, and I am not—"

He waited. She'd almost said something else. He was sure of it.

But when she spoke, her voice had changed tenor,

and she sounded too deliberate. "You will ruin me," she said. "You won't mean to, but you will, and I will lose my position and all I hold dear."

She looked him in the eye as she said that, and he nearly flinched at the emptiness he saw in her face.

"Anne," he said, "I will protect you."

"I don't want your protection," she cried. "Don't you understand? I have learned how to care for myself, to keep myself—" She stopped, then finished with: "I can't be responsible for you, too."

"You don't have to be," he answered, trying to make sense of her words.

She turned away. "You don't understand."

"No," he said harshly. "No, I don't." How could he? She kept secrets, held them to her chest like tiny treasures, leaving him to beg for her memories like some damned dog.

"Daniel . . . ," she said softly, and there it was again. His name, and it was like he'd never heard it before. Because when she spoke, he felt every sound like a caress. Every syllable landed on his skin like a kiss.

"Anne," he said, and he didn't even recognize his voice. It was rough, and hoarse with need, and laced with desire, and . . . and . . .

And then, before he had a clue what he was about, he pulled her roughly into his arms and was kissing her like she was water, air, his very salvation. He needed her with a desperation that would have shaken him to his core if he'd let himself think about it.

But he wasn't thinking. Not right now. He was tired of thinking, tired of worrying. He wanted just to feel. He wanted to let passion rule his senses, and his senses rule his body.

He wanted her to want him the very same way.

"Anne, Anne," he gasped, his hands frantically tugging against the awful wool of her nightgown. "What you do to me—"

She cut him off, not with words but with her body, pressing it against his with an urgency that matched his own. Her hands were on his shirt, tearing at the front, pulling it open until he felt her on his skin.

It was more than he could bear.

With a guttural moan, he half-lifted, half-turned her until they went tumbling to the bed, and finally he had her exactly where he'd wanted her for what felt like a lifetime. Under him, her legs softly cradling him.

"I want you," he said, even though it could hardly have been in doubt. "I want you now, in every way a man can want a woman."

His words were coarse, but he liked them that way. This wasn't romance, this was pure need. She'd almost died. He might die tomorrow. And if that happened, if the end came and he hadn't tasted paradise first . . .

He nearly ripped her nightgown from her body.

And then . . . he stopped.

He stopped to breathe, to simply look at her and revel in the glorious perfection of her body. Her breasts rose and fell with each breath, and with a trembling hand, he reached out and cupped one, nearly shuddering with pleasure from just that simple touch.

"You are so beautiful," he whispered. She must have heard those words before, thousands of times, but he wanted her to hear them from *him*. "You are so . . ."

But he didn't finish, because she was so much more than her beauty. And there was no way he could say it all, no way he could put into words all the reasons his breath quickened every time he saw her.

Her hands rose to cover some of her nakedness, and she blushed, reminding him that this must be new to her. It was new to him, too. He'd made love to women before, probably more than he wanted to admit to, but this was the first time . . . she was the first one . . .

It had never been like this. He couldn't explain the difference, but it had never been like this.

"Kiss me," she whispered, "please."

He did, yanking his shirt over his head right before he settled his body atop hers, skin to glorious skin. He kissed her deeply, then he kissed her neck, and the hollow of her collarbone, and then finally, with a pleasure that tightened every muscle in his body, he kissed her breast. She let out a soft squeal and arched underneath him, which he took as an invitation to move to the other side, kissing and sucking and nipping until he thought he might lose control right then and there.

Dear God, she hadn't even touched him. He still had his breeches fully fastened, and he'd almost lost himself. That hadn't even happened when he was a green boy.

He had to get inside her. He had to get inside her now. It went beyond desire. It went beyond need. It was primal, an urge that rose from deep within him, as if to say that his very life depended on making love to this woman. If that was mad, then *he* was mad.

For her. He was mad for her, and he had a feeling it was never going to go away.

"Anne," he moaned, pausing for a moment to try to gain his breath. His face rested lightly on the tender skin of her belly, and he inhaled the scent of her even as he fought for control of his body. "Anne, I need you." He looked up. "*Now.* Do you understand?"

He rose to his knees, and his hands went to his breeches, and then she said . . .

"No."

His hands stilled. *No, she didn't understand? No, not now?* Or *no, not—*

"I can't," she whispered, and she tugged at the sheet in a desperate attempt to cover herself.

Dear God, not *that* no.

"I'm sorry," she said with an agonized gasp. "I'm so sorry. Oh, my God, I'm so sorry." With frenetic motions she lurched from the bed, trying to pull the sheet along with her. But Daniel was still pinning it down, and she stumbled, then found herself jerked backward toward the bed. Still, she held on, tugging and pulling and over and over again saying, "I'm sorry."

Daniel just tried to breathe, great big gulps of air that he prayed would ease what was now a painful erection. He was so far gone he couldn't even think straight, let alone put together a sentence.

"I shouldn't have," she said, still trying to cover herself with the damned bedsheet. She couldn't get away from the side of the bed, not if she wanted to keep herself covered. He could reach out for her; his arms were long enough. He could wrap his hands around her shoulders and pull her back, tempt her back into his arms. He could make her writhe and squirm with pleasure until she couldn't remember her own name. He knew how to do it.

And yet he didn't move. He was a bloody stupid statue, up there on the four-poster bed, on his knees with his hands clutching at the fastening of his breeches.

"I'm sorry," she said again, for what had to be the fiftieth time. "I'm sorry, I just . . . I can't. It's the only thing I have. Do you understand? It's the only thing I have."

Her virginity.

He hadn't even given it a thought. What kind of man was he? "I'm sorry," he said, and then he almost laughed at the absurdity of it. It was a symphony of apologies, uncomfortable and utterly discordant.

"No, no," she returned, her head still shaking

back and forth, "I shouldn't have. I shouldn't have let you, and I shouldn't have let myself. I know better. *I know better.*"

So did he.

With a muttered curse he got down from the bed, forgetting that he'd been pinning her in place with the sheet. She went stumbling and twirling, tripping over her own feet until she landed in a nearby wing-back chair, wrapped up like a clumsy Roman, toga askew.

It would have been funny if he hadn't been so bloody close to exploding.

"I'm sorry," she said again.

"Stop *saying* that," he practically begged her. His voice was laced with exasperation—no, make that desperation—and she must have heard it, too, for she clamped her mouth shut, swallowing nervously as she watched him pull on his shirt.

"I have to leave for London, anyway," he said, not that *that* would have stopped him if she hadn't done so.

She nodded.

"We will discuss this later," he said firmly. He had no idea what he'd say, but they *would* talk about it. Just not right now, with the entire house waking up around him.

The entire house. Good God, he really *had* lost his head. In his determination to show Anne honor and respect the night before, he'd ordered the maids to put her in the finest guest bedroom, on the same hall as the rest of the family. Anyone could have walked through the door. His *mother* could have seen them. Or worse, one of his young cousins. He couldn't imagine what they would have thought he was doing. At least his mother would have known he wasn't killing the governess.

Anne nodded again, but she wasn't quite looking at him. Some little part of him thought this was curious, but then some other, larger part of him promptly forgot about it. He was far too concerned with the painful results of unfulfilled desire to think about the fact that she wouldn't look him in the eye when she nodded.

"I will call upon you when you arrive in town," he said.

She said something in return, so softly that he couldn't make out the words.

"What was that?"

"I said—" She cleared her throat. Then she did it again. "I said that I don't think that's wise."

He looked at her. Hard. "Would you have me pretend to visit my cousins again?"

"No. I— I would—" She turned away, but he saw her eyes flash with anguish, and maybe anger, and then, finally, resignation. When she looked back up, she met his gaze directly, but the spark in her expression, the one that so often drew him to her . . . It seemed to have gone out.

"I would prefer," she said, her voice so carefully even it was almost a monotone, "that you not call at all."

He crossed his arms. "Is that so?"

"Yes."

He fought for a moment—against himself. Finally he asked, somewhat belligerently, "Because of this?"

His eyes fell to her shoulder, where the sheet had slipped, revealing a tiny patch of skin, rosy pink and supple in the morning light. It was barely an inch square, but in that moment he wanted it so badly he could barely speak.

He wanted *her*.

She looked at him, at his eyes, so firmly fixed to one spot, then down at her bare shoulder. With a little gasp she yanked the sheet back up.

"I—" She swallowed, perhaps summoning her courage, then continued. "I would not lie to you and say that I did not want this."

"Me," he cut in peevishly. "You wanted *me*."

She closed her eyes. "Yes," she finally said, "I wanted you."

Part of him wanted to interrupt again, to remind her that she still wanted him, that it wasn't and would never be in the past.

"But I can't have you," she said quietly, "and because of that, *you* can't have *me*."

And then, to his complete astonishment, he asked, "What if I married you?"

ANNE STARED AT him in shock. Then she stared at him in horror, because he looked just as surprised as she felt, and she was fairly certain that if he could have taken back the words, he would have done.

With haste.

But his question—she couldn't possibly think of it as a proposal—hung in the air, and they both stared at each other, unmoving, until finally her feet seemed to recognize that this was not a laughing matter, and she leapt up, skittering backward until she had managed to put the wingback chair between them.

"You can't," she blurted out.

Which seemed to rouse that masculine don't-you-tell-*me*-what-to-do reaction. "Why not?" he demanded.

"You just can't," she shot back, tugging at the sheet, which had snagged on the corner of the chair. "You should know that. For heaven's sake, you're an earl. You can't marry a nobody." Especially not a nobody with a falsified name.

"I can marry anyone I damn well please."

Oh, for heaven's sake. Now he looked like a three-year-old who'd had his toy snatched away. Didn't he understand that she couldn't *do* this? He might delude himself, but she would never be so naïve. Especially after her conversation with Lady Pleinsworth the night before.

"You're being foolish," she told him, yanking at the damned sheet again. Dear God, was it too much just to want to be *free*? "And impractical. And furthermore, you don't even want to marry me, you just want to get me into your bed."

He drew back, visibly angered by her statement. But he did not contradict.

She let out an impatient breath. She hadn't meant to insult him, and he should have realized that. "I do not think that you meant to seduce and abandon," she said, because no matter how furious he made her, she could not bear his believing that she thought him a scoundrel. "I know that sort of man, and you are not he. But you hardly intended to propose marriage, and I certainly will not hold you to it."

His eyes narrowed, but not before she saw them glint dangerously. "When did you come to know my mind better than I do?"

"When you stopped *thinking*." She pulled at the sheet again, this time with such violence that the chair lurched forward and nearly toppled. And Anne very nearly found herself naked. "Aaargh!" she let out, so frustrated she wanted to punch something. Looking up, she saw Daniel standing there, just watching her, and she nearly screamed, she was so bloody *angry*. At him, at George Chervil, at the damned damned sheet that kept tangling her legs. "Will you just go?" she snapped. "Now, before someone comes in."

He smiled then, but it wasn't anything like the smiles she knew of him. It was cold, and it was mocking, and the sight of it on his face tore through her heart. "What would happen then?" he murmured. "You, dressed in nothing but a sheet. Me, rather rumpled."

"No one would insist upon marriage," she snapped. "That much I can tell you. You'd go back to your merry life, and I would be cast out without a reference."

He stared at her sourly. "I suppose you're going to say that that was my plan all along. To bankrupt you until you had no choice but to become my mistress."

"No," she said curtly, because she could not lie to him, not about this. And then, in a softer voice, she added, "I would never think that of you."

He fell silent, his eyes watching her intently. He was hurting, she could see that. He hadn't proposed marriage, not really, but still she'd somehow managed to reject him. And she *hated* that he was in pain. She hated the look on his face, and she hated the stiff way his arms were held at his sides, and most of all she hated that nothing was ever going to be the same. They would not talk. They would not laugh.

They would not kiss.

Why had she stopped him? She'd been in his arms, skin to skin, and she'd wanted him. She'd wanted him with a fire she'd never dreamed possible. She'd wanted to take him into her, and she'd wanted to love him with her body as she already loved him with her heart.

She loved him.

Dear God.

"Anne?"

She didn't respond.

Daniel's brow knit with concern. "Anne, are you all right? You've gone pale."

She wasn't all right. She wasn't sure she'd ever be all right again.

"I'm fine," she said.

"Anne . . ." Now he looked worried, and he was walking toward her, and if he touched her, if he so much as reached for her, she'd lose her resolve.

"No," she practically barked, hating the way her voice came from deep in her throat. It hurt. The word hurt. It hurt her neck, and it hurt her ears, and it hurt him, too.

But she had to do it.

"Please don't," she said. "I need you to leave me alone. This. . . . This . . ." She fought for a word; she couldn't bear to call it a thing. "This *feeling* between us . . ." she finally settled upon. "Nothing can come of it. You must realize that. And if you care for me at all, you will leave."

But he did not move.

"You will leave now," she practically cried, and she sounded like a wounded animal. Which was what she was, she supposed.

For several seconds more he stood frozen, and then finally, in a voice as low as it was determined, he said, "I am leaving, but not for any of the reasons you request. I am going to London to settle the issue with Ramsgate, and then—and *then*," he said with greater force, "we will talk."

Silently, she shook her head. She could not do this again. It was too painful to listen to him spin stories about happy endings that would never be hers.

He strode to the door. "We will talk," he said again.

It wasn't until after he'd left that Anne whispered, "No. We won't."

Chapter Sixteen

London
One week later

SHE WAS BACK.

Daniel had heard it from his sister, who had heard it from his mother, who had heard it directly from his aunt.

A more efficient chain of communication he could not imagine.

He hadn't really expected the Pleinsworths to remain at Whipple Hill for quite so long after he left. Or perhaps more to the point, he hadn't given any thought to the matter, not until several days had passed and they'd still remained in the country.

But as it turned out, it was probably for the best that they (and by they, he really meant Anne) had stayed out of town. It had been a busy week—busy and frustrating, and the knowledge of Miss Wynter's presence within walking distance would have been a distraction he could not afford.

He had talked to Hugh. Again. And Hugh had talked to his father. Again. And when Hugh had returned, reporting back to Daniel that he still did not think that his father had been involved in the recent attacks, Daniel had flown off the handle. Hugh had done what Daniel should have insisted upon weeks earlier.

He took him to speak with Lord Ramsgate directly.

And now Daniel was at a complete loss, because he, too, did not think that Lord Ramsgate had tried to kill him. Maybe he was a fool, maybe he just wanted to believe that this horrific chapter of his life was finally over, but the fury just hadn't been in Ramsgate's eyes. Not like the last time they'd met, right after Hugh had been shot.

Plus there was the new development of Hugh's threatened suicide. Daniel was not sure if his friend was brilliant or mad, but either way, when he reiterated his vow to kill himself if anything untoward happened to Daniel, it had been chilling. Lord Ramsgate was visibly shaken, even though it was hardly the first time he'd heard his son make the threat. Even Daniel had felt ill, being witness to such an unholy promise.

And he believed him. The look in Hugh's eyes . . . The icy, almost expressionless way he'd delivered the statement . . . It was terrifying.

All this meant that when Lord Ramsgate had practically spat at Daniel, vowing that he would do him no harm, Daniel believed him.

That had been two days earlier, two days during which Daniel had had little to do but think. About who else might wish to see him dead. About what Anne could possibly have meant when she'd said that she couldn't be responsible for him. About the secrets she was hiding, and why she'd said he didn't have all the information.

What in bloody hell had she meant by that?

Could the attack have been directed toward *her*? It wasn't inconceivable that someone might have realized she'd be riding home in his curricle. They'd certainly been inside the inn long enough for someone to sabotage the harness.

He thought back to the day she'd run into Hoby's, wild-eyed and terrified. She'd said there was someone she did not wish to see.

Who?

And didn't she realize that he could help her? He might be recently returned from exile, but he had position, and with that came power, certainly enough to keep her safe. Yes, he had been on the run for three years, but he'd been up against the Marquess of Ramsgate.

Daniel was the Earl of Winstead; there were only so many men who outranked him. A handful of dukes, a few more marquesses, and the royals. Surely Anne had not managed to make an enemy among that exalted population.

But when he had marched up the steps of Pleinsworth House to demand an interview, he had been informed that she was not at home.

And when he had repeated the request the following morning, he was met with the same answer.

Now, several hours later, he was back, and this time his aunt came in person to deliver the refusal.

"You must leave that poor girl alone," she said sharply.

Daniel was not in the mood to be lectured by his aunt Charlotte, so he cut straight to the point. "I need to speak with her."

"Well, she is not here."

"Oh, for God's sake, Aunt, I know she's—"

"I fully admit that she was upstairs when you called this morning," Lady Pleinsworth cut in. "Fortunately, Miss Wynter has the sense to cut off this flirtation, even if you do not. But she is not here now."

"Aunt Charlotte . . ." he warned.

"She's not!" Her chin lifted ever so slightly in the air. "It is her afternoon free. She always goes out on her afternoon free."

"Always?"

"As far as I know." His aunt flicked her hand impatiently through the air. "She has errands, and . . . And whatever it is she does."

Whatever it is she does. What a statement.

"Very well," Daniel said in a curt voice. "I shall wait for her."

"Oh, no, you won't."

"You're going to bar me from your sitting room," he said, giving her a look of mild disbelief.

She crossed her arms. "If I must."

He crossed his. "I am your nephew."

"And amazingly enough, the connection does not seem to have imbued you with common sense."

He stared at her.

"That was an insult," she mentioned, "in case you're having difficulty sorting it out."

Good God.

"If you have any care for Miss Wynter," Lady Pleinsworth continued imperiously, "you will leave her in peace. She is a sensible lady, and I keep her in my employ because I am fully certain that it is you who have pursued her and not the other way around."

"Did you talk with her about me?" Daniel demanded. "Did you threaten her?"

"Of course not," his aunt snapped, but she looked away for a split second, and Daniel knew she was lying. "As if I would threaten her," she continued in a huff. "And furthermore, *she's* not the one who needs a talking to. She knows how the world works, even if you do not. What happened at Whipple Hill can be overlooked—"

"*What happened?*" Daniel echoed, panic rising within him as he wondered to what, precisely, his aunt was referring. Had someone found out about his visit to Anne's bedroom? No, that was impossible. Anne would have been thrown out of the house if that had been the case.

"Your time spent alone with her," Lady Pleinsworth clarified. "Don't think I was unaware.

As much as I would like to believe that you have suddenly taken an interest in Harriet, Elizabeth, and Frances, any fool could see that you've been panting after Miss Wynter like a puppy dog."

"Another insult, I assume," he bit off.

She pursed her lips but otherwise ignored his comment. "I do not want to have to let her go," she said, "but if you pursue the connection, I will have no choice. And you can be sure that no family of good standing would hire a governess who consorts with an earl."

"*Consorts?*" he repeated, his voice somewhere between disbelief and disgust. "Don't insult her with such a word."

His aunt drew back and regarded him with mild pity. "It is not *I* who insults her. In fact, I applaud Miss Wynter for possessing good judgment where you do not. I was warned not to hire such an attractive young woman as a governess, but despite her looks she is extremely intelligent. And the girls quite adore her. Would you have me discriminate against her for her beauty?"

"No," he bit off, ready to climb the walls with frustration. "And what the devil has that to do with anything? I just want to speak with her." His voice rose at the end, coming dangerously close to a roar.

Lady Pleinsworth leveled a long stare at his face. "No," she said.

Daniel practically bit his tongue to keep from snapping at her. The only way his aunt was going to let him see Anne was if he told her that he suspected that *she* had been the target of the attack at Whipple Hill. But anything that hinted at a scandalous past would have her fired immediately, and he would not be the cause of her loss of employment.

Finally, his patience worn down to a threadbare string, he let out a between-the-teeth exhale and said, "I need to speak with her once. One time only. It may be in your sitting room with the door ajar, but I would insist upon privacy."

His aunt regarded him suspiciously. "Once?"

"Once." It was not strictly true; he wished for a great deal more than that, but that was all he was going to request.

"I shall think about it," she sniffed.

"Aunt Charlotte!"

"Oh, very well, just once, and only because I wish to believe that your mother raised a son who has some sense of right and wrong."

"Oh, for the love of—"

"Don't blaspheme in front of me," she warned, "and make me reconsider my judgment."

Daniel clamped his mouth shut, gritting his teeth so hard he fully expected to taste powder.

"You may call upon her tomorrow," Lady Pleinsworth granted. "At eleven in the morning. The girls plan to go shopping with Sarah and Honoria. I would prefer not to have them in the house while you are . . ." She appeared not to know how to describe it, instead flicking her hand distastefully in the air.

He nodded, then bowed, then left.

But like his aunt, he did not see Anne, watching them from a crack in the door to the next room, listening to every word they said.

ANNE WAITED UNTIL Daniel stormed out of the house, then looked down at the letter in her hands. Lady Pleinsworth hadn't been lying; she *had* gone out to run her errands. But she'd returned through the back door, as was her usual practice when she did not have the girls with her. She'd been on her way up to her room when she realized that Daniel was in the front hall. She shouldn't have eavesdropped, but she could not help herself. It wasn't so much what he said; she just wanted to hear his voice.

It would be the last time she would hear it.

The letter was from her sister Charlotte, and it was a bit out of date, as it had been sitting at the receiving house where Anne preferred to pick up her mail since well before she had left for Whipple Hill. The receiving house she *hadn't* gone to that day she'd run into the bootmaker's shop in a panic. If she'd had this letter before she'd thought she'd seen George Chervil, she wouldn't have been frightened.

She'd have been terrified.

According to Charlotte, he'd come by the house again, this time when Mr. and Mrs. Shawcross were out. He'd first tried to cajole her into revealing Anne's whereabouts, then he'd ranted and screamed until the servants had come in, worried for Charlotte's safety. He'd left then, but not until he had revealed that he knew Anne was working as a governess for an aristocratic family, and that this being springtime, she was likely in London. Charlotte did not think he knew which family Anne was working for; else why would he have expended so much energy trying to get the answer from her? Still, she was worried, and she begged Anne to take caution.

Anne crumpled the letter in her hands, then eyed the tidy fire burning in the grate. She always burned Charlotte's letters after she received them. It was painful every time; these wispy slips of paper were her only link to her old life, and more than once she had sat at her small writing table, blinking back tears as she traced the familiar loops of Charlotte's script with her index finger. But Anne had no illusions that she enjoyed perfect privacy as a servant, and she had no idea how she might explain them if they were ever discovered. This time, however, she happily threw the paper into the fire.

Well, not happily. She wasn't sure she would do anything happily, ever again. But she enjoyed destroying it, however grim and furious that joy might be.

She shut her eyes, keeping them tightly closed against her tears. She was almost certainly going to have to leave the Pleinsworths. And she was bloody angry about it. This was the best position she'd ever had. She was not trapped on an island with an aging old lady, caught in a endless circle of endless boredom. She was not bolting her door at night against a crude old man who seemed to think *he* should be educating *her* while his children slept. She liked living with the Pleinsworths. It was the closest she'd ever felt to home, since . . . since . . .

Since she'd had a home.

She forced herself to breathe, then roughly wiped her tears away with the back of her hand. But then, just as she was about to head into the main hall and up the stairs, a knock sounded at the door. It was probably Daniel; he must have forgot something.

She darted back into the sitting room, pulling the door almost shut. She ought to close it completely, she knew that, but this might very well be her last glimpse of him. With her eye to the crack, she watched as the butler went to answer the knock. But as Granby swung the door open, she saw not Daniel but a man she'd never seen before.

He was a rather ordinary-looking fellow, dressed in clothing that marked him as someone who worked for a living. Not a laborer; he was too clean and tidy for that. But there was something rough about him, and when he spoke, his accent held the harsh cadence of East London.

"Deliveries are in the rear," Granby said immediately.

"I'm not here to make a delivery," the man said with a nod. His accent might be coarse but his manners were polite, and the butler did not close the door on his face.

"What, then, is your business?"

"I'm looking for a woman who might live here. Miss Annelise Shawcross."

Anne stopped breathing.

"There is no one here by that name," Granby said crisply. "If you will excuse me—"

"She might call herself something else," the man cut in. "I'm not sure what name she's using, but she has dark hair, blue eyes, and I'm told she is quite beautiful." He shrugged. "I've never seen her myself. She could be working as a servant. But she's gentry, make no mistake of it."

Anne's body tensed for flight. There was no way Granby would not recognize her from that description.

But Granby said, "That does not sound like anyone in this household. Good day, sir."

The man's face tightened with determination, and he shoved his foot in the door before Granby could close it. "If you change your mind, sir," he said, holding something forth, "here is my card."

Granby's arms remained stiffly at his sides. "It is hardly a matter of changing my mind."

"If that's what you say." The man placed the card back in his breast pocket, waited for one more moment, then left the house.

Anne placed her hand over her heart and tried to take deep, silent breaths. If she'd had any doubts that the attack at Whipple Hill had been the work of George Chervil, they were gone now. And if he was willing to risk the life of the Earl of Winstead to carry out his revenge, he wouldn't think twice about harming one of the young Pleinsworth daughters.

Anne had ruined her own life when she'd let him seduce her at sixteen, but she would be damned before she allowed him to destroy anyone else. She was going to have to disappear. Immediately. George knew where she was, and he knew *who* she was.

But she could not leave the sitting room until Granby exited the hall, and he was just *standing* there, frozen in position with his hand on the doorknob. Then he turned, and when he did . . . Anne should have remembered that he missed nothing. If it had been Daniel at the door, he would not have noticed that the sitting room door was slightly ajar, but Granby? It was like waving a red flag in front of a bull. The door should be open, or it should be shut. But it was never left ajar, with a strip of air one inch wide.

And of course he saw her.

Anne did not pretend to hide. She owed him that much, after what he had just done for her. She opened the door and stepped out into the hall.

Their eyes met, and she waited, breath held, but he only nodded and said, "Miss Wynter."

She nodded in return, then dipped into a small curtsy of respect. "Mr. Granby."

"It is a fine day, is it not?"

She swallowed. "Very fine."

"Your afternoon off, I believe?"

"Indeed, sir."

He nodded once more, then said, as if nothing out of the ordinary had just occurred, "Carry on."

Carry on.

Wasn't that what she always did? For three years

on the Isle of Man, never seeing another person her own age except for Mrs. Summerlin's nephew, who thought it good sport to chase her around the dining table. Then for nine months near Birmingham, only to be dismissed without a reference when Mrs. Barraclough caught Mr. Barraclough pounding on her door. Then three years in Shropshire, which hadn't been too bad. Her employer was a widow, and her sons had more often than not been off at university. But then the daughters had had the effrontery to grow up, and Anne had been informed that her services were no longer needed.

But she'd carried on. She'd obtained a second letter of reference, which was what she'd needed to gain a position in the Pleinsworth household. And now that she'd be leaving, she'd carry on again.

Although where she'd carry herself to, she had no idea.

Chapter Seventeen

THE FOLLOWING DAY, Daniel arrived at Pleinsworth House at precisely five minutes before eleven. He had prepared in his mind a list of questions he must ask of Anne, but when the butler admitted him to the house, he was met with considerable uproar. Harriet and Elizabeth were yelling at each other at the end of the hall, their mother was yelling at both of them, and on a backless bench near the sitting room door, three maids sat sobbing.

"What is going on?" he asked Sarah, who was attempting to usher a visibly distraught Frances into the sitting room.

Sarah gave him an impatient glance. "It is Miss Wynter. She has disappeared."

Daniel's heart stopped. "What? When? What happened?"

"I don't know," Sarah snapped. "I'm hardly privy to her intentions." She gave him an irritated glance before turning back to Frances, who was crying so hard she could barely breathe.

"She was gone before lessons this morning," Frances sobbed.

Daniel looked down at his young cousin. Frances's eyes were red-rimmed and bloodshot, her cheeks were streaked with tears, and her little body was shaking uncontrollably. She looked, he realized, like he felt. Forcing down his terror, he crouched next to her so that he could look her in the eye. "What time do you begin lessons?" he asked.

Frances gasped for air, then got out, "Half nine."

Daniel spun furiously back to Sarah. "She has been gone almost two hours and no one has informed me?"

"Frances, please," Sarah begged, "you must try to stop crying. And no," she said angrily, whipping her head back around to face Daniel, "no one informed you. Why, pray tell, would we have done?"

"Don't play games with me, Sarah," he warned.

"Do I look like I'm playing games?" she snapped, before softening her voice for her sister. "Frances, please, darling, try to take a deep breath."

"I should have been told," Daniel said sharply. He was losing patience. For all any of them knew, Anne's enemy—and he was now certain she had one—had snatched her from her bed. He needed answers, not sanctimonious scoldings from Sarah. "She's been gone at least ninety minutes," he said to her. "You should have—"

"What?" Sarah cut in. "What should we have done? Wasted valuable time notifying *you*? You, who have no connection or claim to her? You, whose intentions are—"

"I'm going to marry her," he interrupted.

Frances stopped crying, her face lifting up toward his, eyes shining with hope. Even the maids, still three abreast on the bench, went silent.

"What did you say?" Sarah whispered.

"I love her," he said, realizing the truth of it as the words left his lips. "I want to marry her."

"Oh, Daniel," Frances cried, leaving Sarah's side and throwing her arms around him. "You must find her. You must!"

"What happened?" he asked Sarah, who was still staring at him slackjawed. "Tell me everything. Did she leave a note?"

She nodded. "Mother has it. It did not say much, though. Just that she was sorry but she had to leave."

"She said she sent me a hug," Frances said, her words muffling into his coat.

Daniel patted her on her back even as he kept his eyes firmly on Sarah. "Did she give any indication that she might not have left of her own volition?"

Sarah gaped at him. "You don't think someone kidnapped her?"

"I don't know what to think," he admitted.

"Nothing was out of place in her room," Sarah told him. "All of her belongings were gone, but nothing else was amiss. Her bed was neatly made."

"She always makes her bed," Frances sniffled.

"Does anyone know when she left?" Daniel asked.

Sarah shook her head. "She did not take breakfast. So it must have been before that."

Daniel swore under his breath, then carefully disentangled himself from Frances's grasp. He had no idea how to search for Anne; he didn't even know where to start. She had left so few clues as to her background. It would have been laughable if he weren't so terrified. He knew . . . what? The color of her parents' eyes? Well, now, *there* was something that was going to help him find her.

He had nothing. Absolutely nothing.

"My lord?"

He looked up. It was Granby, the long-standing Pleinsworth butler, and he looked uncharacteristically distraught.

"Might I have a word with you, sir?" Granby asked.

"Of course." Daniel stepped away from Sarah, who was watching the two men with curiosity and confusion, and motioned to Granby to follow him into the sitting room.

"I heard you speaking with Lady Sarah," Granby said uncomfortably. "I did not intend to eavesdrop."

"Of course," Daniel said briskly. "Go on."

"You . . . care for Miss Wynter?"

Daniel regarded the butler carefully, then nodded.

"A man came yesterday," Granby said. "I should have said something to Lady Pleinsworth, but I wasn't sure, and I did not want to tell tales about

Miss Wynter if it turned out to be nothing. But now that it seems to be certain that she is gone . . ."

"What happened?" Daniel asked instantly.

The butler swallowed nervously. "A man came asking for a Miss Annelise Shawcross. I sent him away instantly; there is no one here by that name. But he was insistent, and he said Miss Shawcross might be using a different name. I did not like him, my lord, I can tell you that. He was . . ." Granby shook his head a little, almost as if trying to dislodge a bad memory. "I did not like him," he said again.

"What did he say?"

"He described her. This Miss Shawcross. He said she had dark hair, and blue eyes, and that she was quite beautiful."

"Miss Wynter," Daniel said quietly. Or rather— *Annelise Shawcross*. Was that her real name? Why had she changed it?

Granby nodded. "It is exactly how I might have described her."

"What did you tell him?" Daniel asked, trying to keep the urgency out of his voice. Granby was feeling guilty enough for not having come forward sooner, he could see that.

"I told him that we had no one in residence who matched that description. As I said, I did not like his aspect, and I would not jeopardize Miss Wynter's welfare." He paused. "I like our Miss Wynter."

"I do, too," Daniel said softly.

"That is why I am telling you this," Granby said,

his voice finally finding some of the vigor with which it was usually imbued. "You must find her."

Daniel took a long, unsteady breath and looked down at his hands. They were shaking. This had happened before, several times back in Italy, when Ramsgate's men had come particularly close. Something had rushed through his body, some kind of terror in the blood, and it had taken him hours to feel normal again. But this was worse. His stomach churned, and his lungs felt tight, and more than anything, he wanted to throw up.

He knew fear. This went beyond fear.

He looked at Granby. "Do you think this man has taken her?"

"I do not know. But after he left, I saw her." Granby turned and looked off to the right, and Daniel wondered if he was re-creating the scene in his mind. "She had been in the sitting room," he said, "right over there by the door. She heard everything."

"Are you sure?" Daniel asked.

"It was right there in her eyes," Granby said quietly. "She is the woman he seeks. And she knew I knew."

"What did you say to her?"

"I believe I remarked upon the weather. Or something of equal unimportance. And then I told her to carry on." Granby cleared his throat. "I believe she understood that I did not intend to turn her in."

"I'm sure she did," Daniel said grimly. "But she may have felt that she must leave, nonetheless." He didn't know how much Granby knew about the curricle accident at Whipple Hill. Like everyone else, he probably thought that it had been Ramsgate's work. But Anne obviously suspected otherwise, and it was clear that whoever had tried to hurt her did not care if anyone else was injured, too. Anne would never allow herself to put one of the Pleinsworth girls at risk. Or . . .

Or him. He closed his eyes for a moment. She probably thought she was protecting him. But if anything happened to her . . .

Nothing would destroy him more completely.

"I will find her," he told Granby. "You can be sure of it."

ANNE HAD BEEN lonely before. In fact, she'd spent most of the past eight years feeling lonely. But as she sat huddled on her hard boardinghouse bed, wearing her coat over her nightgown to keep out the chill, she realized that she had never known misery.

Not like this.

Maybe she should have gone to the country. It was cleaner. Probably less dangerous. But London was anonymous. The crowded streets could swallow her up, make her invisible.

But the streets could also chew her to bits.

There was no work for a woman like her. Ladies with her accent did not work as seamstresses or shopgirls. She'd walked up and down the streets of her new neighborhood, a marginally respectable place that squeezed itself in between middle-class shopping areas and desperate slums. She'd entered every establishment with a Help Wanted sign, and quite a few more without. She'd been told she wouldn't last long, that her hands were too soft, and her teeth too clean. More than one man had leered and laughed, then offered a different type of employment altogether.

She could not obtain a gentlewoman's position as a governess or companion without a letter of reference, but the two precious recommendations she had in her possession were for Anne Wynter. And she could not be Anne Wynter any longer.

She pulled her bent legs even tighter against her and let her face rest against her knees, closing her eyes tight. She didn't want to see this room, didn't want to see how meager her belongings looked even in such a tiny chamber. She didn't want to see the dank night through the window, and most of all, she didn't want to see herself.

She had no name again. And it hurt. It hurt like a sharp, jagged slice in her heart. It was an awful thing, a heavy dread that sat upon her each morning, and it was all she could do to swing her legs over the side of the bed and place her feet on the floor.

This wasn't like before, when her family had thrown her from her home. At least then she'd had somewhere to go. She'd had a plan. Not one of her choosing, but she'd known what she was supposed to do and when she was supposed to do it. Now she had two dresses, one coat, eleven pounds, and no prospects save prostitution.

And she could not do that. Dear God, she couldn't. She'd given herself too freely once before, and she would not make the same mistake twice. And it would be far, far too cruel to have to submit to a stranger when she'd stopped Daniel before they had completed their union.

She'd said no because . . . She wasn't even sure. Habit, possibly. Fear. She did not want to bear an illegitimate child, and she did not want to force a man into marriage who would not otherwise choose a woman like her.

But most of all, she'd needed to hold onto herself. Not her pride, exactly; it was something else, something deeper.

Her heart.

It was the one thing she still had that was pure and utterly hers. She had given her body to George, but despite what she had thought at the time, he had never had her heart. And as Daniel's hand had gone to the fastening of his breeches, preparing to make love to her, she had known that if she let him, if she let *herself*, he would have her heart forever.

But the joke was on her. He already had it. She'd gone and done the most foolish thing imaginable. She had fallen in love with a man she could never have.

Daniel Smythe-Smith, Earl of Winstead, Viscount Streathermore, Baron Touchton of Stoke. She didn't want to think about him, but she did, every time she closed her eyes. His smile, his laugh, the fire in his eyes when he looked at her.

She did not think he loved her, but what he felt must have come close. He had cared, at least. And maybe if she'd been someone else, someone with a name and position, someone who didn't have a madman trying to kill her . . . Maybe then when he had so foolishly said, "What if I married you?" she would have thrown her arms around him and yelled, "Yes! Yes! Yes!"

But she didn't have a *Yes* sort of life. Hers was a series of Noes. And it had finally landed her here, where she was finally as alone in body as she had been for so many years in spirit.

Her stomach let out a loud groan, and Anne sighed. She'd forgotten to buy supper before coming back to her boardinghouse, and now she was starving. It was probably for the best; she was going to have to make her pennies last as long as she could.

Her stomach rumbled again, this time with anger, and Anne abruptly swung her legs over the side of the bed. "*No*," she said aloud. Although what she really meant was *yes*. She was hungry, damn it, and she was going to get something to eat. For once in her life she was going to say yes, even if it was only to a meat pasty and a half pint of cider.

She looked over at her dress, laid neatly over her chair. She really didn't feel like changing back into it. Her coat covered her from head to hem. If she put on some shoes and stockings and pinned up her hair, no one would ever know she was out in her nightgown.

She laughed, the first time she'd made such a sound in days. What a strange way to be wicked.

A few minutes later she was out on the street, making her way to a small food shop she passed every day. She'd never gone inside, but the smells that poured forth every time the door opened . . . oh, they were heavenly. Cornish pasties and meat pies, hot rolls, and heaven knew what else.

She felt almost happy, she realized, once she had her hands around her toasty meal. The shopkeeper had wrapped her pasty in paper, and Anne was taking it back to her room. Some habits died hard; she was still too much of a proper lady to ever eat on the street, despite what the rest of humanity seemed to be doing around her. She could stop and get cider across the street from her boardinghouse, and when she got back to her room—

"You!"

Anne kept walking. The streets in this neighborhood were so loud, filled with so many voices, that it never occurred to her that a stray "You!" might actually be directed at her. But then she heard it again, closer.

"Annelise Shawcross."

She didn't even turn around to look. She knew that voice, and more to the point, that voice knew her real name. She ran.

Her precious supper slipped from her fingers and she ran faster than she would have ever thought herself capable. She darted around corners, shoved her way through crowds without so much as a begging of pardon. She ran until her lungs burned and her nightgown stuck to her skin, but in the end, she was no match for George's simple yell of—

"Catch her! Please! My wife!"

Someone did, probably because he sounded like he'd be *ever* so grateful, and then, when he arrived at her side, he said to the man whose burly arms were holding her like a vise, "She's not well."

"I'm not your wife!" Anne yelled, struggling against her captor's grasp. She twisted and turned, smacking his leg with her hip, but he would not be swayed. "I'm not his wife," she said to him, trying to sound reasonable and sane. "He's mad. He's been chasing after me for years. I'm not his wife, I swear."

"Come now, Annelise," George said in a soothing voice. "You know that's not true."

"No!" she howled, bucking against both of the men now. "I am not his wife!" she yelled again. "He's going to kill me!"

Finally, the man who had caught her for George began to look unsure. "She says she's not yer wife," he said with a frown.

"I know," George said with a sigh. "She has been this way for several years. We had a baby—"

"What?" Anne howled.

"Stillborn," George said to the other man. "She never got over it."

"He lies!" Anne yelled.

But George just sighed, and his duplicitous eyes brimmed with tears. "I have had to accept that she will never again be the woman I married."

The man looked from George's sad noble face to Anne's, which was contorted with rage, and he must have decided that of the two, George was more likely to be sane, so he handed her over. "God-speed," he said.

George thanked him profusely, then accepted his aid *and* his handkerchief to combine with his own to form bindings for Anne's hands. When that was done, he gave her a vicious yank, and she stumbled up against him, shuddering with revulsion as her body pressed up against the length of his.

"Oh, Annie," he said, "it is so nice to see you again."

"You cut the harness," she said in a low voice.

"I did," he said with a proud smile. Then he frowned. "I thought you'd be more seriously injured."

"You could have killed Lord Winstead!"

George just shrugged, and in that moment he confirmed all of Anne's darkest suspicions. He was mad. He was utterly, completely, loonlike mad. There could be no other explanation. No sane individual would risk killing a peer of the realm in order to get to *her*.

"What about the attack?" she demanded. "When we thought it was just petty thieves?"

George looked at her as if she were speaking in tongues. "What are you talking about?"

"When Lord Winstead was attacked!" she practically yelled. "Why would you do such a thing?"

George drew back, his upper lip curling with condescension and contempt. "I don't know what you're talking about," he sneered, "but your precious Lord Winstead has enemies of his own. Or don't you know *that* sordid story?"

"You're not fit to speak his name," she hissed.

But he only laughed, then crowed, "Do you have any idea how long I have been waiting for this moment?"

About as long as she'd been living as a castoff from society.

"Do you?" he growled, grabbing the knotted handkerchiefs and twisting them viciously.

She spat in his face.

George's face mottled with rage, his skin turning so red that his blond eyebrows nearly glowed in relief. "That was a mistake," he hissed, and he pulled her furiously toward a darkened alley. "Convenient of you to choose such a disreputable neighborhood," he cackled. "No one will even look twice when I—"

Anne started to scream.

But no one paid her notice, and anyway, she only made noise for a moment. George slugged her in the stomach, and she stumbled against a wall, gasping for breath.

"I've had eight years to imagine this moment," he said in a terrifying murmur. "Eight years to remember you every time I look in the mirror." He pressed his face close to hers, his eyes wild with rage. "Take a good look at my face, Annelise. I've had eight years to heal, but look! *Look!*"

Anne tried to escape, but her back was jammed up against a brick wall, and George had grabbed her chin and was forcing her to face his ruined cheek. The scar had healed better than she would have thought, white now instead of red, but it still puckered and pulled, distorting his cheek into a strange bisection of skin.

"I'd thought I'd have some fun with you first," he said, "since I never got to that day, but I didn't envision myself in a filthy alleyway." His lips twisted into a monstrous leer. "Even I didn't think you'd be brought so low."

"What do you mean, first?" Anne whispered.

But she didn't know why she asked. She knew. She'd known all along, and when he pulled out a knife, they both knew exactly what he planned to do with it.

Anne didn't scream. She didn't even think. She couldn't have said what she did, except that ten seconds later, George was lying on the cobbles, curled up like a fetus, unable to make a sound. Anne stood over him for one final moment, gasping for breath, and then she kicked him, hard, right where she'd kneed him before, and then, her hands still bound, she ran.

This time, however, she knew exactly where she was going.

Chapter Eighteen

At ten that evening, after another fruitless day of searching, Daniel headed home. He watched the pavement as he walked, counting his steps as he somehow pulled each foot in front of the other.

He'd hired private investigators. He'd combed the streets himself, stopping at every receiving house with Anne's description and both of her names. He'd found two men who said they remembered someone of that description dropping off letters, but they didn't recall where she sent them to. And then finally there was one who said that she matched a description of someone else altogether, someone named Mary Philpott. Lovely lady, the proprietor of the receiving house said. She never posted letters, but she came by once per week like clockwork to see if she'd received any, except for that one time . . .

was it two weeks ago? He'd been surprised not to see her, especially since she hadn't received a letter the week before, and she almost never went more than two weeks without one.

Two weeks. That would correspond with the day Anne had come running into Hoby's looking as if she'd seen a ghost. Had she been on her way to pick up her mail when she'd run into the mysterious person she had not wished to see? He had driven her to a receiving house to post the letter she'd held in her reticule, but it had not been the same one "Mary Philpott" used to receive her letters.

At any rate, the man at the receiving house had continued, she'd come back a few weeks later. Tuesday, it was. Always Tuesday.

Daniel frowned. She had disappeared on a Wednesday.

Daniel had left his name at all three receiving houses, along with a promise of a reward should they notify him of her appearance. But beyond that, he didn't know what to do. How was he supposed to find one woman in all of London?

And so he just walked and walked and walked, constantly searching faces in crowds. It would have been like the proverbial needle in the haystack, except that it was worse. At least the needle was *in* the haystack. For all he knew, Anne had left town entirely.

But it was dark now, and he needed sleep, and so he dragged himself back to Mayfair, praying that his mother and sister would not be at home when he arrived. They had not asked what he was doing each day from dawn to late evening, and he had not told them, but they knew. And it was easier if he did not have to see the pity on their faces.

Finally, he reached his street. It was quiet, blessedly so, and the only sound was his own groan as he lifted his foot to the first stone step at the entrance to Winstead House. The only sound, that was, until someone whispered his name.

He froze. "Anne?"

A figure stepped out of the shadows, trembling in the night. "Daniel," she said again, and if she said anything more, he did not hear it. He was down the stairs in an instant, and she was in his arms, and for the first time in nearly a week, the world felt steady on its axis.

"Anne," he said, touching her back, her arms, her hair. "Anne, Anne, Anne." It seemed the only thing he could say, just her name. He kissed her face, the top of her head. "Where have you—"

He stopped, suddenly realizing that her hands had been bound. Carefully, very carefully so as not to terrify her with the extent of his fury, he began to work at the knots at her wrists.

"Who did this to you?" he asked.

She just swallowed, nervously wetting her lips as she held out her hands.

"Anne . . ."

"It was someone I used to know," she finally told him. "He— I— I will tell you later. Just not now. I can't— I need—"

"It's all right," he said soothingly. He squeezed one of her hands, then went back to work on the knots. They had been tied furiously tight, and she had probably made it worse with her struggles. "It'll just be a moment," he said.

"I didn't know where else to go," she said tremulously.

"You did the right thing," he assured her, yanking the cloth from her wrists and tossing it aside. She had started to shake, and even her breath began to tremble.

"I can't stop them," she said, staring down at her quivering hands as if she did not recognize them.

"You will be fine," he said, covering her hands with his. He held them tight, trying to keep her steady. "It is only your nerves. The same thing has happened to me."

She looked up at him, her eyes huge and questioning.

"When Ramsgate's men were chasing me in Europe," he explained. "When it was through, and I knew I was safe. Something inside of me let go, and I shook."

"It will stop, then?"

He gave her a reassuring smile. "I promise."

She nodded, in that moment looking so terribly fragile that it was all he could do not to wrap his arms around her and try to protect her from the entire world. Instead he allowed himself to place his arm around her shoulders and steer her toward his home. "Let's get you inside," he said. He was so overcome—with relief, with dread, with fury—but no matter what, he had to get her inside. She needed care. She probably needed food. And everything else could sort itself out later.

"Can we go in the back?" she said haltingly. "I'm not— I can't—"

"You will always use the front door," he said fiercely.

"No, it's not that, it's—please," she begged. "I'm in such a state. I don't want anyone to see me like this."

He took her hand. "I see you," he said quietly.

Her eyes met his, and he could swear he saw some of the bleakness wash away. "I know," she whispered.

He brought her hand to his lips. "I was terrified," he told her, laying his soul bare. "I did not know where to find you."

"I'm sorry," she said. "I won't do it again."

But there was something in her apology that unsettled him. Something too meek, too nervous.

"I have to ask you something," she said.

"Soon," he promised. He guided her up the steps, then held up a hand. "Wait one moment." He peered inside the hall, ascertained that all was quiet, then motioned to her to come inside. "This way," he whispered, and together they silently dashed up the stairs to his room.

Once he shut the door behind him, however, he found himself at a loss. He wanted to know everything—Who had done this to her? Why had she run? Who *was* she, really? He wanted answers, and he wanted them now.

No one treated her this way. Not while he took breath.

But first she needed to get warm, and she needed to simply breathe, and allow herself to realize that she was safe. He had been in her place before. He knew what it was like to run.

He lit a lamp, and then another. They needed light, the both of them.

Anne stood awkwardly near the window, rubbing at her wrists, and for the first time that evening, Daniel really looked at her. He'd known she was disheveled, but in his relief to have finally found her he had not realized how much. Her hair was pinned up on one side but hung loose on the other, her coat was missing a button, and there was a bruise on her cheek that made his blood run cold.

"Anne," he said, trying to find the words for the question that must be asked. "Tonight . . . Whoever this was . . . Did he . . . ?"

He couldn't get the word out. It sat at the back of his tongue, tasting like acid and rage.

"No," she said, holding herself with quiet dignity. "He would have done, but when he found me, I was outside, and—" She looked away then, squeezing her eyes shut against the memory. "He told me that— He said he was going to—"

"You don't have to say anything," he said quickly. At least not now, when she was so upset.

But she shook her head, and her eyes held a determination that he could not contradict. "I want to tell you everything," she said.

"Later," he said gently. "After you take a bath."

"No," she said, her voice barely a choke. "You have to let me speak. I stood outside for hours, and I have only so much courage."

"Anne, you don't need courage with—"

"My name is Annelise Shawcross," she blurted out. "And I would like to be your mistress." And then, while he was staring at her in stunned disbelief, she added, "If you'll have me."

ALMOST AN HOUR later, Daniel was standing by his window, waiting for Anne to finish with her bath. She had not wanted anyone to know that she was in the house, so he had hidden her in a wardrobe while several footmen saw to the task of filling a tub, and now she was presumably still soaking in it, waiting for the chill of fear to leave her body.

She had tried to talk to him about her proposition, insisting that it was her only option, but he had not been able to listen. For her to have offered herself up to him in such a way . . . She could only have done so if she felt herself to be completely without hope.

And that was something he could not bear to imagine.

He heard the door to his bathroom open, and when he turned he saw her, scrubbed clean and new, her wet hair combed away from her face and hanging down over her right shoulder. She'd twisted it somehow; not a braid but more of a spiral that kept the strands in one thick cord.

"Daniel?" She said his name quietly as she peered out into the room, her bare feet padding along the plush carpet. She was wearing his dressing gown, the deep midnight blue almost the same color as her eyes. It was huge on her, falling nearly to her ankles, and she had her arms wrapped around her waist just to keep it in place.

He thought she'd never looked so beautiful.

"I'm right here," he said when he realized she didn't see him standing by the window. He'd removed his coat while she was bathing, his neckcloth and boots, too. His valet had been put out that he had not wished for assistance, so Daniel had set the boots outside the door, hoping he'd take that as an invitation to take them back to his quarters and polish them.

Tonight was not a night for interruptions.

"I hope you don't mind that I took your dressing gown," Anne said, hugging her arms more tightly to her body. "There was nothing else . . ."

"Of course not," he replied, motioning to nothing in particular. "You may use anything you wish."

She nodded, and even from ten feet away, he saw her swallow nervously. "It occurred to me," she said, her voice catching as she spoke, "that you probably already knew my name."

He looked at her.

"From Granby," she clarified.

"Yes," he said. "He told me about the man who

was looking for you. It was all I had to go on when I was searching for you."

"I imagine it wasn't much help."

"No." His lips twisted into a wry smile. "I did find Mary Philpott, though."

Her lips parted with momentary surprise. "It was the name I used to write to my sister Charlotte so that my parents would not realize she was corresponding with me. It was through her letters that I knew that George was still—" She cut herself off. "I'm getting ahead of myself."

Daniel's hands clenched at the sound of another man's name. Whoever this George was, he had tried to hurt her. To kill her. And the urge to swing out his arms and punch something was overwhelming. He wanted to find this man, to hurt *him*, to make him understand that if anything—anything—happened to Anne again, Daniel would tear him apart with his bare hands.

And he had never considered himself to be a violent man.

He looked up at Anne. She was still standing in the center of the room, her arms hugging her body. "My name is— My name *was* Annelise Shawcross," she said. "I made a terrible mistake when I was sixteen, and I've been paying for it ever since."

"Whatever you did—" he began, but she held up her hand.

"I'm not a virgin," she said to him, the words blunt in the air.

"I don't care," he said, and he realized he didn't.

"You should."

"But I don't."

She smiled at him—forlornly, as if she was preparing to forgive him for changing his mind. "His name was George Chervil," she said. "Sir George Chervil now that his father has died. I grew up in Northumberland, in a medium-sized village in the western part of the county. My father is a country gentleman. We were always comfortable, but not particularly wealthy. Still, we were respected. We were invited everywhere, and it was expected that my sisters and I would make good matches."

He nodded. It was an easy picture to paint in his mind.

"The Chervils were very rich, or at least they were in comparison to everyone else. When I look at this . . ." She glanced around his elegant bedchamber, at all the luxuries he used to take for granted. He'd not had so many material comforts while in Europe; he would not fail to appreciate such things again.

"They were not of this status," she continued, "but to us—to everyone in the district—they were unquestionably the most important family we knew. And George was their only child. He was very handsome, and he said lovely things, and I thought I loved him." She shrugged helplessly and glanced up at the ceiling, almost as if begging forgiveness for her younger self.

"He said he loved me," she whispered.

Daniel swallowed, and he had the strangest sensation, almost a premonition of what it must like to be a parent. Someday, God willing, he'd have a daughter, and that daughter would look like the woman standing in front of him, and if ever she looked at him with that bewildered expression, whispering, "He said he loved me . . ."

Nothing short of murder would be an acceptable response.

"I thought he was going to marry me," Anne said, bringing his thoughts back to the here and now. She seemed to have regained some of her composure, and her voice was brisk, almost businesslike. "But the thing is, he never said he would. He never even mentioned it. So I suppose, in a way, I bear some of the blame myself—"

"No," Daniel said fiercely, because whatever happened, he knew it could not be her fault. It was all too easy to guess what would happen next. The rich, handsome man, the impressionable young girl . . . It was a terrible tableau, and terribly common.

She gave him a grateful smile. "I don't mean to say I blame myself, because I don't. Not any longer. But I should have known better."

"Anne . . ."

"No," she said, stopping his protest. "I *should* have known better. He did not mention marriage. Not once. I assumed he would ask. Because . . . I don't know. I just did. I came from a good family. It never occurred to me that he wouldn't want to marry me. And . . . Oh, it sounds horrible now, but the truth was, I was young and I was pretty and I knew it. My God, it sounds so silly now."

"No, it doesn't," Daniel said quietly. "We have all been young."

"I let him kiss me," she said, then quietly added, "and then I let him do a great deal more."

Daniel held himself very still, waiting for the wave of jealousy that never came. He was furious with the man who'd taken advantage of her innocence, but he did not feel jealous. He did not need to be her first, he realized. He simply needed to be her last.

Her only.

"You don't have to say anything about it," he told her.

She sighed. "No, I do. Not because of that. Because of what happened next." She walked across the room in a burst of nervous energy and grasped the back of a chair. Her fingers bit into the upholstery, and it gave her something to look at when she said, "I must be honest, I did like what he did up to a point, and after that, well, it wasn't dreadful. It just seemed rather awkward, really, and a bit uncomfortable."

She looked back up at him, her eyes meeting his with stunning honesty. "But I did like the way it seemed to make *him* feel. And that made *me* feel powerful, and the next time I saw him, I was fully prepared to let him do it all again."

She closed her eyes, and Daniel could practically see the memory washing over her face. "It was such a lovely night," she whispered. "Midsummer, and so very clear. You could have counted the stars forever."

"What happened?" he quietly asked.

She blinked, almost as if waking from a dream, and when she spoke, it was with an offhandedness that was almost disconcerting. "I found out he had proposed marriage to someone else. The day after I gave myself to him, as a matter of fact."

The fury that had been building within began to crackle. He had never, not once in his life, felt such anger on behalf of another person. Was this what love meant? That another person's pain cut more deeply than one's own?

"He tried to have his way with me, anyway," she continued. "He told me I was . . . I can't even remember the exact words, but he made me feel like a whore. And maybe that's what I was, but—"

"No," Daniel said forcefully. He could accept that she should have known better, that she could have been more sensible. But he would never allow her to think such a thing of herself. He strode across the room, and his hands came down on her shoulders. She tilted her face toward his, her eyes . . . those bottomless, deep blue eyes . . . He wanted to lose himself. Forever.

"He took advantage of you," he said with quiet intensity. "He should have been drawn and quartered for—"

A horrified bubble of laughter burst from her mouth. "Oh, dear," she said, "just wait until you hear the rest of the story."

His brows rose.

"I cut him," she said, and it took him a moment

to understand what she meant. "He came at me, and I was trying to get away, and I suppose I grabbed the first thing my hand touched. It was a letter opener."

Oh, dear God.

"I was trying to defend myself, and I only meant to wave the thing at him, but he lunged at me, and then—" She shuddered, and the blood drained from her face. "From here to here," she whispered, her finger sliding from her temple to her chin. "It was awful. And of course there was no hiding it. I was ruined," she said with a little shrug. "I was sent away, told to change my name, and sever all ties with my family."

"Your parents allowed this?" Daniel asked in disbelief.

"It was the only way to protect my sisters. No one would have married them if it got out that I had slept with George Chervil. Can you imagine? Slept with him and then *stabbed* him?"

"What I cannot imagine," he bit off, "is a family who would turn you out."

"It's all right," she said, even though they both knew it wasn't. "My sister and I have corresponded clandestinely all this time, so I wasn't completely alone."

"The receiving houses," he murmured.

She smiled faintly. "I always made sure I knew where they were," she said. "It seemed safer to send and receive my mail from a more anonymous location."

"What happened tonight?" he asked. "Why did you leave last week?"

"When I left . . ." She swallowed convulsively, turning her head away from his, her eyes finding some unknown spot on the floor. "He was enraged. He wanted to take me before the magistrate and have me hanged or transported or something, but his father was quite stern. If George made a spectacle of me, he'd lose his engagement with Miss Beckwith. And she was the daughter of a viscount." She looked up with a wry expression. "It was quite the coup."

"Did the marriage go forward?"

Anne nodded. "But he has never let go of his vow for revenge. The scar healed better than I might have expected, but he is still marked most visibly. And he was so very handsome before. I used to think he wanted to kill me, but now . . ."

"What?" Daniel demanded when she did not finish the sentence.

"He wants to cut me," she said, very quietly.

Daniel let out a vicious curse. It did not matter that he was in the presence of a lady. There was no way he could stop the foul language that spat from his mouth. "I'm going to kill him," he said.

"No," Anne said, "you're not. After what happened with Hugh Prentice—"

"No one would mind if I removed Chervil from the face of this earth," he cut in. "I have no worries on that score."

"You will not kill him," Anne said sternly. "I have already injured him grievously—"

"Surely you do not make *excuses* for him?"

"No," she replied, with enough alacrity to set his

mind at ease. "But I do think he has paid for what he did to me that night. He will never escape what I did to him."

"As well he shouldn't," Daniel bit off.

"I want this to *stop*," she said firmly. "I want to live my life without looking over my shoulder. But I don't want revenge. I don't need it."

Daniel rather thought *he* might need it, but he knew it was her decision to make. It took him a moment to stuff down his anger, but he managed it, and finally he asked, "How did he explain the injury?"

Anne looked relieved that he had changed the subject. "A riding accident. Charlotte told me no one believed it, but they said that he'd been thrown by his horse and his face had been cut open by the branch of a tree. I don't think anyone suspected the truth—I'm sure people thought the worst of me when I disappeared so suddenly, but I can't imagine anyone thought I would stab him in the face."

Much to his surprise, Daniel felt himself smile. "I'm glad you did."

She looked at him with surprise.

"You should have cut him somewhere else."

Her eyes widened, and then she let out a snort of laughter.

"Call me bloodthirsty," he murmured.

Her expression grew a little bit wicked. "You'll be pleased to know that tonight, while I was getting away . . ."

"Oh, tell me you kneed him in the balls," he begged. "Please please *please* tell me that."

She pressed her lips together, trying not to laugh again. "I might have done."

He tugged her close. "Hard?"

"Not as hard as I kicked him once he was on the ground."

Daniel kissed one of her hands, and then the other. "May I say that I'm very proud to know you?"

She flushed with pleasure.

"And I'm very *very* proud to call you mine." He kissed her, lightly. "But you will never be my mistress."

She drew back. "Dan—"

He stopped her with a finger to her lips. "I have already announced that I plan to marry you. Would you make me a liar?"

"Daniel, you can't!"

"I can."

"No, you—"

"I *can*," he said firmly. "And I will."

Her eyes searched his face with frantic movement. "But George is still out there. And if he hurts you . . ."

"I can take care of the George Chervils of the world," he assured her, "as long as you can take care of me."

"But—"

"I love you," he said, and it felt as if the whole world settled into place when he finally told her. "I love you, and I cannot bear the thought of a moment without you. I want you at my side and in my bed. I want you to bear my children, and I want every bloody person in the world to know that you are mine."

"Daniel," she said, and he couldn't tell if she was protesting or giving in. But her eyes had filled with tears, and he knew he was close.

"I won't be satisfied with anything less than everything," he whispered. "I'm afraid you're going to have to marry me."

Her chin trembled. It might have been a nod. "I love you," she whispered. "I love you, too."

"And . . . ?" he prodded. Because he was going to make her say it.

"Yes," she said. "If you're brave enough to want me, I will marry you."

He pulled her against him, kissing her with all of the passion, and fear, and emotion he'd been holding inside of him for a week. "Bravery has nothing to do with it," he told her, and he almost laughed, he was so exquisitely happy. "It's self-preservation."

Her brow furrowed.

He kissed her again. He couldn't seem to stop. "I believe I would die without you," he murmured.

"I think . . . ," she whispered, but she didn't finish, at least not right away. "I think that before . . . with George . . . I don't think it counts." She lifted her face to his, her eyes shining with love and promise. "Tonight is going to be my first time. With you."

Chapter Nineteen

AND THEN ANNE said one word. Just one.

"Please."

She didn't know *why* she said it; it certainly wasn't the result of rational thought. It was just that she had spent the last five years of her life reminding people that it never hurt to use good manners and say please for the things one wanted.

And she wanted this very badly.

"Then I," Daniel murmured, bowing his head in a courtly gesture, "can say only 'thank you.'"

She smiled then, but not the smile of amusement or humor. It was a different thing altogether, the kind of smile that took a body by surprise, that wobbled on the lips until it found its bearing. It was the smile of pure happiness, coming so deep from within that Anne had to remind herself to breathe.

One tear rolled down her cheek. She reached up to wipe it away, but Daniel's fingers found it first. "A happy tear, I hope," he said.

She nodded.

His hand cupped her cheek, the pad of his thumb brushing lightly over the faint bruise near her temple. "He hurt you."

Anne had seen the bruise when she had looked at her reflection in the bathroom looking glass. It didn't hurt much, and she couldn't even remember exactly how she'd got it. The fight with George was a blur, and she decided it was better that way.

Still, she smiled slyly, murmuring, "He looks worse."

It took Daniel a moment, but then his eyes flared with quiet humor. "Does he?"

"Oh, yes."

He kissed her softly behind her ear, his breath hot on her skin. "Well, that's very important."

"Mmm-hmm." She arched her neck as his lips moved slowly toward her collarbone. "I was told once that the most important part of a fight is making sure your opponent looks worse than you do when you're through."

"You have very wise advisors."

Anne sucked in her breath again. His hands had moved to the silken tie of the dressing gown, and she could feel the belt grow loose as he undid the knot. "Just one," she whispered, trying not to lose herself completely when she felt his large hands slide along the tender skin of her belly and then around to her back.

"Just one?" he asked, cupping her bottom.

"One advisor, but he's—oh, my!"

He squeezed again. "Was *this* the 'oh my'?" Then he did something entirely different, something that involved just one very wicked finger. "Or this?"

"Oh, Daniel . . ."

His lips found her ear again, and his voice was hot and husky on her skin. "Before the night is through, I'm going to make you scream."

She had just enough sense left to say, "No. You can't."

He lifted her against him, with just enough roughness that her feet left the ground and she had no choice but to wrap her legs around his. "I assure you, I can."

"No, no . . . I'm not . . ."

His finger, which had been drawing lazy circles on her mound, dipped in a little further.

"No one knows that I am here," Anne gasped, clutching desperately at his shoulders. He was moving within her now, languid and slow, but every touch seemed to send shivers of desire to the very center of her body. "If we wake someone up . . ."

"Oh, that's right," he murmured, but she could hear a wicked smile in his voice. "I suppose I shall have to be prudent and save a few things for when we're married."

Anne couldn't even begin to imagine what he was talking about, but his words were having just as much effect on her as his hands, spinning her into a heated coil of passion.

"For tonight," he said, carrying her to the edge of

the bed, "I will have no choice but to make sure that you are a very good girl indeed."

"A good girl?" she echoed. She was backed up against the edge of a sinfully large bed, wearing a man's dressing gown that was hanging open to reveal the curve of her breasts, and there was a finger inside of her, making her pant with pleasure.

There was nothing good about her just then.

Nothing good, and everything wonderful.

"Do you think you can be quiet?" he teased, kissing her throat.

"I don't know."

He slid another finger inside of her. "What if I do this?"

She let out a little squeak, and he smiled diabolically.

"What about this?" he said huskily, nudging one side of the dressing gown with his nose. It fell over her shoulder, baring her breast, but only for a split second before his mouth closed over the tip.

"Oh!" She was a little louder that time, and she heard him chuckle against her skin. "You are wicked," she told him.

He flicked against her with his tongue, then looked up wolfishly. "I never said I wasn't." He moved to her other breast, which was impossibly even more sensitive than the first, and Anne barely noticed when the dressing gown fell completely away from her body.

He looked up again. "Wait until you see what else I can do."

"Oh, my God." She couldn't imagine what could be more wicked than this.

But then his mouth slid to the hollow between her breasts, and he moved down . . . down . . . over her belly, her navel, down to . . .

"Oh, my God," she gasped. "You can't."

"Can't I?"

"Daniel?" She didn't know what she was asking him, but before she knew it, he had lifted her up so that she was now sitting on the very edge of the bed, and his mouth was where his fingers had just been, and the things he was doing with his tongue, and his lips, and his breath . . .

Dear God, she was going to melt. Or explode. She clutched at his head so hard that he actually had to loosen her grasp, and then finally, unable to support herself any longer, she fell back, landing on the soft mattress, her legs still hanging over the side of the bed.

Daniel's head poked up, and he looked very pleased with himself.

She watched as he stood, then gasped, "What are you doing to me?" Because he couldn't possibly be finished. She ached for him, for something, for—

"When you reach it," he said, yanking his shirt over his head, "it will be with me inside of you."

"Reach it?" What in heaven did he mean, *reach it*?

His hands went to his breeches, and within seconds he was naked, and Anne could only stare at him in wonder as he stepped between her legs. He was magnificent, but surely, *surely* he didn't think that was going to—

He touched her again, his hands wrapping around her thighs, pulling her open to greet him.

"Oh, my God," she whispered. She did not think she'd ever said those words so many times as she had in the last few minutes, but if there had ever been a time to praise the Lord's creation, this had to be it.

The tip of him nudged against her opening, but he didn't push forward. Instead he seemed content merely to touch her, letting his manhood rub against her most sensitive skin, circling one way and then another. With every tiny stroke she felt herself open for him a little bit more, and then, seemingly without pressure, the entire tip slid inside of her.

She clutched at the bed, barely able to fathom the strangeness of the sensation. It felt as if he'd rip her apart if he pushed forward, and yet at the same time she wanted more. She had no idea how this could be so, but she couldn't seem to stop her hips from pressing against him.

"I want all of you," she whispered, shocking herself with her words. "Now."

She heard his sharply indrawn breath, and when she looked up at him, his eyes were unfocused and glazed with desire. He groaned her name, and then he pushed forward, not all the way, but enough so that she once again felt that strange, marvelous sensation of being opened to him, being opened *by* him.

"More," she said, and she wasn't begging. She was commanding.

"Not yet." He pulled out a little, then pushed back in. "You're not ready."

"I don't care." And she didn't. There was a pressure building inside of her, and it was making her greedy. She wanted all of him, pulsing within her. She wanted to feel him slide inside of her, sheathing himself to the hilt.

He moved again, and this time she grasped his hips, trying to force him closer to her. "I need you," she moaned, but he strained against her, determined to take this at his chosen pace. His face was contorted with barely leashed desire, though, and Anne knew he wanted this as much as she did. He was holding back because he thought it was what she needed.

But she knew better.

He must have awakened something within her, some wicked, wanton, womanly part of her soul. She had no idea how she knew what to do; she didn't even know that she was going to do it until it happened, but her hands came to her body and she grasped her breasts, pushing them together, squeezing them, all the while watching him watching her . . .

He stared at her with desire so palpable she could feel it on her skin. "Do it again," he said hoarsely, and she did, boosting herself like a naughty corset, until she looked huge and plump and deliciously ripe.

"Do you like that?" she whispered, just to tease him.

He nodded, his breath coming so fast that his movements were jerky and rough. He was still trying so hard to go slowly, and Anne knew she had to send him over the edge. He couldn't stop watching her hands on her breasts, and the pure, primitive need in his eyes made her feel like a goddess, powerful and strong.

She licked her lips and let her hands roam to her nipples, catching each rosy tip between her middle and forefingers. The sensation was amazing, almost as electric as it had been when Daniel had been suckling her there. She felt a new jolt of pleasure, sparking between her legs, and she realized with surprise that she had caused this, with her own wicked fingers. Her head lolled back, and she moaned with desire.

Daniel, too, was caught on the wave of need, and he finally thrust forward, hard and fast, until their bodies were fully joined. "You're going to do that again," he growled. "Every night. And I'm going to watch you . . ." He shuddered with pleasure as he moved within her. "I'm going to watch you every night."

She smiled, reveling in her newfound power, and she wondered what else she might do that would make him so weak with desire.

"You are the most beautiful thing I've ever seen," he said. "Right now. This moment. But that's— that's—" He moved again, groaning at the sensitive friction of it. Then he planted his hands on the mattress, on either side of her head.

He was trying to hold himself still, she realized.

"That's not what I wanted to say," he said, each word requiring its own ragged breath.

She looked at him, into his eyes, and she felt one of his hands take hers, their fingers entwining in a lovers' knot.

"I love you," he said. "*I love you.*" And then he said it again, and again, with his mouth, with his voice. With every motion of his body, she felt it. It was overwhelming, amazing, and utterly humbling, to feel so magnificently a part of another person.

She squeezed his hand. "I love you, too," she whispered. "You are the first man . . . The first man I've . . ."

She didn't know how to say it. She wanted him to know every moment of her life, every triumph and disappointment. Most of all, she wanted him to know that he was the first man she had ever trusted completely, the only man to win her heart.

He took her hand and brought it to his lips. Right then, in the midst of the most carnal, erotic coupling she could imagine, he kissed her knuckles, as gently and honorably as an ancient knight.

"Don't cry," he whispered.

She hadn't realized she was.

He kissed away her tears, but as he bent over he moved again within her, restoking the turbulent fire at her core. She stroked his calves with her feet, lifting her hips in a feminine squirm, and then he was moving, and she was moving, and something was changing within her, stretching and tightening until she could not possibly bear it, and then—

"Oooooh!" She let out a little cry as the world burst around her, and she grabbed him, clutching his shoulders so hard she lifted from the bed.

"Oh, my God," he panted. "Oh, my God, oh my—" With one final thrust he cried out, jerking forward and then finally collapsing as he spilled himself within her.

It was done, Anne thought dreamily. It was done, and yet her life was finally beginning.

LATER THAT NIGHT, Daniel lay on his side, leaning on his elbow with his head propped in his hand as he idly toyed with the loose strands of Anne's hair. She was sleeping—or at least he thought she was. If not, she was being remarkably indulgent, letting him stroke through the soft curls, marveling at the way the flickering candlelight reflected on each strand.

He hadn't realized her hair was so long. When she had it done up, with her pins and combs and whatever else it was women used, it looked like any other hair bun. Well, any other hair bun when worn by a woman so beautiful it made his heart stop.

But down, her hair was glorious. It spilled over her shoulders like a sable blanket, rippling into soft, luxurious waves that came to an end at the tops of her breasts.

He allowed himself a wicked little smile. He liked that her hair didn't cover her breasts.

"What are you smiling about?" she murmured, her voice thick and lazy with sleep.

"You're awake," he said.

She let out a little mewl as she stretched, and he happily watched as the bedsheet slipped from her body. "Oh!" she chirped, yanking it back up.

He covered her hand with his, tugging it down. "I like you that way," he murmured huskily.

She blushed. It was too dark for him to see the pink on her skin, but her eyes looked down for just a moment, the way they always did when she was embarrassed. And then he smiled again, because he hadn't even realized he'd known that about her.

He liked knowing things about her.

"You didn't say what you were smiling about," she said, gently pulling the sheet back up and tucking it under her arm.

"I was thinking," he said, "that I rather like it that your hair is not quite long enough to cover your breasts."

This time he *did* see her blush, even in the dark.

"You did ask," he murmured.

They fell into a companionable silence, but soon Daniel saw worry lines begin to form on Anne's forehead. He wasn't surprised when she asked, softly, "What happens now?"

He knew what she was asking, but he didn't want to answer. Snuggled together in his four-poster bed with the canopy pulled closed around them, it was easy to pretend that the rest of the world did not exist. But morning would come soon enough, and with it, all of the dangers and cruelties that had brought her to this point.

"I will pay a call upon Sir George Chervil," he

finally said. "I trust it will not be difficult to determine his address."

"Where will I go?" she whispered.

"You will stay here," Daniel said firmly. He could hardly believe she'd think he'd allow her to go anywhere else.

"But what will you tell your family?"

"The truth," he said. Then, when her eyes widened with shock, he quickly added, "Some of it. There is no need for anyone to know precisely where you slept tonight, but I will have to tell my mother and sister how you came to be here without so much as a change of clothing. Unless you can think of a reasonable story."

"No," she agreed.

"Honoria can lend you a wardrobe, and with my mother here as chaperone, it will not be untoward in the least for you to be installed in one of our guest bedrooms."

For a split second she looked as if she might protest, or perhaps suggest an alternative plan. But in the end she nodded.

"I will see to a special license right after I see to Chervil," Daniel said.

"A special license?" Anne echoed. "Aren't they terribly extravagant?"

He nudged a little closer. "Do you really think I'm going to be able to wait a proper engagement period?"

She started to smile.

"Do you really think *you* can wait?" he added huskily.

"You've turned me into a wanton," she whispered.

He pulled her against him. "I can't quite summon the will to complain."

As he kissed her, he heard her whisper, "I can't, either."

All would be right with the world. With a woman like this in his arms, how could it be otherwise?

Chapter Twenty

THE FOLLOWING DAY, after getting Anne settled as a proper guest in his household, Daniel set out to pay a call upon Sir George Chervil.

As expected, it hadn't been difficult to find his address. He lived in Marylebone, not far from his father-in-law's Portman Square residence. Daniel knew who Viscount Hanley was; indeed, Daniel had been at Eton at the same time as two of Hanley's sons. The connection was not terribly deep, but the family would know who he was. If Chervil did not come around to his way of thinking with appropriate speed, Daniel had every confidence that a call upon his father-in-law—who undoubtedly controlled the purse strings, including the deed for the tidy little Marylebone home upon whose steps Daniel was now ascending—would do the trick.

Within moments of knocking on the front door, Daniel was ushered into a sitting room decorated in muted shades of green and gold. A few minutes later, a woman came in. From her age and attire, he could only deduce that she was Lady Chervil, the viscount's daughter George Chervil had chosen to marry instead of Anne.

"My lord," Lady Chervil said, offering him an elegant curtsy. She was quite pretty, with light brown curls and clear, peaches-and-cream skin. She could not compare to Anne's dramatic beauty, but then again, few could. And Daniel was, perhaps, somewhat biased.

"Lady Chervil," he said in return. She looked surprised by his presence, and more than a little bit curious. Her father was a viscount, so she must be used to receiving high-ranking visitors, but at the same time, he imagined it had been some time since an earl had called upon her in her own home, especially if it had been only recently that her husband had become a baronet.

"I have come to call upon your husband," Daniel told her.

"I am afraid he is not home just now," she said. "Is there anything with which I may assist you? I am surprised that my husband did not mention your connection."

"We have not been formally introduced," Daniel explained. There seemed no reason to pretend otherwise; Chervil would make as much clear when he returned home and his wife mentioned that the Earl of Winstead had paid a call.

"Oh, I'm so sorry," she said, not that there was anything for which to apologize. But she seemed like the sort of woman who said *I'm sorry* whenever she wasn't sure what else to say. "Is there anything with which I might assist you? Oh, I'm so sorry, I asked that already, didn't I?" She motioned to a seating area. "Would you care to sit? I can have tea brought out immediately."

"No, thank you," Daniel said. It was an effort to keep his manners polite, but he knew that this woman bore no blame for what had happened to Anne. She likely had never even heard of her.

He cleared his throat. "Do you know when your husband is expected back?"

"I shouldn't think it would be too long," she replied. "Would you like to wait?"

Not really, but Daniel didn't see any other alternative, so he thanked her and took a seat. Tea was brought out, and much small conversation was made, interspersed with long pauses and unconcealed glances at the mantel clock. He tried to distract himself with thoughts of Anne, and what she must be doing at that precise moment.

While he was sipping tea, she was trying on clothing lent to her by Honoria.

While he was tapping his fingers impatiently against his knee, she was sitting down to dinner with his mother, who had, much to Daniel's pride and relief, not batted so much as an eyelash when he announced that he planned to marry Miss Wynter, and oh, by the way, she would be staying at Winstead House as their guest, since she couldn't very well continue on as a governess to the Pleinsworths.

"Lord Winstead?"

He looked up. Lady Chervil had her head tilted to the side and was blinking expectantly. She had clearly asked him a question—one he had not heard. Fortunately, she was the sort of woman in whom good manners had been ingrained since birth, and so she drew no attention to his lapse, instead saying (and presumably repeating), "You must be terribly excited about your sister's upcoming nuptials." At his blank look, she added, "I read about it in the newspaper, and of course I attended your family's lovely musicales when I was having my season."

Daniel wondered if that meant that she was no longer receiving invitations. He hoped so. The thought of George Chervil sitting in his home made his skin crawl.

He cleared his throat, trying to keep his expression pleasant. "Yes, very much so. Lord Chatteris has been a close friend since childhood."

"How lovely for you, then, that he will now be your brother."

She smiled, and Daniel was struck by a tiny arrow of unease. Lady Chervil seemed to be a most pleasant woman, someone with whom his sister—or Anne—would be friendly were she not married to Sir George. She was innocent of everything, save for marrying a scoundrel, and he was going to upend her life completely.

"He is at my house right now," Daniel said, trying to assuage his disquietude by offering her slightly more charming conversation. "I believe he has been dragged over to help plan the wedding."

"Oh, how lovely."

He gave her a nod, using the opportunity to play the game of *What-Must-Anne-Be-Doing-Now?* He hoped she was with the rest of his family, offering her opinion on lavender-blue and blue-lavender and flowers and lace and everything else that went into a family celebration.

She deserved a family. After eight years, she deserved to feel as if she belonged.

Daniel glanced at the mantel clock again, trying to be a bit more discreet about it. He had been here an hour and a half. Surely Lady Chervil was growing restless. No one remained in a sitting room for an hour and a half, waiting for someone to come home. They both knew that propriety dictated that he offer his card and depart.

But Daniel wasn't budging.

Lady Chervil smiled awkwardly. "Truly, I did not think Sir George would be gone so long. I can't imagine what is keeping him."

"Where did he go?" Daniel asked. It was an intrusive question, but after ninety minutes of chit-chat, it no longer seemed importune.

"I believe he visited a doctor," Lady Chervil said. "For his scar, you know." She looked up. "Oh, you said you had not been introduced. He has . . ." She motioned to her face with a sad expression. "He has a scar. It was a riding accident, just before we were married. I think it makes him look dashing, but he is forever trying to minimize it."

Something unsettling began to roil in the pit of Daniel's belly. "He went to see a doctor?" he asked.

"Well, I think so," Lady Chervil replied. "When he left this morning, he said that he was going to see someone about his scar. I just assumed it was a doctor. Who else would he see?"

Anne.

Daniel stood so quickly he upset the teapot, sending lukewarm dregs running across the table.

"Lord Winstead?" Lady Chervil asked, her voice laced with alarm. She came to her feet, too, hurrying after him as he strode for the door. "Is something wrong?"

"I beg your pardon," he said. He did not have time for niceties. He'd already sat here for ninety bloody minutes, and God only knew what Chervil was planning.

Or had already done.

"May I help you in some way?" she asked, hurrying after him as he made his way to the front door. "Perhaps I can convey a message to my husband?"

Daniel turned around. "Yes," he said, and he did not recognize his own voice. Terror had made him unsteady; rage was making him bold. "You may tell him that if he touches so much as a hair on my fiancée's head, I shall personally see to it that his liver is extracted through his mouth."

Lady Chervil went very pale.

"Do you understand?"

She nodded unsteadily.

Daniel stared at her. Hard. She was terrified, but that was nothing compared to what Anne would be feeling if she was now in the clutches of George Chervil. He took another step toward the door, then paused. "One more thing," he said. "If he comes home tonight alive, I suggest you have a talk with him about your future here in England. You might find life more comfortable on another continent. Good day, Lady Chervil."

"Good day," she said. Then she fainted dead away.

"ANNE!" DANIEL BELLOWED as he ran into the front hall of Winstead House. "Anne!"

Poole, the longtime butler at Winstead House, materialized as if from nowhere.

"Where is Miss Wynter?" Daniel demanded, struggling for breath. His landau had been stalled in traffic, and he'd run the last few minutes of the journey, tearing through the streets like a madman. It was a wonder he had not been run down by a carriage.

His mother emerged from the sitting room, followed by Honoria and Marcus. "What is going on?" she asked. "Daniel, what on earth—"

"Where is Miss Wynter?" he panted, still gasping for air.

"She went out," his mother said.

"Out? She went *out*?" Why the devil would she

do that? She knew that she was supposed to remain at Winstead House until he returned.

"Well, that's what I understand," Lady Winstead looked over at the butler for help. "I wasn't here."

"Miss Wynter had a visitor," Poole said. "Sir George Chervil. She left with him an hour ago. Perhaps two."

Daniel turned on him in horror. "What?"

"She did not seem to care for his company," Poole began.

"Well, then why on earth would she—"

"He was with Lady Frances."

Daniel stopped breathing.

"Daniel?" his mother said with rising concern. "What is going on?"

"Lady Frances?" Daniel echoed, still staring at Poole.

"Who is Sir George Chervil?" Honoria asked. She looked at Marcus, but he shook his head.

"She was in his carriage," Poole told Daniel.

"Frances?"

Poole nodded. "Yes."

"And Miss Wynter took his word on this?"

"I do not know, my lord," the butler said. "She did not confide in me. But she walked out to the pavement with him, and then she entered the carriage. She appeared to do so of her own volition."

"Bloody hell," Daniel swore.

"Daniel," Marcus said, his voice rock solid and steady in a room that was spinning. "What is going on?"

Daniel had told his mother some of Anne's past earlier that morning; now he told all of them the rest.

The blood drained from Lady Winstead's face, and when she grabbed Daniel's hand, it felt like a panicked claw. "We must go tell Charlotte," she said, barely able to speak.

Daniel nodded slowly, trying to think. How had Chervil gotten to Frances? And where would he—

"Daniel!" his mother nearly screamed. "We must go tell Charlotte now! That madman has her daughter!"

Daniel jerked to attention. "Yes," he said. "Yes, at once."

"I'm coming, too," Marcus said. He turned to Honoria. "Will you stay? Someone needs to remain here in case Miss Wynter comes back."

Honoria nodded.

"Let's go," Daniel said. They raced out of the house, Lady Winstead not even bothering to don a coat. The carriage that Daniel had abandoned five minutes earlier had arrived, and so he put his mother inside with Marcus and took off running. It was only a quarter mile, and if the roads were still clogged with traffic, he could reach Pleinsworth House faster on foot.

He arrived moments ahead of the carriage, breathing hard as he raced up the steps to Pleinsworth House. He slammed the knocker down three times and was reaching for the fourth when Granby opened the door, stepping quickly aside as Daniel practically tumbled in.

"Frances," he gasped.

"She's not here," Granby told him.

"I know. Do you know where—"

"Charlotte!" his mother yelled, yanking her skirts up well over her ankles as she ran up the steps. She turned to Granby with wild eyes. "Where is Charlotte?"

Granby motioned toward the back of the house. "I believe she is seeing to her correspondence. In the—"

"I'm right here," Lady Pleinsworth said, hurrying out of a room. "My heavens, what is going on? Virginia, you look—"

"It's Frances," Daniel said grimly. "We think she may have been kidnapped."

"What?" Lady Pleinsworth looked at him, and then at his mother, and then finally at Marcus, who was standing silently by the door. "No, that can't be," she said, sounding far more confused than worried. "She was just—" She turned to Granby. "Wasn't she out for a walk with Nanny Flanders?"

"They have not yet returned, my lady."

"But surely they have not been gone so long as to cause concern. Nanny Flanders doesn't move very quickly any longer, so it will take them some time to get 'round the park."

Daniel exchanged a grim glance with Marcus before telling Granby, "Someone needs to go look for the nurse."

The butler nodded. "At once."

"Aunt Charlotte," Daniel began, and then he related the events of the afternoon. He gave her only a very brief account of Anne's background; there would be time for that later. But it did not take long to tell her enough so that her face went ashen.

"This man . . ." she said, her voice shaking with terror. "This madman . . . You think he has Frances?"

"Anne would never have gone with him otherwise."

"Oh, my heavens." Lady Pleinsworth swayed and became unsteady on her feet. Daniel quickly helped her to a chair. "What will we do?" she asked him. "How can we find them?"

"I'll go back to Chervil's house," he said. "It's the only—"

"Frances!" Lady Pleinsworth shrieked.

Daniel turned around just in time to see Frances come tearing through the hall and hurl herself at her mother. She was dusty, and dirty, and her dress was torn. But she did not appear to have been injured, at least not deliberately.

"Oh, my dear girl," Lady Pleinsworth sobbed, clutching Frances to her with frantic hands. "What happened? Oh, dear God, have you been hurt?" She touched her arms, and her shoulders, and then finally showered her small face with kisses.

"Aunt Charlotte?" Daniel said, trying to keep the urgency from his voice. "I'm sorry, but I really do need to talk with Frances."

Lady Pleinsworth turned on him with furious eyes, shielding her daughter with her body. "Not now," she snarled. "She's been through a fright. She needs to bathe, and eat, and—"

"She is my only hope—"

"She is a child!"

"And Anne might die!" he nearly roared.

The hall went silent, and from behind his aunt, Daniel heard Frances's voice. "He has Miss Wynter."

"Frances," he said, reaching for her hands and pulling her toward a bench. "Please, you must tell me everything. What happened?"

Frances took a few deep breaths and looked to her mother, who gave her a terse nod of approval. "I was in the park," she said, "and Nanny had fallen asleep on the bench. She does that almost every day." She looked back up to her mother. "I'm sorry, Mama. I should have told you, but she's getting so old, and she's tired in the afternoon, and I think it's a long way for her to walk to the park."

"It's all right, Frances," Daniel said, trying to keep the urgency out of his voice. "Just tell us what happened next."

"I wasn't paying attention. I was playing one of my unicorn games," she explained, and she looked at Daniel as if she knew he would understand. "I had galloped off quite a ways from where Nanny was." She turned to her mother, her expression earnest. "But she would still have been able to see me. If she were awake."

"Then what?" Daniel urged.

Frances looked at him with the most bewildered expression. "I don't know. I looked up, and she was gone. I don't know what happened to her. I called for her several times, and then I went over to the pond where she likes to feed the ducks, but she wasn't there, and then—"

She started to shake uncontrollably.

"That is enough," Lady Pleinsworth said, but Daniel shot her a pleading look. He knew this was upsetting for Frances, but it had to be done. And surely his aunt would realize that Frances would be far more upset if Anne were killed.

"What happened next?" Daniel asked gently.

Frances swallowed convulsively, and she hugged her arms to her small body. "Someone grabbed me. And he put something into my mouth that tasted horrid, and the next thing I knew I was in a carriage."

Daniel shared a concerned glance with his mother. Next to her, Lady Pleinsworth had begun to silently cry.

"It was probably laudanum," he said to Frances. "It was very, very wrong for someone to force it upon you, but it will not hurt you."

She nodded. "I felt funny, but I don't now."

"When did you first see Miss Wynter?"

"We went to your house. I wanted to get out, but the man—" She looked up at Daniel as if only just then remembering something very important. "He had a scar. A really big one. Right across his face."

"I know," he said softly.

She looked up at him with huge, curious eyes, but she didn't question him. "I couldn't get out of the carriage," she said. "He said he would hurt Miss Wynter if I did. And he made his driver watch me, and he didn't look very nice."

Daniel forced down his rage. There had to be a special place in hell for people who hurt children. But he managed to remain calm as he said, "And then Miss Wynter came out?"

Frances nodded. "She was very angry."

"I'm sure she was."

"She yelled at him, and he yelled at her, and I didn't understand most of what they were talking about, except that she was really, really angry with him for having me in the carriage."

"She was trying to protect you," Daniel said.

"I know," Frances said softly. "But . . . I think . . . I think she might have been the one to cause his scar." She looked over at her mother with a tortured expression. "I don't think Miss Wynter would do something like that, but he kept talking about it, and he was so angry with her."

"It was a long time ago," Daniel said. "Miss Wynter was defending herself."

"Why?" Frances whispered.

"It doesn't matter," he said firmly. "What matters is what happened today, and what we can do to save her. You have been very brave. How did you get away?"

"Miss Wynter pushed me from the carriage."

"What?" Lady Pleinsworth shrieked, but Lady Winstead restrained her when she tried to rush forward.

"It wasn't going very fast," Frances said to her mother. "It only hurt a little when I hit the ground. Miss Wynter had whispered to me to curl up like a ball before I hit the ground."

"Oh, dear God," Lady Pleinsworth sobbed. "Oh, my baby."

"I'm all right, Mama," Frances said, and Daniel was amazed at her resilience. She had been kidnapped and then tossed from a carriage, and now *she* was comforting her mother. "I think Miss Wynter chose the spot she did because I wasn't very far from home."

"Where?" Daniel asked urgently. "Where were you, exactly?"

Frances blinked. "Park Crescent. The far end."

Lady Pleinsworth gasped through her tears. "You came all that distance yourself?"

"It wasn't that far, Mama."

"But all the way through Marylebone!" Lady Pleinsworth turned to Lady Winstead. "She walked all the way through Marylebone on her own. She's just a child!"

"Frances," Daniel asked urgently. "I must ask you. Do you have any idea where Sir George might be taking Miss Wynter?"

Frances shook her head, and her lips quivered. "I wasn't paying attention. I was so scared, and most of the time they were yelling at each other, and then he hit Miss Wynter—"

Daniel had to force himself to draw breath.

"—and then I was even more upset, but he did say—" Frances looked up sharply, her eyes wide with excitement. "I remember something. He mentioned the heath."

"Hampstead," Daniel said.

"Yes, I think so. He didn't say that specifically, but we were heading in that direction, weren't we?"

"If you were at Park Crescent, yes."

"He also said something about having a room."

"A room?" Daniel echoed.

Frances nodded vigorously.

Marcus, who had been silent throughout the questioning, cleared his throat. "He might be taking her to an inn."

Daniel looked over at him, gave a nod, then turned back to his young cousin. "Frances, do you think you would recognize the carriage?"

"I do," she said, her eyes wide. "I really do."

"Oh, no!" Lady Pleinsworth thundered. "She is not going with you to search for a madman."

"I have no other choice," Daniel told her.

"Mama, I want to help," Frances pleaded. "Please, I love Miss Wynter."

"So do I," Daniel said softly.

"I will go with you," Marcus said, and Daniel shot him a look of deep gratitude.

"No!" Lady Pleinsworth protested. "This is madness. What do you think you're going to do? Let her ride on your back as you go traipsing into some public house? I'm sorry, I cannot allow—"

"He can bring outriders," Daniel's mother interrupted.

Lady Pleinsworth turned to her in shock. "Virginia?"

"I am a mother, too," Lady Winstead said. "And if anything happens to Miss Wynter . . ." Her voice fell to a whisper. "My son will be broken."

"You would have me trade my child for yours?"

"No!" Lady Winstead took both of her sister-in-law's hands fiercely in her own. "I would never. You know that, Charlotte. But if we do this properly, I don't think Frances will be in any danger."

"No," Lady Pleinsworth said. "No, I cannot agree. I will not risk the life of my child—"

"She won't leave the carriage," Daniel said. "You can come, too."

And then . . . he saw it on her face . . . She was beginning to relent.

He took her hand. "Please, Aunt Charlotte."

She swallowed, her throat catching on a sob. And then, finally, she nodded.

Daniel nearly sagged with relief. He had not found Anne yet, but Frances was his only hope, and if his aunt had forbidden her to accompany him to Hampstead, all would have been lost.

"There is no time to lose," Daniel said. He turned to his aunt. "There is room for four in my landau. How fast can you have a carriage readied to follow? We will need seats for five on the return."

"No," his aunt said. "We will take our coach. It can seat six, but more importantly, it will support outriders. I am not allowing you to take my daughter anywhere near that madman without armed guards on the carriage."

"As you wish," Daniel said. He could not argue. If he had a daughter, he would be just as fiercely protective.

His aunt turned to one of the footmen who had been witness to the entire scene. "Have it brought 'round at once."

"Yes, ma'am," he said, before taking off at a run.

"Now there will be room for me," Lady Winstead announced.

Daniel looked at his mother. "You're coming, too?"

"My future daughter-in-law is in danger. Would you have me anywhere else?"

"Fine," Daniel acceded, because there was little point in arguing. If it was safe enough for Frances, it was certainly safe enough for his mother. Still—

"You are not coming in," he said sternly.

"I wouldn't dream of it. I have skills, but they do not include fighting madmen with weapons. I am sure I would only get in the way."

As they rushed outside to wait for the carriage, however, a phaeton rounded the corner of the square at far too fast a speed. It was only due to the skill of the driver—Hugh Prentice, Daniel realized with shock—that it did not tip over.

"What the devil?" Daniel strode forward and took the reins as Hugh awkwardly got himself down.

"Your butler told me you were here," Hugh said. "I've been looking for you all day."

"He called at Winstead House earlier," his mother said. "Before Miss Wynter left. She claimed not to know where you went."

"What is going on?" Daniel asked Hugh. His friend, whose face was normally an emotionless mask, was pinched tight with worry.

Hugh handed him a piece of paper. "I received this."

Daniel quickly read the missive. The handwriting was neat and tidy, with an angular masculinity to the letters. *We have an enemy in common,* it read, then gave instructions for how to leave a reply at a public house in Marylebone.

"Chervil," Daniel said under his breath.

"Then you know who wrote this?" Hugh asked.

Daniel nodded. George Chervil was unlikely to know that he and Hugh were not, and never had been, enemies. But there was ample gossip that might lead one to reach that conclusion.

He quickly related the events of the day to Hugh, who glanced up at the Pleinsworth carriage as it rolled up and said, "You have room for one more."

"It's not necessary," Daniel said.

"I'm coming," Hugh stated. "I may not be able to run, but I'm a bloody good shot."

At that, both Daniel and Marcus swiveled their heads toward him in disbelief.

"When I'm sober," Hugh clarified, having the grace to blush. A little. Daniel doubted his cheeks knew how to do more than that.

"Which I am," Hugh added, obviously feeling the need to make this clear.

"Get in," Daniel said, jerking his head toward the carriage. He was surprised that Hugh hadn't noticed—

"We'll put Lady Frances on her mother's lap on the way home to make room for Miss Wynter," Hugh said.

Never mind, Hugh did notice everything.

"Let's go," Marcus said. The ladies were already in the carriage, and Marcus had one foot on the step.

It was a strange band of rescuers, but as the coach sped away, four armed footmen serving as outriders, Daniel could not help but think that his was a most marvelous family. The only thing that could make it better would be Anne, by his side, and with his name.

He could only pray that they reached Hampstead in time.

Chapter Twenty-one

Anne had, in her life, known moments of terror. When she'd stabbed George and realized what she'd done—that had been paralyzing. When Daniel's curricle had run wild and she'd felt herself sailing through the air after being thrown from the vehicle—that, too, had been terrifying. But nothing—*nothing*—had ever or would ever compare to the moment when, realizing that the horses pulling George Chervil's carriage had slowed to a walk, she had leaned down to Frances and whispered, "Run home." And then, before she had had a chance to second-guess herself, she'd wrenched open the carriage door and pushed Frances out, yelling for her to curl up in a ball when she hit the ground.

She had only a second to make sure that Frances scrambled to her feet before George yanked her back into the carriage and slapped her across her face.

"Do not think you can cross me," he hissed.

"Your war is with me," she spat, "not that child."

He shrugged. "I wouldn't have hurt her."

Anne was not so sure she believed him. Right now George was so obsessed with ruining Anne that he could not see past the next few hours. But eventually, once the rage in his blood had cooled, he would realize that Frances could identify him. And while he might think he could get away with injuring—or even killing—Anne, even he had to know that kidnapping the daughter of an earl would not be treated so lightly.

"Where are you taking me?" Anne asked.

His brows rose. "Does it matter?"

Her fingers clenched the seat of his carriage. "You won't get away with this, you know," she said. "Lord Winstead will have your head."

"Your new protector?" he sneered. "He won't be able to prove anything."

"Well, there's—" She stopped herself before she reminded him that Frances could easily recognize his face. The scar took care of that.

But George was instantly suspicious of an unfinished sentence. "There's what?" he demanded.

"There's me."

His lips twisted into a cruel mockery of a smile. "Is there?"

Her eyes widened with horror.

"Well, there is," he murmured. "But there won't be."

So he planned to kill her, then. Anne supposed she shouldn't be surprised.

"But don't worry," George added, almost casually. "It won't be quick."

"You are mad," Anne whispered.

He grabbed her, his fingers grasping the fabric of her bodice and yanking her until they were nearly nose to nose. "If I am," he hissed, "it is because of you."

"You brought this on yourself," she shot back.

"Oh, really?" he spat, tossing her back against the far wall of the carriage. "I did *this*." He motioned sarcastically to his face. "I took a knife and sliced myself up, making a monster of—"

"Yes!" she cried out. "You did! You were a monster before I ever touched you. I was only trying to defend myself."

He snorted with disdain. "You had already spread your legs for me. You don't get to say no after you've done it once."

She gaped at him. "You really believe that?"

"You liked it the first time."

"I thought you loved me!"

He shrugged. "That's your stupidity, not mine." But then he turned sharply, regarding her with an expression that approached glee. "Oh, my," he said, grinning with the worst sort of schadenfreude. "You did it again, didn't you? You let Winstead plow you. Tsk tsk tsk. Oh, Annie, haven't you learned anything?"

"He asked me to marry him," she said, eyes narrowing.

George burst into raucous laughter. "And you believed him?"

"I said yes."

"I'm sure you thought you did."

Anne tried to take a deep breath, but her teeth were clenched so hard together that she shook when she tried to draw air. She was so . . . bloody . . . *angry*. Gone was the fear, the apprehension, the shame. Instead all she felt was blood-boiling fury. This man had stolen eight years of her life. He had made her scared, and he had made her lonely. He had taken the innocence of her body, and he had smashed the innocence of her spirit. But this time, he was not going to win.

She was finally happy. Not just secure, not even just content, but happy. She loved Daniel, and by some miracle he loved her in return. Her future spread before her in lovely sunrise shades of pink and orange, and she could actually see herself— with Daniel, with laughter, with children. She was not giving that up. Whatever her sins, she had long since paid for them.

"George Chervil," she said, her voice strangely calm, "you are a blight on humanity."

He looked at her with mild curiosity, then shrugged, turning back to the window.

"Where are we going?" she asked again.

"It's not far."

Anne looked out her own window. They were

moving much faster now than when she'd pushed Frances from the carriage. She did not recognize the area, but she thought they were heading north. Or at least mostly north. They'd long since left behind Regent's Park, and although she'd never taken the girls there, she knew that it was located north of Marylebone.

The carriage kept up its brisk pace, slowing just enough at intersections for Anne to read some of the signs on the shops. *Kentish Town*, one of them said. She'd heard of that. It was a village on the outskirts of London. George had said they weren't going far, and maybe that was true. But still, Anne did not think there was any way that anyone would find her before George tried to carry out his plan. She did not think he had said anything in front of Frances that might indicate where they were going, and in any case, the poor girl would surely be a wreck by the time she reached home.

If Anne was going to be saved, she would have to do it herself.

"It is time to be your own heroine," she whispered.

"What was that?" George said in a bored voice.

"Nothing." But inside, her brain was spinning. How would she do this? Was there any sense in planning, or would she need to wait and see how events unfolded? It was hard to know just how she might escape without first seeing the lay of the land.

George turned toward her with growing suspicion. "You look rather intent," he said.

She ignored him. What were his weaknesses? He was vain—how might she use that to her advantage?

"What are you thinking about?" he demanded.

She smiled secretly. He did not like to be ignored—that, too, might be useful.

"Why are you smiling?" he screamed.

She turned, her expression carefully constructed to appear as if she'd only just heard him. "I'm sorry, did you say something?"

His eyes narrowed. "What are you up to?"

"What am I up to? I'm sitting in a carriage being kidnapped. What are *you* up to?"

A muscle in his good cheek began to twitch. "Don't talk to me in that tone of voice."

She shrugged, accompanying the motion with a dismissive roll of her eyes. He would hate that.

"You're planning something," he accused.

She shrugged again, deciding that with George, most anything that worked once would work even better the second time.

She was right. His face grew mottled with rage, sending his scar into sharp white contrast with his skin. It was gruesome to watch, and yet she could not tear her eyes away.

George caught her staring and grew even more agitated. "What are you planning?" he demanded, his hand shaking with fury as he jabbed her with his forefinger.

"Nothing," she said quite honestly. Nothing specific at least. Right now all she was doing was setting him on edge. And it was working beautifully.

He was not used to women treating him with disdain, she realized. When she had known him, the girls had fawned and hung on his every word. She did not know what sort of attention he drew now, but the truth was, when he was not red-faced with fury he was not unhandsome, even with his scar. Some women would pity him, but others would probably find him dashing, mysterious even, with what looked like a valiant war wound.

But disdain? He would not like that, especially from her.

"You're smiling again," he accused.

"I'm not," she lied, her voice but a quip.

"Don't try to cross me," he raged, poking her shoulder again with his finger. "You cannot win."

She shrugged.

"What is wrong with you?" he roared.

"Nothing," she said, because by now she had realized that nothing would infuriate him more than her calm demeanor. He wanted her to cower with terror. He wanted to see her shake, and he wanted to hear her beg.

So instead she turned away from him, keeping her eyes firmly on the window.

"Look at me," George ordered.

She waited for a moment, then said, "No."

His voice dropped to a growl. "Look at me."

"No."

"Look at me," he screamed.

This time she did. His voice had reached a pitch of instability, and she realized that she was already tensing her shoulders, waiting for a blow. She stared at him without speaking.

"You cannot win against me," he snarled.

"I shall try," Anne said softly. Because she was not giving up without a fight. And if he managed to destroy her, then as God was her witness, she was taking him down, too.

THE PLEINSWORTH COACH sped along the Hampstead Road, the team of six pulling the carriage with speeds not often seen on the route. If they looked out of place—a large, opulent coach going breakneck speed with armed outriders—Daniel did not care. They might attract attention, but not from Chervil. He was at least an hour ahead of them; if he was indeed going to an inn in Hampstead, he would be there already, inside and thus unlikely to see them on the street.

Unless the room was facing the street . . .

Daniel let out a shaky breath. He would have to cross that bridge if he came to it. He could either get to Anne quickly or stealthily, and given what she'd told him of Chervil, he was opting for speed.

"We will find her," Marcus said in a quiet voice.

Daniel looked up. Marcus did not radiate power and swagger, but then again, he never had. Marcus was dependable, and quietly confident, and right then, his eyes held a resoluteness that Daniel found comforting. Daniel gave a nod, then turned back to the window. Beside him his aunt was keeping up a steady stream of nervous chatter as she clutched

Frances's hand. Frances kept saying, "I don't see it. I don't see his carriage yet," even though Daniel had more than once told her that they had not yet reached Hampstead.

"Are you sure you will be able to recognize the carriage?" Lady Pleinsworth asked Frances with a dubious frown. "One looks very much like another to me. Unless there is a crest . . ."

"It's got a funny bar on it," Frances said. "I will know it."

"What do you mean, a funny bar?" Daniel asked.

"I don't know," she said with a shrug. "I don't think it does anything. It's just for decoration. But it's gold, and it swirls." She made a motion in with her hand, and it brought to mind Anne's hair the night before, when she had twisted her wet locks into a thick coil.

"Actually," Frances said, "it reminded me of a unicorn's horn."

Daniel felt himself smile. He turned to his aunt. "She will recognize the carriage."

They sped past several of London's outlying hamlets, finally reaching the quaint village of Hampstead. Off in the distance, Daniel could see the wild green of the famed heath. It was a huge expanse of land, putting the London parks to shame.

"How do you want to do this?" Hugh asked. "It might be best to go on foot."

"No!" Lady Pleinsworth turned on him with visible hostility. "Frances is not getting out of the carriage."

"We will go up the high street," Daniel said. "Everyone shall look for inns and public houses—anyplace where Chervil might have hired a room. Frances, you search for the carriage. If we don't find anything, we shall start on the smaller alleys."

Hampstead seemed to have a remarkable number of inns. They passed the King William IV on the left, the Thatched House on the right, and then the Holly Bush on the left again, but even though Marcus hopped out to peer around the backs to look for anything resembling the "unicorn" carriage Frances had described, they found nothing. Just to be sure, Marcus and Daniel went inside each of the inns and asked if they had seen anyone matching Anne's and George Chervil's descriptions, but no one had.

And given the description Frances had given him of Chervil's scar, Daniel rather thought Chervil would have been noticed. And remembered.

Daniel hopped back into the coach, which was waiting on the high street, attracting a fair bit of attention from the townspeople. Marcus had already returned, and he and Hugh were talking about something in animated, yet quiet, tones.

"Nothing?" Marcus asked, looking up.

"Nothing," Daniel confirmed.

"There's another inn," Hugh said. "It's inside the heath, on Spaniards Road. I have been there before." He paused. "It's more remote."

"Let's go," Daniel said grimly. It was possible they had missed an inn near the high street, but they could always come back. And Frances had said that Chervil had specifically mentioned "the heath."

The carriage sped away, arriving five minutes later at The Spaniards Inn, which sat practically within the heath, its white-painted brick and black shutters elegant amidst the wilderness.

Frances pointed her arm and started to shriek.

ANNE SOON FOUND out why George had chosen this particular inn. It was on a road that went right through Hampstead Heath, and while it wasn't the only building on the road, it was considerably more isolated than the establishments in the center of the village. Which meant that if he timed it right (which he did), he could drag her out of the carriage, through a side door, and up to his room without anyone noticing. He had help, of course, in the form of his driver, who guarded her while George went in to retrieve his key.

"I don't trust you to keep your mouth shut," George growled as he shoved a gag in her mouth. It went without saying, Anne thought, that he couldn't very well ask the innkeeper for his key while accompanied by a woman who had a smelly old rag in her mouth. Not to mention hands tied behind her back.

George seemed eager for her to know all of his plans, and so he kept up a boastful monologue as he arranged the room to his liking.

"I've had this room for a week," he said, shoving a chair in front of the door. "I wasn't supposed to find you on the street last night without my carriage."

Anne stared at him in horrified fascination from her spot on the floor. Was he going to blame her for that?

"Yet another thing you've managed to ruin for me," he muttered.

Apparently, he was.

"It doesn't matter, though," he said. "It all worked out in the end. I found you at your lover's house, just as I expected I would."

Anne watched as he glanced around the room, looking for something else with which to block the door. There wasn't much, not unless he moved the entire bed.

"How many have you had since I knew you?" he asked, turning slowly around.

Anne shook her head. What was he talking about?

"Oh, you'll tell me," he snapped, and he strode forward and yanked the gag from her mouth. "How many lovers?"

For about one second Anne considered screaming. But George was holding a knife, and he'd locked the door and put a chair in front of it. If anyone was near, *and* if that person cared to save her, George would still be able to slice her to ribbons before help arrived.

"How many?" George demanded.

"None," Anne said automatically. It seemed amazing that she might forget her night with Daniel when faced with such a question, but what came to mind first were all those years of loneliness, of having not so much as a friend, much less a lover.

"Oh, I think Lord Winstead would have something else to say about that," George sneered. "Unless . . ." His mouth slid into an unpleasantly gleeful smile. "Are you telling me he couldn't perform?"

It was very tempting to give George a catalogue of all the ways Daniel had outperformed him, but instead Anne just said, "He is my fiancé."

George laughed at that. "Yes, so you believe. Good God, the man has my admiration. What a trick. And no one will take your word over his after the fact." He paused for a moment, looking almost wistful. "It must be convenient to be an earl. I couldn't have got away with that." He brightened. "Still, as it turns out, I didn't even have to ask. All I had to do was say, 'I love you,' and you not only believed me, you thought it meant I'd marry you."

He looked over at her and tsk tsked. "Foolish girl."

"I will not disagree with you on that point."

His head tilted, and he regarded her approvingly. "My my, we've grown wise in our old age."

By this point Anne had realized that she had to keep George talking. It delayed his attack, and it gave her time to plot. Not to mention that when George was talking, he was generally boasting, and when he was boasting, he was distracted.

"I've had time to learn from my mistakes," she said, taking a quick glance at the window when he walked to the wardrobe to get something out. How high up were they? If she jumped, could she survive?

He turned around, apparently not finding what he was looking for, and crossed his arms. "Well, that's nice to hear."

Anne blinked in surprise. He was regarding her with an expression that was almost paternal. "Do you have children?" she blurted out.

His expression turned to ice. "No."

And just like that, Anne knew. He had never consummated his marriage. Was he impotent? And if so, did he blame her for it?

She gave her head a tiny shake. What a stupid question. Of course he blamed her for it. And dear God above, she finally comprehended the extent of his rage. It wasn't just his face; in his eyes, she had unmanned him.

"Why are you shaking your head?" George demanded.

"I'm not," she replied, then realized she was shaking her head again. "Or I didn't mean to. It's just something I do when I'm thinking."

His eyes slitted. "What are you thinking about?"

"You," she said, quite honestly.

"Really?" For a moment he looked pleased, but this quickly gave way to suspicion. "Why?"

"Well, you're the only other person in the room. It makes sense that I'd be thinking about you."

He took a step toward her. "What were you thinking?"

How on earth could she not have noticed how utterly self-absorbed he was? Granted, she'd been only sixteen, but surely, she'd had more sense than that.

"What were you thinking?" he persisted when she did not immediately reply.

She considered how to answer this. She certainly could not tell him that she had been pondering his impotence, so instead she said, "The scar is not as dreadful as I think you think it is."

He snorted and turned back to whatever it was he was doing. "You're just saying that to get on my good side."

"I *would* say it to get on your good side," she admitted, craning her neck to get a better look at his activities. He seemed to be rearranging everything again, which seemed rather pointless, as there wasn't much in the hired room to rearrange. "But as it happens," Anne continued, "I think it's the truth. You're not as pretty as you were when we were young, but a man doesn't want to be pretty, does he?"

"Perhaps not, but I don't know a soul who'd want *this*." George made a grand, sarcastic gesture to his face, his hand sweeping down from ear to chin.

"I am sorry I hurt you, you know," Anne said, and to her great surprise, she realized she meant it. "I'm not sorry I defended myself, but I am sorry you were injured in the process. If you'd just let me go when I asked, none of this would have happened."

"Oh, so now it's my fault?"

She shut her mouth. She shouldn't have said the last bit, and she was not going to compound her error by saying what she *wanted* to say, which was, *Well, yes*.

He waited for a response, and when he didn't get one, he muttered, "We're going to have to move this."

Oh dear God, he *did* want to move the bed.

But it was a huge, heavy piece of furniture, not

something he could move on his own. After a minute or so of shoving and grunting and a good deal of cursing, he turned to Anne and snapped, "Help, for God's sake."

Her lips parted in disbelief. "My hands are tied," she reminded him.

George cursed again, then strode over and yanked her to her feet. "You don't need your hands. Just wedge yourself against it and push."

Anne could do nothing but stare.

"Like this," he bit off, leaning his bottom against the side of the bed. He planted his feet on the thread-bare rug, then used his body weight to shove against it. The big bed lurched forward, about an inch.

"You really think I'm going to do that?"

"I *think* that I still have the knife."

Anne rolled her eyes and walked over. "I really don't think this will work," she told him over her shoulder. "For one thing, my hands are in the way."

He looked down to where her hands were bound, still behind her back. "Oh, bloody hell," he muttered. "Get over here."

She *was* over there, but Anne thought it best to hold that quip in.

"Don't try anything," he warned her, and with a tug, she felt him slice through her bindings, nicking the base of her thumb in the process.

"Ow!" she yelped, bringing her hand to her mouth.

"Oh, that hurts, does it?" George murmured, his eyes taking on a glaze of bloodlust.

"Not any longer," she said quickly. "Shall we move the bed?"

He chuckled to himself and took up position. Then, just as Anne was preparing to pretend to be trying with all her might to push the bed against the door, George suddenly straightened.

"Should I cut you first?" he wondered aloud. "Or have a spot of fun?"

Anne glanced at the front of his breeches. She couldn't help herself. *Was* he impotent? She didn't see any evidence of an erection.

"Oh, so that's what you want to do," he crowed. He grabbed her hand and pulled it to him, forcing her to feel him through the fabric. "Some things never change."

Anne tried not to gag as he rubbed her left hand roughly over his crotch. Even with his clothes on, it was making her sick, but it was far better than having her face cut open.

George began to groan with pleasure, and then, to Anne's horror, she felt something begin to . . . happen.

"Oh, God," George moaned. "Oh, that feels good. It's been so long. So bloody long . . ."

Anne held her breath as she watched him. His eyes were closed, and he looked almost trancelike. She looked down at his hand—the one holding the knife. Was it her imagination, or was he not holding it so tightly? If she grabbed it . . . *Could* she grab it?

Anne grit her teeth. She let her fingers wiggle a bit, and then, just as George let out a deeper, longer groan of pleasure, she made her move.

Chapter Twenty-two

"T HAT'S IT!" FRANCES shrieked. Her thin arm jutted forth wildly. "That's the carriage. I'm sure of it."

Daniel twisted his body around to follow Frances's direction. Sure enough, a small yet well-made carriage was parked near the inn. It was standard black, with a gold decorative bar around the top. Daniel had never seen anything quite like it before, but he could see exactly why Frances had said it reminded her of a unicorn's horn. If one chopped off the correct length of it and sharpened the end, it would make a marvelous addition to a costume.

"We will remain in the carriage," Lady Winstead reaffirmed just as Daniel was turning to the ladies to issue instructions.

Daniel gave her a nod, and the three men hopped

down. "You will guard this carriage with your lives," he said to the outriders, and then he swiftly entered the inn.

Marcus was right behind him, and Hugh caught up by the time Daniel had finished questioning the innkeeper. Yes, he had seen a man with a scar. He'd had a room here for a week, but he didn't use it every night. He'd come to the desk for his key just a quarter of an hour earlier, but there was no woman with him.

Daniel slapped a crown on the counter. "Which room is his?"

The innkeeper's eyes widened. "Number four, your lordship." He placed his hand on the crown and slid it along the counter to the edge until he could scoop it up. He cleared his throat. "I might have a spare key."

"Might you?"

"I might."

Daniel produced another crown.

The innkeeper produced a key.

"Wait," Hugh said. "Is there any other entrance into the room?"

"No. Just the window."

"How high off the ground is it?"

The innkeeper's brows rose. "Too high to sneak in unless you climb the oak tree."

Hugh immediately turned to Daniel and Marcus.

"I'll do it," Marcus said, and he headed out the door.

"It will probably be unnecessary," Hugh said as

he followed Daniel up the stairs, "but I prefer to be thorough."

Daniel was not going to argue with "thorough." Especially not from Hugh, who noticed everything. And forgot nothing.

When they saw the door to Room Four at the end of the hall, Daniel immediately barreled forward, but Hugh laid a restraining hand on his shoulder. "Listen first," he advised.

"You've never been in love, have you?" Daniel replied, and before Hugh could respond, he turned the key in the lock and kicked the door open, sending a chair clattering into the room.

"Anne!" he shouted, even before he saw her.

But if she called out his name, it was lost in a shriek of surprise as the chair caught her straight at the knees and she went flying, her hand scrabbling madly for something that flew from its grasp.

A knife.

Daniel lunged for it. Anne lunged for it. George Chervil, who had been doing a desperate dance with Anne, bouncing his weight from foot to foot as he swiped his hands out for the knife, did an all-out dive for it.

In fact, everyone went for the knife except Hugh, who, unnoticed to all, was standing in the doorway with a pistol trained on Chervil, looking almost bored.

"I wouldn't if I were you," Hugh said, but George grabbed the knife anyway, and then jumped atop Anne, who was still scrabbling on the floor, having lost the race for the weapon by mere inches.

"Shoot me and she dies," George said, holding the blade perilously close to Anne's throat.

Daniel, who had instinctively rushed forward, skidded to a stop. He set his gun down and then slid it behind him.

"Step away," George said, clutching his knife like a hammer. "Do it!"

Daniel nodded, holding his hands high as he backed up a step. Anne was lying belly down on the floor, and George was straddling her, one hand on the hilt of his knife, the other clutching onto her hair. "Don't hurt her, Chervil," Daniel warned. "You don't want to do this."

"Ah, but that's where you're wrong. I very much do want to do this." He tapped the blade lightly against Anne's cheek.

Daniel's gut twisted.

But George hadn't drawn blood. He seemed to be enjoying his moment of power, and he yanked harder on Anne's hair, pulling her head up in what looked to be an agonizingly uncomfortable position.

"You will die," Daniel promised.

George shrugged. "So will she."

"What about your wife?"

George looked at him sharply.

"I spoke with her this morning," Daniel said, keeping his gaze firmly on George's face. He wanted desperately to look at Anne, to meet her eyes. He could tell her he loved her without any words. She would know; he had only to look at her.

But he did not dare. As long as he was looking

at George Chervil, George Chervil was looking at him. And not at Anne. Or the knife.

"What did you say to my wife?" George hissed, but a flicker of unease passed over his face.

"She seems a lovely woman," Daniel said. "What will happen to her, I wonder, if you die here, in a public inn, at the hands of two earls and the son of a marquess?"

George's head jerked as he turned to Hugh, only just then realizing who he was. "But you hate him," he said. "He shot you."

Hugh just shrugged.

George paled, and he started to say something, only to interrupt himself with "Two earls?"

"There's another one," Daniel said. "Just in case."

George started breathing hard, his eyes darting from Daniel to Hugh, and occasionally down to Anne. Daniel could see that he was starting to perspire. He was reaching his edge, and an edge was always a dangerous place to be.

For everyone.

"Lady Chervil will be ruined," Daniel said. "Cast out of society. Even her father will not be able to save her."

George began to tremble. Daniel finally allowed himself to steal a glance at Anne. She was breathing hard, clearly frightened, and yet, when their eyes met . . .

I love you.

It was as if she'd said it aloud.

"The world is not kind to women who have been cast out of their homes," Daniel said softly. "Just ask Anne."

George was beginning to waver; Daniel could see it in his eyes. "If you let her go," he promised, "you will live."

He would live, but not anywhere in the British Isles. Daniel would see to that.

"And my wife?"

"I shall leave all explanations up to you."

George's head twitched, as if his collar had grown too tight. His eyes were blinking furiously, and then, for one moment, he squeezed them shut, and—

"He shot me! Oh, my God, he shot me!"

Daniel's head snapped around as he realized that Hugh had fired his gun. "Are you bloody insane?" he snapped, even as he rushed forward to snatch Anne away from George, who was now rolling on the floor, howling with pain as he clutched his bleeding hand.

Hugh limped into the room and looked down at George. "It's just a nick," he said dispassionately.

"Anne, Anne," Daniel said hoarsely. The whole time she'd been captive to George Chervil he'd held all of his terror at bay. He'd stood straight, muscles tense, but now, now that she was safe . . .

"I thought I might lose you," he gasped, holding her as close as he possibly could. He buried his face in the crook of her shoulder, and to his mortification, he realized he was soaking her dress with his tears. "I didn't know— I don't think I knew—"

"I wouldn't have shot her, by the way," Hugh said, walking over to the window. George screamed when he "accidentally" stepped on his hand.

"You are a bloody madman," Daniel said, his outrage cutting right through his tears.

"Or," Hugh said plainly, "I've never been in love." He looked down at Anne. "It does leave one more clearheaded." He motioned to his gun. "Better aim, too."

"What is he talking about?" Anne whispered.

"I rarely know," Daniel admitted.

"Got to let Chatteris in," Hugh said, whistling as he wrenched the window open.

"He's crazy," Daniel said, pulling just far enough away from Anne to cradle her face in his hands. She looked so beautiful, and precious, and *alive*. "He's plumb crazy."

Her lips trembled into a smile. "But effective."

Daniel felt something begin to rumble in his belly. Laughter. Dear God, maybe they were all crazy.

"Need a hand?" Hugh called out, and they both turned to the window.

"Is Lord Chatteris in a *tree*?" Anne asked.

"What in God's name is going on?" Marcus demanded, even as he tumbled into the room. "I heard gunshots."

"Hugh shot him," Daniel said, jerking his head toward Chervil, who was attempting to crawl to the door. Marcus immediately strode over and blocked his way. "While he was holding Anne."

"I haven't heard you say thank you yet," Hugh

said, peering out the window for no reason Daniel could discern.

"Thank you," Anne said. Hugh turned around, and she gave him a smile so brilliant, he actually started.

"Well, now," he said awkwardly, and Daniel had to smile. The air *did* change when Anne was in the room.

"What are we going to do with him?" Marcus asked, always one to see to the practical matters at hand. He reached down and picked something off the floor, regarded it for a moment, and crouched next to George.

"Ow!" George howled.

"Tying his hands," Marcus confirmed. He glanced at Anne. "I'm assuming this was what he used to tie yours?"

She nodded.

"That hurts!"

"Shouldn't have got yourself shot," Marcus said. With no compassion whatsoever. He looked back at Daniel. "We do have to figure out what to do with him."

"You promised you wouldn't kill me," George whined.

"I promised I wouldn't kill you if you let her go," Daniel reminded him.

"Which I did."

"After I shot you," Hugh retorted.

"He's not worth killing," Marcus said, yanking the bindings tight. "There will be questions."

Daniel nodded, grateful for his friend's level head. Still, he was not quite ready to allow Chervil to let go of his fear. With a quick kiss to the top of Anne's head, Daniel stood up. "May I?" he said to Hugh, holding out his hand.

"I reloaded," Hugh said, handing him his gun.

"I knew you would," Daniel murmured. He walked over to George.

"You said you wouldn't kill me!" George shrieked.

"I won't," Daniel stated. "Not today, at least. But if you come anywhere near Whipple Hill again, I will kill you."

George nodded furiously.

"In fact," Daniel continued, reaching down and scooping up the knife, which Hugh had kicked over to him, "if you come anywhere near London, I will kill you."

"But I live in London!"

"Not any longer, you don't."

Marcus cleared his throat. "I have to say, I don't much want him in Cambridgeshire."

Daniel glanced over at his friend, gave him a nod, then turned back to Chervil. "If you come anywhere near Cambridgeshire, *he'll* kill you."

"If I might make a suggestion," Hugh said smoothly, "it might be easier for all concerned if we extend the ban to the whole of the British Isles."

"What?" George cried. "You can't—"

"Or we could kill you," Hugh said. He glanced over at Daniel. "You could offer advice on living in Italy, couldn't you?"

"But I don't know Italian," George whimpered.

"You'll learn," Hugh snapped.

Daniel looked down at the knife in his hands. It was dangerously sharp. And it had been but an inch away from Anne's throat.

"Australia," he said firmly.

"Right," Marcus said, yanking George to his feet. "Shall we take care of him?"

"Please do."

"We'll take his carriage," Hugh said. And then he gave them a rare smile. "The one with the unicorn horn."

"The unicorn . . . ," Anne repeated in bewilderment. She turned to Daniel. "Frances?"

"She saved the day."

"Then she's unhurt? I had to push her from the carriage, and I—"

"She's fine," Daniel assured her, pausing for a moment to watch Hugh and Marcus bid them farewell and drag Chervil away. "A bit dusty, and I think my aunt may have lost five years from her life, but she is well. And once she sees you—" But he couldn't finish. Anne had started to cry.

Daniel immediately knelt at her side, pulling her close. "It's all right," he murmured. "Everything is going to be all right."

Anne shook her head. "No, it's not." She looked up, her eyes shining with love. "It's going to be so much better."

"I love you," he said. He had a feeling he would be saying this frequently. For the rest of his life.

"I love you, too."

He took her hand and brought it to his lips. "Will you marry me?"

"I already said yes," she said with a curious smile.

"I know. But I wanted to ask you again."

"Then I accept again."

He pulled her close, needing to feel her in his arms. "We should probably go down. Everyone's worried."

She nodded, her cheek brushing lightly against his chest.

"My mother is in the carriage, and Aunt—"

"Your mother?" Anne yelped, pulling back. "Oh, my heavens, what must she think of me?"

"That you must be amazing, and lovely, and that if she's very very nice to you, you'll give her a bushel of grandchildren."

Anne smiled slyly. "If *she's* very nice to me?"

"Well, it goes without saying that I'll be very nice to you."

"How many children in a bushel, do you think?"

Daniel felt his soul grow light. "Quite a few, I imagine."

"We will have to be most industrious."

He amazed himself by maintaining a serious expression. "I am quite a hardworking fellow."

"It's one of the reasons I love you." She touched his cheek. "One of the many, many reasons."

"That many, eh?" He smiled. No, he was already smiling. But maybe now he was smiling just a little bit more. "Hundreds?"

"Thousands," she confirmed.

"I might have to request a full accounting."

"Now?"

And who said women were the only ones who liked to fish for compliments? He was more than happy to sit here and listen to her say lovely things about him. "Perhaps just the primary five," he demurred.

"Well . . ." She paused.

And paused.

He gave her a dry look. "Is it really so difficult to come up with five?"

Her eyes were so wide and innocent that he almost believed her when she said, "Oh, no, it's just that it's a challenge to pick my favorites."

"At random, then," he suggested.

"Very well." Her mouth scrunched up on one side as she thought. "There is your smile. I adore your smile."

"I adore your smile, too!"

"You have a lovely sense of humor."

"So do you!"

She gave him a stern look.

"I can't help it if you're taking all the good reasons," he said.

"You *don't* play a musical instrument."

He looked at her blankly.

"Like the rest of your family," she clarified. "I just don't know if I could bear it, having to listen to you practice."

He leaned forward with a roguish tilt of his head.

"What makes you think I *don't* play an instrument?"

"You don't!" she gasped, and he almost thought she might be ready to reconsider having accepted him.

"I don't," he confirmed. "Which is not to say I haven't taken lessons."

She gazed at him questioningly.

"The boys of the family are not required to continue lessons once they leave for school. Unless they show exceptional talent."

"Have any shown exceptional talent?"

"Not a one," he said cheerfully. He rose to his feet and held out his hand. It was time to go home.

"Wasn't I supposed to give you two more reasons?" she asked, letting him help her to her feet.

"Oh, you can tell me later," he said. "We have lots of time."

"But I just thought of one."

He turned with a quizzical brow. "You say that like it took a great effort."

"It's actually more of a moment," she said.

"A moment?"

She nodded, following him out the door into the hallway. "On the night we first met. I was prepared to leave you in the back hall, you know."

"Bruised and bleeding?" He tried for outrage, but he rather thought his smile ruined the effect.

"I would lose my position if I were caught with you, and I'd already been trapped in that storage closet for heaven knows how long. I really didn't have time to help tend to your wounds."

"But you did."

"I did," she said.

"Because of my charming smile and lovely sense of humor?"

"No," she said plainly. "It was because of your sister."

"Honoria?" he asked in surprise.

"You were defending her," she said with a helpless shrug. "How could I abandon a man who defended his sister?"

To Daniel's embarrassment, his cheeks grew warm. "Well, anyone would have done so," he mumbled.

Halfway down the stairs, Anne exclaimed, "Oh, I thought of another one! When we were practicing Harriet's play. You *would* have been the wild boar if she'd asked."

"No, I wouldn't."

She patted his arm as they stepped outside. "Yes, you would."

"Very well, I would," he lied.

She looked at him shrewdly. "You think you're just saying that to placate me, but I know you would have been a good sport."

Good gracious, it was like they were an old married couple already.

"Oh, I thought of another one!"

He looked at her, at her shining eyes, so full of love, and hope, and promise. "Two, actually," she said.

He smiled. He could think of thousands.

Epilogue

Another year, another Smythe-Smith musicale . . .

"I THINK DAISY HAD better step to the right," Daniel murmured into his wife's ear. "Sarah looks as if she might bite her head off."

Anne cast a nervous glance at Sarah, who, having used up her only possible excuse the year before, was back up on the stage, at the piano . . .

Murdering the keys.

Anne could only deduce that she'd decided that fury was preferable to abject misery. Heaven only knew if the piano would survive the encounter.

Even worse was Harriet, who'd been conscripted that year to replace Honoria, who, as the new Lady Chatteris, no longer had to perform.

Marriage or death. Those were the only avenues

of escape, Sarah had grimly told Anne the day before when Anne had stopped by to see how the rehearsals were going.

Whose death, Anne wasn't sure. When Anne had arrived, Sarah had somehow got hold of Harriet's violin bow and was brandishing it like a sword. Daisy was shrieking, Iris was moaning, and Harriet had been gasping with delight as she wrote it all down for future use in a play.

"Why is Harriet talking to herself?" Daniel asked, his whispered voice bringing Anne back to the here and now.

"She doesn't know how to read music."

"*What?*"

Several people looked their way, including Daisy, whose glare could only be described as homicidal.

"What?" Daniel repeated, far more quietly.

"She can't read music," Anne whispered back, keeping her eyes politely on the unfolding concert. "She told me she's never been able to learn. She got Honoria to write the notes out and then she memorized them." She looked over at Harriet, who was mouthing the notes so clearly that even the guests in the back row would surely realize she'd just played—or rather, attempted to play—B-flat.

"Why couldn't she just read the letters Honoria wrote out for her?"

"I don't know," Anne admitted. She smiled encouragingly at Harriet, who grinned back.

Ah, Harriet. One really had to love her. And Anne did, even more so now that she was a member of the family. She loved being a Smythe-Smith. She loved the noise, and the constant stream of cousins in her drawing room, and how lovely they'd all been to her sister Charlotte when she'd come for a visit earlier that spring.

But most of all, she loved being a Smythe-Smith who did *not* have to perform at the musicale. Because unlike the rest of the audience, whose groans and grumbles Anne could clearly hear around her, she knew the truth:

It was far, far worse up on the stage than it was in the seats.

Although . . .

"I cannot bring myself to lose all affection for the concert," she whispered to Daniel.

"Really?" He winced when Harriet did something unspeakable with her violin. "Because I cannot bring myself to lose all affection for my hearing."

"But without the musicale, we should never have met," she reminded him.

"Oh, I think I would have found you."

"But not on a night like this."

"No." He smiled and took her hand. It was incredibly gauche, and not at all what married couples were supposed to do in public, but Anne did not care. She twined her fingers through his and smiled. And it no longer mattered that Sarah was pounding the piano keys or that Harriet had started to recite her notes so loudly that the first row of the audience could hear her speak.

She had Daniel, and she was holding his hand.

That was really all that mattered.

THE DUKE AND I by Julia Quinn – now a
series created for Netflix by Shondaland

Praise for Julia Quinn's Bridgerton series:

'Quinn is a master of historical romance'
Entertainment Weekly

'A smart, funny touch ... reminiscent of Helen Field
Time Magazine

AVAILABLE FROM PIATKUS NOW!

Do you love historical fiction?

Want the chance to hear news about your favourite authors (and the chance to win free books)?

Suzanne Allain
Mary Balogh
Lenora Bell
Charlotte Betts
Manda Collins
Joanna Courtney
Grace Burrowes
Evie Dunmore
Lynne Francis
Pamela Hart
Elizabeth Hoyt
Eloisa James
Lisa Kleypas
Jayne Ann Krentz
Sarah MacLean
Terri Nixon
Julia Quinn

Then visit the Piatkus website
www.yourswithlove.co.uk

And follow us on Facebook and Instagram
www.facebook.com/yourswithlovex | @yourswithlovex

PIATKUS